the mystery
of the
missing nun

And Other Famous
Michigan Murder Mysteries

Larry Wakefield

Published by Horizon Books
Traverse City, Michigan

The Mystery of the Missing Nun

Printed in the United States of America by Horizon Books, 243 East Front Street, Traverse City, Michigan 49684

FIRST EDITION
ISBN: 0-915937-10-7

On the Cover: Larry Wakefield at the front door gate of the historic old Leelanau County Jail in Leland, Michigan, where the murder suspect of the Felician nun was incarcerated while awaiting her trial. Design by Judy Albaugh.

CONTENTS

INTRODUCTORY NOTE

This book is a collection of seventeen fascinating stories of famous Michigan murders. All of them are true—they really happened. Each one has become a kind of classic in that part of the state where it occurred. Each is the kind of story that is handed down from generation to generation—possibly at night by the family fireside after the little kids have been put to bed. Each is unique.

I am fascinated by murder. Maybe that says something sinister about me, but I really don't think so. I think most people are interested in murder. I think that, with the possible exception of treason, it's the most interesting of crimes. At an early impressionable age I read Edmund Pearson's *Studies in Murder*, with it's famous Lizzie Borden case, and I've been hooked on murder ever since.

I don't mean detective stories. I don't care who killed Roger Ackroyd. For me, the difference between the true murder story and Agatha Christie's fiction is the difference between Dr. Crippen and his waxwork at Madame Tussaud's famous museum in London.

But not all murders make good stories. Most murders are squalid affairs, simple slaughter. In the preface to his book *More Studies in Murder* Pearson wrote, "Of all the murders in the whole world in any given year, not more than one or two are worthy of the connoisseur's attention...The Borden case is without parallel in the criminal history of America. It is the most interesting, and perhaps, the most puzzling murder that has occurred in this country."

1

I am inclined to agree, but I also think that the murder of the Felician nun at Isadore in 1907—the centerpiece of this book—runs the Borden case a very close second. It has all the elements of a great murder story—mystery, suspense, drama, a strong story line—and even the added titillation of an illicit love affair.

DEATH BATTLE
AT RATTLE RUN

Fifty years ago, every motorist who traveled from Mt. Clemens to Port Huron on old U.S. 25 had to pass through Rattle Run, though some may hardly have been aware of it. The town itself is insignificant—in fact, if you happened to be lighting a cigarette or engaged in conversation with a companion, you might miss it altogether: just an aimless congregation of old frame houses and, at a crossroads a little farther on, a small wooden church; it was known as Columbus Church, after the name of the township.

Today a new four-lane federal highway bypasses it to the south, and Rattle Run, named for a small meandering stream nearby, is more isolated and insignificant than ever. Yet the place has one claim to distinction. It was the scene of one of Michigan's most bizarre and mysterious murder cases.

One wintry evening—Tuesday, January 5, 1909—two men were seen making their way separately through snow to the little Methodist church at the crossroads, one in a horse-drawn buggy, one afoot. They were the Reverend John Haviland Carmichael, the church's pastor, and Gideon Browning, a local handyman. Just what happened there that night will never be known exactly, but the next morning, two men who lived across the road from the church noticed the front door of the building swinging open. They investigated and discovered a scene of horror.

It was evident at a glance that a terrible struggle had taken place here. Pews were overturned and broken. The organ was hacked and splintered by sharp, heavy blows. A small stained-glass window was shattered. Blood was everywhere—pools of it on the floor, splashes on the walls.

Bloody footprints told the course of the battle, how it swayed back and forth from one end of the small room to the other. The carpet in the center aisle was scuffed and bunched as though a heavy object had been dragged along it. And in the ashes of the big wood stove, which was still warm to the touch, they found a pile of smouldering bones. A large piece of skull made it evident that these were human remains. Crying murder, the two men went running to telephone the sheriff.

In their preliminary investigation an hour later, County Sheriff W. F. Wagensell and his deputy found the following objects: a bloody knife and hatchet on the floor, a pair of blood-spattered men's trousers and underpants, and an eye-glasses case bearing the inscription "J. H. Carmichael, Adair, Mich." on a card pasted inside.

The clothing appeared to be of a size that Carmichael, a big man, would wear. Sifting through the ashes in the stove, the sheriff found several steel frog overcoat buttons, which were believed to have come from the minister's overcoat. The contents of the stove, along with the other articles found, were packaged and sent to Port Huron for professional examination.

Questioned at their home in Adair, Carmichael's wife said her husband had left the house early Tuesday morning for Rattle Run, where he planned to make arrangements for a series of revival meetings. His failure to return home that night hadn't alarmed her—he often stayed overnight with friends there. Nor did she for one moment believe that the remains of the body in the stove were those of her husband, for who would want to kill a man of the cloth? Yet, when she was told about the glasses case, Mrs. Carmichael, a big woman weighing over 200 pounds, fainted dead away.

4

At about this same time, it was learned that a handyman named Gideon Browning, also of Adair, had likewise gone to Rattle Run on Tuesday evening, and was missing. He had taken the train and gotten off at Hickey, a little station two and a half miles from Rattle Run. Earlier he told his sister and her husband, with whom he boarded, that he had an appointment to meet the Reverend Carmichael there that evening.

Although nobody yet knew the identity of the body in the stove, the weight of suspicion now fell on "Gid" Browning. Police at all points in southern Michigan, particularly along the railroad and the St. Clair River, were alerted to be on the lookout for him. A description of Carmichael was also sent out. Oddly enough, the two men had often been seen together and seemed to be friends of a sort, though people wondered what they could possibly have in common.

Carmichael was a big, powerful man of fifty-five, with craggy features and a large brown beard. He had the evangelical fervor of an Old Testament prophet and a booming voice to match. He was known to suffer terribly from headaches. Perhaps that is what made him so restless. In his twenty-six years in the ministry he had served at more than a dozen parishes, seldom staying more than a year or two at any one place.

Browning, fifty-one, was a smaller man, but wiry and strong, with a thick walrus mustache. Considered somewhat simple minded, he had been a sailor, carpenter, and roustabout; at present he was doing odd jobs. The only thing noteworthy about Browning was his eyes. They were small, dark, and beady—"penetrating," some people said. They reminded others of a snake's eyes, and gave them the "creeps."

On the evidence of the blood-stained clothing, which had now been positively identified as Carmichael's, the police were almost certain that Browning was the murderer, but they were at a loss as to the motive. A bloody dollar bill in one of the pockets and a silver dollar on the floor seemed to rule out robbery. But the preacher's gold watch was missing.

Meanwhile, a nameless fear had descended upon the little community of Rattle Run. A madman seemed to be loose in their midst—where might he strike next? People who had never bothered to do so before now took pains to lock their doors and windows at night. And everyone avoided the vicinity of the church after dark.

On Friday, January 8, the remains of the body in the stove were definitely identified as Gideon Browning's. There could be no doubt about it. Three teeth in the ashes were identified by a dentist in St. Clair as part of a set of false teeth he had made for Browning. And Browning's sister recognized the steel buttons and a tie pin as belonging to her brother; also a piece of scalp and tuft of hair found on the floor.

Now that the identity of the victim was known, gossipers at the village store in Adair castigated the police for their stupidity in believing that the poor, loony handyman could have committed such a horrible crime. Sure, "Gid" was a little "queer," and he had "funny-looking" eyes, but everyone knew he was harmless — wouldn't hurt a fly. The preacher, on the other hand, was characterized as a "blood-thirsty fiend."

On Saturday, a Grand Trunk Railroad ticket agent in Port Huron told police he was sure he had sold a ticket for Chicago to the Reverend Carmichael. He now recognized the preacher from the description circulated by the police. He said Carmichael had boarded the five o'clock, westbound train early Wednesday morning.

This was corroborated by a baggage master at the railroad station, who said he was accosted early Wednesday morning by a big man wearing a fur overcoat who asked that his suitcase be checked for Chicago.

"There," the stranger had said, dropping the valise to the floor, "I have carried that for several miles and am glad to get a chance to set it down."

Two Detroit detectives were hired to get on Carmichael's trail and stay there until they found him, dead or alive. The hunt for the preacher was now in full cry.

But it came to a sudden end on Monday. Sheriff Wagensell got word from the police in Carthage, Illinois that Rev. John Haviland Carmichael had committed suicide there early that morning. In the little backwater town where the Mormon prophet Joseph Smith had met his end in 1844 at the hands of a lynch mob, the preacher had cut his throat with a penknife and bled to death.

6

According to the owner of a rooming house in Carthage, Moranda Hughes, Carmichael had arrived there on Saturday morning. He signed the register as John Elder, and said he was a carpenter who had come to see about starting a small wood-products factory in the city.

For the next two days he seemed to have wandered aimlessly about town — undoubtedly in torment. Early Monday morning he told Miss Hughes he had decided against the factory and was leaving town on the morning train. An hour later he was found in a privy behind the rooming house, unconscious but still alive. However, he died at the hospital without ever regaining consciousness.

The doctor who examined his body said that the wound in his throat was not necessarily fatal. Carmichael evidently had felt with his fingers for the carotid artery and then made a small incision rather than a slash. He had succeeded only in nicking the artery. Death was caused by loss of blood and exposure to the near-zero degree weather. If found half an hour earlier, he might have been saved.

Two letters were found in his overcoat pocket. One was addressed to his wife, begging her forgiveness. "I have always been a coward," he wrote. "It robbed me of my judgement, and I ran."

The other letter was an eight-page confession addressed to Sheriff Wagensell. Carmichael wrote that he had killed the handyman in self-defense. "Browning always had a strange, hypnotic power over me that gave me the horrors," he wrote.

"Once in the depot in Adair he came out of his house in his shirt sleeves and exercised me, compelling me to walk the railroad track rails. I felt like a small bantam chicken."

Carmichael wrote that Browning had asked him to come to Columbus Church and conduct his wedding ceremony that fatal evening. "When I got there, he was alone and I felt uneasy. He said, 'It is all right, Elder. The others are coming in a carriage.' " Carmichael wrote that Browning had helped him build a fire in the stove while they were waiting.

Carmichael continued: "Presently he took a hearty laugh and said, 'There's no use looking, Elder, for there ain't going to be no wedding.' He was sitting there where the gleams of light from the stove shone on his face, and his eyes were so brilliant I was thrilled through and through with the queerest feeling.

"I then asked him why he had made the present arrangements with me, and he said, 'Well, Elder, I just wanted to have a little fun. You consider yourself an educated man and I thought I would show you what I could do.' "

Carmichael then noticed that Browning had a weapon of some sort up his sleeve.

"Instantly, I made a grab for it and got the hatchet from him and asked him what he meant to do with it.

"He said, 'I'll show you,' and from his overcoat pockets drew out a knife in each hand. He came at me, striking with both hands while I backed across the church and down the side aisle and across the front.

"Then I threw the hatchet and struck him and he fell. I turned to open the door when he grabbed me by the leg and threw me down where my hands came upon the hatchet. There was a desperate struggle in which I used the hatchet until he laid quiet and still."

Carmichael wrote that then he fell into a blind rage and dragged the body to the stove. He removed the clothing, cut up the body, and put it in the stove. He said the stove was hot enough to make the stovepipe cherry red almost to the elbow.

"Then I saw that my clothing was torn and bloody while some of his were yet whole, and I exchanged and took all but a few of mine and piled them in along with his body. Then I went up to the tunnel station, where I turned my rig about and started the horse on the back track. My big coat hid my torn and bloody garments until I got to Chicago, where I purchased others."

Carmichael concluded his confession: "I am tired of trying to hide, though I have succeeded in eluding the detectives so far. If you get this while I am still alive, come and get me. I shall be not far from Carthage, Illinois." The letter was signed, "J. H. Carmichael."

Sheriff Wagensell didn't bother to conceal his scorn. The "confession," he said, was nothing but a pack of lies. Far from confessing the truth, Carmichael had chosen to carry his awful secret with him to the grave. No more need be said.

The Port Huron *Daily Times* in a story on Tuesday, January 12, indicated that it, too, understood the real nature of the crime: "The public mind for six days mirrored the lonely church at the corners, one half mile from the village of Rattle Run — has seen in a mental picture the two men, one a minister, whose disordered mind was kindled with the fires of a demon-like passion. . . ."

Although neither the sheriff nor the newspaper mentioned the word (it is unthinkable that they would have done so in those days), it is clear, nonetheless, that they knew this was a homosexual crime.

Carmichael's body was returned to Michigan by railroad train. An autopsy conducted in Port Huron revealed that Carmichael was a drug addict — his arms and legs were covered with punctures from hypodermic needles. Perhaps the preacher had used morphine to ease the pain of his terrible headaches.

The funeral was held in Romulus, where Carmichael's oldest daughter had been buried five years earlier. At the open casket, Carmichael's brother, a mail carrier in another little town in southern Michigan, pointed out several small scars on his brother's face. They had been caused, he said, by a sledding accident when he and his brother were small boys. They had slid into a tree while coasting down a hill near their homes in West Virginia.

He gazed sadly down at his brother's face, and murmured, "Poor boy. Poor boy."

It was a fitting epitaph.

THE DYING SPARLINGS
AT UBLY

Somebody must have put a curse on the men of the Sparling family at Ubly, for they kept dying, one by one. Anyhow, that's the story that began to circulate among people in the little farming community on Michigan's Thumb. It didn't seem possible that one family could have so much bad luck. There had to be a reason.

First to die was John Wesley Sparling, a ruggedly handsome man of forty-eight, seemingly in perfect health. He took sick while plowing his corn field one spring day in 1908 and died in a Port Huron hospital a few weeks later. The cause of his illness was puzzling. His friend and family physician, Dr. Robert A. MacGregor, diagnosed it tentatively as "creeping paralysis due to acute inflamation of the spine." But even he had to admit he was perplexed.

Sparling, a hardworking farmer, was well liked, and practically the whole community turned out for his funeral. His widow and the five grown children—four boys and a girl—were left to work the large and prosperous farm. Fortunately, Carrie Sparling, a beautiful woman two years younger than her husband, was considered quite capable of looking after the business end. Indeed, she had handled most of the business affairs when her husband was alive.

Two years later, Peter, the oldest son, died. He, too, was stricken suddenly while working in the hay fields and died five days later at the hospital. Dr. MacGregor, a handsome, square-jawed man of thirty-six, said his death was due to sunstroke and blood poisoning. The hospital doctors apparently concurred.

Although his death seemed strange, little was said openly.

Tongues began to wag in earnest, though, when in May of the following year, son Albert—the next oldest at twenty-three, suddenly came down with the same symptoms that had stricken his father and brother: gripping stomach pains and a terrible nausea. He died two days later. Dr. MacGregor said Albert's death had probably been caused by an injury to his stomach. He was known to have taken a bad fall while chasing some stray cows shortly before his illness.

Albert's death left only Ray, twenty-one, Scyrel, twenty, and their mother to work the farm; the daughter had married and moved away.

The two young men were frightened. Terrible things were happening to the Sparling family—their turn might be next. For advice they went to their great-uncle, John Sparling, a wealthy and prominent citizen of Bad Axe and former member of the state legislature. He advised them to leave home immediately and seek their fortunes in the Canadian northwest, as his own two sons had done successfully. Ray and Scyrel promised to take his advice, telling him it might be a while, however, before they could raise the necessary funds.

John Sparling feeling uneasy after talking with the two boys, went to see the county prosecutor, Xenophon A. Boomhower. He told Boomhower that he feared the Sparling boys were in mortal danger. It seemed that somebody was trying to wipe out the whole family.

"Do you have any idea who that might be?" Boomhower asked.

"Nothing definite," Sparling said. But he was sure a great evil was afoot. That was all he cared to say.

Boomhower said he'd look into the matter. "Nothing is going to happen to those boys if I can help it," he promised.

12

But Scyrel was taken sick a few weeks later. At first, his illness didn't seem very serious—just a stomach ache and a general malaise. It was nothing, he said. He blamed his upset stomach on some oranges he'd bought from a peddler that morning. And he was angry when his mother called the doctor.

Dr. MacGregor examined the boy. Although he didn't seem very ill, the doctor was worried. Some of the symptoms were quite similar to those experienced by his dead father and brothers preceding their deaths. He left some medicine and said he'd call again in the morning.

Next day, MacGregor brought along another physician for consultation, Dr. W. J. Herrington of Bad Axe. After examining Scyrel, Herrington said he didn't think the boy was seriously ill. But Dr. MacGregor shook his head gloomily and said that all the other Sparlings had been taken the same way; he said he believed that Scyrel would die, too.

Dr. MacGregor brought in still another doctor the next day, Dr. Daniel Conboy, also of Bad Axe. They found that Scyrel had taken a turn for the worse. He had severe abdominal pains, an inflamed mouth, and a fast, feeble pulse. Curiously, his temperature was normal. And Dr. Conboy could find no sign of an infectious disease.

After leaving the sick room, Dr. MacGregor asked him: "Are you thinking arsenic?"

Conboy admitted that he was.

"Isn't it strange," MacGregor said, "that both of us are thinking the same thing? You know, I'm beginning to believe that all the others died of arsenic poisoning, too."

Dr. Conboy was shaken; he didn't like the sound of this at all. He went straightway to Prosecutor Boomhower and reported the strange conversation. Then both men called on Dr. MacGregor at his office in Ubly.

Boomhower and Dr. MacGregor were friends and former neighbors in Bad Axe. After discussing Scyrel's illness Boomhower told MacGregor that he would be obliged to order a postmortem if the boy were to die. They all agreed that there was strong evidence that Scyrel was being poisoned. MacGregor made some remarks that seemed to cast suspicion on Mrs. Sparling. Boomhower demanded

13

that a full-time nurse be hired to oversee the boy's food, drink, and medication. MacGregor agreed and telephoned an agency in Port Huron for the services of a nurse. She arrived at the Sparling household the next day.

At Boomhower's request Dr. Conboy also called at the Sparling home that day. Dr. MacGregor was there when he arrived. He stopped Conboy and asked why he had come. "It must be something important or you wouldn't be here," MacGregor said.

Conboy told him that Boomhower had suggested that he "throw a scare into Mrs. Sparling."

MacGregor replied, "You don't have to do that. I have already scared the devil out of her. She is in a state of collapse and will be in an asylum inside of four months."

Later that day MacGregor found that Scyrel was dying. Piteously, the boy said, "My God, doctor, I don't want to die. Isn't there something you can do for me?"

Dr. MacGregor told the boy not to fear, that he would soon be well. But Scyrel died two days later.

MacGregor immediately telephoned Boomhower. Now, at long last, the law swung into action. Boomhower told MacGregor to prepare for an autopsy at the farm next morning; he would bring Dr. Conboy and the coroner, Dr. C. B. Morden, to perform it. Dr. MacGregor, however, decided not to wait until morning. He and another Ubly doctor, W. B. Holdship, performed the autopsy that evening.

Next morning Boomhower was furious that his orders had not been followed. He took charge of the body and a second postmortem was conducted by Conboy and Morden. The latter expressed surprise that the stomach had not been removed. MacGregor explained that he had cut into it and found it "absolutely normal." Strange, Dr. Morden said. How did he explain the fact that the nurse's chart showed that the boy had vomited clots of blood?

MacGregor said he couldn't explain it.

The vital organs were sent to the forensic medicine laboratory at the University of Michigan for analysis. It reported, a few days later, that the organs contained measurable amounts of arsenic, more than enough to have caused death. There was no sign of any other disease.

Boomhower immediately ordered the examination of Albert Sparling's body.

Meanwhile, Dr. MacGregor had begun to make some strange statements. To a *Detroit News* reporter, he made the following revelation:

"I'm going to tell you something that no one on earth knows except members of the Sparling family. All four of the family died of syphilis."

Astonished, the reporter asked, "What about the poison?"

"Poison will be found in all those bodies," MacGregor said. "It was the chief ingredient of some patent medicines they were taking for the disease."

Dr. Holdship was among those present at the examination. Afterward, MacGregor asked him:

"How did he look?"

"Not very good," Holdship said.

"Do you think they will find arsenic?"

"I shouldn't be surprised."

"I wouldn't be surprised if they find arsenic in all of them. I would give my left leg up to the hip to find out who is giving it to them."

Later, MacGregor told the county sheriff that he was terribly upset. "This thing is killing me," he said.

"You mustn't worry so much," Sheriff Donald McAuley told him. "Everything will work out all right."

"You don't know what I'm up against," MacGregor replied. "I'll be boarding with you some day."

On another occasion—before the laboratory report had been received—he told the sheriff, "I know they will find poison. If you take up the other Sparlings, you will find poison in all of them. I know of a fellow who can tell you who gave it to them and can make Mrs. Sparling confess."

"Then, for God's sake, man, why don't you get busy?" McAuley exclaimed.

"I would just have to look in a mirror to see him," MacGregor said. "Do you understand?"

MacGregor also told the sheriff that, at the time of the inquest, Mrs. Sparling had sent him the present of a dressed goose. "I threw

15

it away," he said, "because I thought it was full of arsenic." He went on to say that all the Sparlings had syphilis and that Ray, the one surviving son, was going to die of it too. He said that Mrs. Sparling had once gone stone blind from the disease.

All these remarks would soon come back to haunt Dr. MacGregor. Sheriff McAuley had a good memory.

At the coroner's inquest—convened in Ubly to investigate Albert's death—it was learned that insurance policies of $1,000 each had been taken on the lives of John Wesley Sparling and his four sons. They were written by Dr. MacGregor's father, Alexander MacGregor, a life insurance agent in London, Ontario. All of them named Mrs. Sparling as beneficiary. It was also learned that Mrs. Sparling had turned over one of the $1,000 checks to Dr. MacGregor. The coroner's jury returned a verdict that death was caused by arsenic poison administered by a person or persons unknown.

Prosecutor Boomhower issued a warrant for Dr. MacGregor's arrest on the following day, and he was taken into custody by Sheriff McAuley. The doctor appeared curiously resigned, as if he had expected this to happen.

From his jail cell in Bad Axe the doctor issued a statement for the press. "This comes after seven years' hard work here," he wrote. "And while my pride is stung by even the hint of a warrant, I will see this thing through to the end."

He went on to say that in the case of John Sparling and his son Albert, the death certificates had been signed by physicians at the hospital, and he pointed out that he had brought several other doctors in for consultation about Peter and Scyrel. In spite of his apparent composure, it was reported that the doctor broke down several times in his prison cell, protesting his innocence with tears streaming down his face.

Mrs. Sparling was also arrested but later was released to the custody of her husband's cousin, Peter S. Sparling, of Colfax. Though her eyes were red and swollen from weeping, she too showed some composure during an interview with a newspaper reporter on the train to Colfax.

"Do you believe that Dr. MacGregor is held unjustly?" the reporter asked.

"I'm so completely dumbfounded and stricken by today's events I can't think of anything," she said. "I can't imagine anyone so vile as to want to poison my boys." She went on to reaffirm her faith in the doctor's innocence.

Charged with the murder of Scyrel Sparling, MacGregor was arraigned in circuit court on December 13, 1911. Sheriff McAuley was one of the first witnesses. In addition to relating Dr. MacGregor's strange remarks, he reported another conversation he had had with the doctor.

"I met MacGregor in town and he asked if Boomhower and I had been out at the Sparling farm the day before. I said, 'Yes,' and he said: 'Do you know that Mrs. Sparling sent word to me that you fellows were there and told me to stick to the same story she told Boomhower?' He said that that was the first time in his life he had ever lost confidence in Mrs. Sparling."

Even more damaging to the defense was the testimony of Annie Pieruski, a domestic servant hired by Mrs. Sparling after her husband's death. Asked if Dr. MacGregor was in the habit of calling at the house at that time, she said he came quite often.

"When the doctor came, what did Mrs. Sparling do?"

"She went to the bedroom."

"What did the doctor do?"

"He went to the bedroom. They shut the door and stayed there for quite a while."

Under cross examination Piernski was asked if the doctor came to treat Mrs. Sparling medically, and she said she didn't know.

"Wasn't it true," the defense attorney asked, "that the doctor would go into the kitchen, roll up his sleeves, and wash his hands before going into the bedroom?"

"No, he would go right into the bedroom," the girl answered.

At the close of testimony, Dr. MacGregor was bound over to trial by jury in circuit court on a charge of murder in the first degree. Meanwhile, the bodies of John Wesley Sparling and Peter Sparling were disinterred and found to contain large quantities of strychnine. The laboratory technicians could find no trace of any other poison or disease and concluded that death in both cases had resulted from strychnine poisoning.

17

The trial of Dr. Robert MacGregor for the murder of Scyrel Sparling opened in Bad Axe on Monday, May 6, 1912. It lasted almost four weeks. Most of the witnesses called by the prosecution had testified at the inquest and the examination; their testimony here was virtually unchanged.

Among the new witnesses was an Ubly banker who was knowledgeable about Mrs. Sparling's financial affairs. He testified that when the man from whom MacGregor was renting his house refused to sell it to him, Mrs. Sparling bought the house for $1,800 and turned it over to the doctor. He said also that one of the $1,000 life insurance checks was endorsed over to the doctor by Mrs. Sparling, and he used it to buy an automobile. Later, the banker said, she gave MacGregor money for a vacation trip in the East and sent him more money during the trip.

Also damaging to the defense was the testimony of the Reverend Henry Bacon, who had been pastor of the church at Tyre from 1907 to 1909. During that time he had sometimes helped out in the fields on the Sparling farm. He was there during John Sparling's last illness, he said, and had helped take care of the sick man.

"Were you in the house with Mr. Sparling?" Bacon was asked.

"Yes, quite frequently."

"Did you see MacGregor go into any room beside the sick room?"

"I remember being there one day when the doctor came and went in and examined Mr. Sparling, and then he came out and went with Mrs. Sparling into a bedroom off the kitchen and shut the door. They were in there about twenty minutes."

The witness went on to say that after Mr. Sparling's death, MacGregor came at least once or twice a week.

"Who was sick at that time?"

"I don't know of anybody being sick then."

After the testimony of two doctors from the forensic laboratory in Ann Arbor — who declared unequivocally that both Scyrel and Albert Sparling died of arsenic poisoning and that they could find no trace of cancer or syphilis — the prosecution rested. It had a strong case; Prosecutor Boomhower had touched all the bases.

Among the first witnesses for the defense was the doctor's wife, Ida MacGregor. Her modesty and straightforwardness won general approval. It was clear from her testimony that if there was anything more than friendship between her husband and Mrs. Sparling, she knew nothing of it, and that she never for a moment doubted his innocence. She explained that she and her husband had been very close friends with the Sparlings; they visited together often and exchanged Christmas gifts.

Dr. MacGregor took the stand on Friday, May 24, and proved to be an excellent witness in his own defense. For five grueling days under direct questioning and cross examination he maintained a calm and dignified demeanor, speaking in soft undertones. Only once did the doctor lose his composure. When asked if there had been improper relations between himself and Mrs. Sparling, he shouted, "No, absolutely not!"

MacGregor denied some of the statements attributed to him by State witnesses, and admitted others. He chose his words with care. On several points, his interpretation of events and conversations differed from that of the prosecution.

He denied making some of the statements referred to by Sheriff MacAuley. He explained his remark about "looking in a mirror" by saying that he was referring not to himself but to the sheriff. He denied that he told Dr. Conboy he had "already scared the devil out of Mrs. Sparling"—at least he was sure he hadn't used those words.

As to his financial dealings with Mrs. Sparling, he said that all the money and property had been given to him in payment for medical services. He said there was nothing sinister about the insurance policies: Mr. Sparling and the boys had come to him for advice, and he had recommended his father's insurance company because it was the least expensive among several choices. In this he was merely acting as a friend of the family.

As to his private meetings with Mrs. Sparling, evil be to him who thinks evil. The meetings were entirely innocent, he said, having to do only with medical treatment for her eyes and discussions about the illness of other members of the family.

19

Altogether it was an impressive performance.

But the jury didn't buy it. On June 1, after only three hours of deliberation, the foreman announced a verdict of "guilty as charged for murder in the first degree."

The doctor took it calmly. There was no perceptible change of expression in his face. His wife, however, threw herself into his arms and wept. "Oh God, it can't be true that you are guilty!" she cried.

He kissed her and pulled away. "It's too late now," he said.

The Sparling case has become a classic in Michigan jurisprudence; it is often cited by lawyers in murder trials where poison is involved. If MacGregor was guilty, then he was one of the clumsiest of poison murderers. Not only did he fail to cover his tracks, but, after the Scyrel Sparling inquest, he dropped all kinds of clues pointing to his guilt. It was almost as if he had wanted to be caught.

Nevertheless, many people never ceased to believe in MacGregor's innocence. Among them was Michigan governor Woodbridge Ferris. He conducted an investigation of his own and — convinced that the doctor was innocent — granted him a full pardon in 1916. He also appointed him as prison physician at Jackson, a post MacGregor held until his death of typhoid fever in 1928. He was fifty-three.

Mrs. Sparling was never brought to trial. Boomhower explained later that he lacked sufficient evidence to get a conviction and that it would be difficult to convince a jury that any mother could participate in or even close her eyes to the deliberate poisoning of her own children.   .

But it is also difficult to believe that some inkling of what was happening had never crossed her mind.

THE MYSTERY OF THE MISSING NUN

The Lady Vanishes

The time: late autumn, 1918. The place: Isadore, a tiny hamlet in Michigan's Leelanau County. The scene: the basement of Holy Rosary Church.

(The basement is not a proper basement. Rather, it is the area between ground level and the floor of the church, no excavation having been dug. The church was built on a gentle slope and the basement is of varying height, in most places not more than five feet. The church rests on cedar posts, and the cellar area, about thirty by forty feet, is enclosed by wainscotting. A door opens to the west, at the rear of the building.)

Two men are digging by lantern light. They have been told that a body is buried here, and they are looking for it. One of them is Father Edward Podlaszewski, the parish priest; the other, Jacob Flees, the church sexton. Flees digs with a potato fork while the priest holds a flashlight. The lantern rests on the ground near the hole, its yellow light casting a huge moving shadow on the wall.

The potato fork strikes something solid. Flees casts it aside and drops to his knees. Digging with his hands, he unearths a long white bone: a human arm bone. He hands it to the priest, who places it in a small wooden box. Other bones follow. Finally, the skull comes to light; carefully the sexton hands it to the priest, who gently puts it in the box. Its cavernous eyes glare balefully in the yellow light. Soon the search is complete: a pile of dirty white bones and a skull, wads of rotted brown woolen cloth, a pair of woman's shoes.

The hole where the body was buried is surprisingly small: about three feet wide and three feet deep. It is apparent to both men that the body must have been jammed into the hole in a sitting position, the head resting on the knees.

Flees fills the hole and smooths it over. The two men depart, leaving the box of bones in the cellar. Two nights later, Flees will transfer the bones to a smaller box, which he has made for the purpose, and carry it to the church graveyard. There he will bury the bones at the foot of a big wooden cross that stands near the center of the cemetery.

By this clandestine action, the two men, though they do not know it, have set in motion a train of events that will lead to the arrest, trial, and conviction of a killer whose crime might otherwise have gone undetected forever.

The village of Isadore lies near the geographic center of Leelanau County in the northern part of lower Michigan. At no time, past or present, has it consisted of more than the church buildings and a few neighboring farm dwellings and outbuildings. The church stands on the summit of a smooth glacial hill. There are woods to the south and northwest; and, a mile to the west, a long, narrow swamp — actually a continuation of the great cedar swamp that lies at the foot of Lake Leelanau. Keep the swamp and its location in mind: it plays a role in our story.

Holy Rosary Church is the center of the community's social and spiritual life. From its eminence on the hill it watches over and inspires its people, most of whom are devoutly religious. It christens them at birth, receives them into its bosom at puberty, marries them when they wed, gives them spiritual sustenance during the course of their lives, and when they die, tucks them away in the grassy church graveyard to sleep peacefully until judgment day.

The parishioners are predominately Slavs — Polilsh and Bohemian farming folk. They came late to Leelanau County, in the last quarter of the nineteenth century, after much of the best land had been gobbled up by other ethnic groups — English, French, German, Scandinavian. For this reason they had to settle for a strip of land between Lake Leelanau and Lime Lake, bounded on the south by the great cedar swamp. Good farmers and husbandmen, they nonetheless prospered and raised big families. From Europe they also brought with them master skills in carpentry, stonecutting, masonry, and blacksmithing. All of the church buildings, past and present, were built by volunteer labor in the parish.

An unfriendly attitude on the part of some of their neighbors has made them draw closely together and helped to maintain their ethnic purity (to use President Jimmy Carter's unfortunate, but now forgotten, phrase). Most of the families are bilingual and the children grow up speaking both Polish and English.

In general, they are an earthy, hardworking, fun-loving people. They care for and help each other: to rebuild a house or barn destroyed by fire, to comfort the bereaved, to lend a helping hand to the needy.

To this close-knit, isolated, Roman Catholic farm community came Sister Mary Janina to teach in the convent school. She arrived at Isadore in the summer of 1906, wearing the brown habit of a Felician nun, a teaching order. Within a year she would play the principal role in a tragedy.

Orphaned at the age of nine by the death of her father and her mother's commitment to an insane asylum, Sister Janina (born Josephine Mezek) was taken in by the Felician sisters at the Mother Home in Detroit. She became a great favorite with the nuns there, who fawned over and coddled her. At eighteen she took her final vows and became a nun. For several years she taught at a parochial school in Detroit. But her health declined (she was slightly tubercular) and in 1906 the Mother Superior sent her to Isadore with the hope that the bracing northern Michigan climate would restore her to good health. She was thirty-two years old, not pretty, but warm and outgoing — and the people of Isadore took to her from the start.

The only physical description of her that survives is the one given to the authorities by the parish priest, Father Andrew Bieniawski, in 1907: "Medium stature, about five feet, five inches; delicate in appearance, olive complexion, brown eyes, mild and amenable disposition. Large pores about the nose; wears glasses; long, bony fingers."

At the time of her arrival at Isadore, the church "family" consisted of seven people: Father Bieniawski and his teenage sister, Susan; his Polish housekeeper, Stanislawa Lipczynska, and her young daughter Mary; two other nuns, Angelina and Josephine; and a chore boy named Gruba. The nuns had quarters above the convent school; the others lived at the rectory — except Gruba, who took his meals there but slept in the school basement.

The two girls, Susan and Mary, helped Mrs. Lipczynska with her housekeeping duties at the rectory. The housekeeper was a short, stocky woman of thirty-seven, who spoke little English. In addition to her housekeeping chores, she tended a large vegetable garden and looked after what Father Bieniawski called his "menagerie." It consisted of geese, guinea hens, pheasants, pigeons, ducks, a parrot, a badger, two rabbits, a horse, and a crocodile. The parrot and crocodile had quarters in the rectory; all the others were kept outside.

Father Bieniawski was a tall, powerful man of thirty-three, with a long, high-cheek-boned equine face, square jaw, and deep-set eyes that some people called "inscrutable" — some, indeed, thought he was partly oriental. He was a stern, humorless disciplinarian; some of his pupils complained that he boxed their ears until they rang. He was respected by all, feared by many, loved by a few.

Sister Mary Janina — or Mary Johns, as she was sometimes called — was a much more sociable person. She seemed happy and contented in the new environment and made many friends throughout the parish. She had a sweet singing voice, clear and strong, and was much in demand for church socials and family gatherings. She often sang at her work.

Although city born and bred, she had a great love of the outdoors. She took frequent walks in the nearby fields and woods, watching the birds and gathering wild flowers. She sometimes wandered far and was late in returning. On Friday, August 23, 1907, she disappeared.

In addition to being a lover of animals, Father Bieniawski was an avid fisherman. Winter or summer, it was unusual if he didn't manage to go fishing at least twice a week. He was fond of repeating a saying he said he'd read somewhere: "God does not subtract the time I spend fishing from my allotted time on earth."

On Friday afternoon, August 23, 1907, Father Bieniawski, together with his sister and Gruba, went fishing on Lake Leelanau, then called Carp Lake. In a horse-drawn wagon they left the parish about an hour past noon. The three sisters and the housekeeper and her daughter stood near the school and waved goodbye as they drove off down the hill. The lake was about four miles to the east, a leisurely half hour's drive.

It was the custom of all three nuns to nap in the afternoon during school vacation; Angelina and Josephine were tubercular, too. After seeing the fishing party off, they retired to their separate rooms over the school, drawing the curtains. The housekeeper and her daughter returned to the rectory, which stood some 150 feet west of the church. Mary was making a blouse for herself. Her mother helped with the fitting and then went off to other duties.

Sister Mary Johns had been busy that morning. She was making preparations for a visit from the head of the diocese, Bishop Richter of Grand Rapids. He was soon to come and bless the new school, which had been completed that summer. (The old school had burned down two years before). She hadn't yet gotten around to decorating the school with some artificial flowers that were stored in boxes under the church.

At about three-thirty that afternoon the two nuns awoke from their naps. They discovered that Sister Janina was already up and gone. They thought she might have gone for a walk and were not unduly alarmed — until they found that the back door of the school was ajar; that wasn't right, it was always kept locked.

25

It wasn't like Janina to be careless about such things. Her prayer book lay open on a windowsill near the door, as if she'd put it down there to answer a summons. The two nuns walked over to the rectory and asked Mrs. Lipczynska and her daughter if they'd seen Janina.

Not since just after noon, they were told.

"Maybe Nigger got her," one of the nuns suggested.

The other women smiled; they understood the joke. "Nigger" was the name of a small, black, stray dog that hung around the church grounds, looking for handouts.

Together, the women began a search of the church buildings and premises. It was possible, they thought, that Janina had fainted and was lying helpless somewhere. Or perhaps she'd become deranged, like her mother, and wandered off. It wasn't like Janina to leave the premises without telling somebody where she was going.

They were still searching when the fishing party returned shortly after dark. By that time it was clear that something was wrong. The priest was angry. He scolded the women for not having roused the neighborhood. Then, by lantern light, he led a search, peering into every nook and cranny, behind every church pew. They also looked under the school and the church. The church cellar was littered with scraps of lumber, seldom-used tools, and broken furniture. In one corner there was a pile of lumber, left over from the construction of the new school. The cardboard boxes containing the artificial flowers were piled near the door, seemingly untouched. There was no trace of Janina. It was after midnight when they broke off the search.

It continued early the next day. Word had gotten around about the missing sister and people began to come in from all around, their numbers increasing as the day wore on. Search parties tramped the woods and fields a mile or so around the church and found nothing. The priest notified Deputy Sheriff John Nolan in Cedar and requested his help. Nolan promised to look into it but didn't show up until Monday morning.

After the short mass on Sunday, Father Bieniawski left on the train for Detroit. He wanted to talk personally with Sister Janina's superiors at the Felician Mother House. He thought it was possible that Janina had confided in one of them — perhaps she wanted to leave her vocation.

But Mother Superior Antonina in Detroit could shed no light on the matter. She had heard nothing unusual from Janina and doubted that the young nun would take such a drastic step. There was nothing to indicate that she was dissatisfied or unhappy at Isadore. She was as surprised at Janina's disappearance as anyone.

Before leaving Detroit, Father Bieniawski hired private detective J. R. Castle to assist in the search. They returned to Isadore together on the train.

Deputy John Nolan was waiting at the rectory when the two men arrived late Monday afternoon. Nolan was annoyed that the priest had hired outside help. It was an affront to the local authorities, he said. He left in a huff, and Castle took charge of the investigation. He organized groups of volunteers in a systematic search of the whole township.

There was plenty of tips. It seemed that almost everyone had a pet theory. A reporter for the Traverse City *Record Eagle* got completely carried away, writing:

SISTER MARY DISAPPEARED

It may be that as Sister Mary walked the halls of the convent, prayer book in hand and with her heart open in supplication for humanity, the sound of a knock echoed through the building from the rear door . . .

Closing her book, she probably quickened her step toward the rear of the building, drew a key from her garments, fitted it in the hole, with visions of a call from some dying brother or sister, or some hungry wayfarer at the door . . .

As the door swung open, there are a hundred things that might have confronted her. It might have been a lover of her younger days . . . They might have quarreled and she, heartbroken, might have turned to the church, where she found comfort in the truest sense.

He may have regretted, found that the fire still burned in his bosom, might have found her whereabouts after years of search and, maddened at his loss, come into Northern Michigan and, taking a desperate chance, kidnapped the woman of his heart . . .

There was more of this, equally overblown and absurd. Father Bieniawski angrily scouted all such speculation that the nun had "run off" or been abducted.

"Sister Mary would no more take off her habit than I would remove my cassock," he said.

On August 30, a week after the nun's disappearance, Father Bieniawski discharged Detective Castle and turned the investigation over to the County Sheriff Martin Brown and his men. Castle's efforts, though strenuous, had been unproductive: he had turned up nothing in the way of a solid clue.

Father Bieniawski's efforts had been equally strenuous. Every day he had tramped the woods and fields with the searching parties, driving himself almost to the point of exhaustion, with little food and sleep. He said he would not rest until Sister Janina had been found, alive or dead.

Saturday morning brought an unexpected development. Sisters Angelina and Josephine packed their bags and left on a train for Manistee. They were frightened.

"What happened to Janina might happen to us," they said. And nothing that Father Bieniawski could say would change their minds.

That evening a small party of men from Traverse City arrived in Isadore to help in the search. With them came Antrim County Sheriff William Kittle and his famous tracking dog, Tom. The sheriff and his bloodhound had been successful in many criminal investigations around the state.

Father Bieniawski welcomed the newcomers. He led them in a search at the convent for something of Janina's that would give the dog her scent. By the light of a flickering candle, Kittle pried open her trunk. It was filled with books and other things that obviously hadn't been handled in months. A box of clothing in her closet was likewise disappointing: everything had been washed recently and neatly folded away. That left the prayer book and a crucifix found in her room.

At five o'clock the next morning the party reassembled. The dog

28

was taken to the nun's room and given the prayer book and the crucifix to smell. Immediately giving tongue, Tom raced downstairs and out the back door. Then, after circling about on the church grounds the dog made a beeline westward through a field of corn and into the woods beyond.

Sheriff Kittle and the search party raced behind, across fields, over fences, through woods and swamp. They could hear the hound's deep, rolling bay as it followed the trail. But then the sound petered out as the dog seemed to lose the scent.

Meanwhile, Pete Bowse, one of the Traverse City men, had been making a search on his own. Deep in the swamp to the west he had found fresh prints of what appeared to be a woman's shoe. The tracks wandered in a curious, aberrant way. He also found other, similar tracks that appeared to be several days old.

The fresh tracks led to a small pool of water where the grass was crushed along the edge in one place as if someone had knelt there to drink. From there the tracks led to the area under a fallen tree only three feet above the ground. They continued along the edge of the swamp — and always in the swamp, although a few paces to the east would have led to dry footing. Comparing the footprints with his own, Bowse concluded that they must have been made by a woman weighing about one hundred pounds.

He found Kittle, who had meanwhile caught up with Tom, and led them to the spot. But the dog paid no attention to the tracks and took off for the woods to the east, baying disconsolately. Presently, however, he broke into full cry, and the sheriff was encouraged. This was the place, he said excitedly, that he had heard a woman's voice earlier that morning: under the necessity of following the dog, he hadn't been able to investigate. The party followed Tom for another half hour. This, however, led to nothing, and the bedraggled men returned to the rectory for breakfast.

That morning, a Sunday, Father Bieniawski cut short his church services and appealed to the congregation for help in the search. Almost 250 people joined in — men, women and children. Deputy Sheriff Nolan organized them into two parties. One swept through the cornfield and the woods to the west, then turned north. The other went south. They walked twenty feet apart, while the leaders raced up and down the line, keeping them in approximate formation. They advanced uphill and down, across fields, swamp and thickets, poking into every possible place of concealment in the hope of finding at least some sign of the missing nun.

Around noon they began coming back, boys with their fathers, old men leaning on canes, women in mud-stained dresses. All were tired and downhearted. No trace had been found of Janina.

Meanwhile, Sheriff Kittle and his party had been making another run with the bloodhound. The dog had been running loose for an hour or more in silence. But now they heard his long, rolling howl, punctuated by a series of sharp yelps that seemed to indicate a fresh trail.

"Circling!" his owner cried. "Come on, boys. He's after her."

They ran toward the sound, crossing a stand of timber where the hound had first been working. The woods were bounded on the south by a barbed wire fence and an east-west road. One of the men found tracks on the south side of the road. Another, working along the fence, found a bit of brown wool hanging from one of the barbs.

They found more tracks in a stretch of swamp. Following these, they came upon the dog, lying stretched out on the ground with his tongue hanging out. Sheriff Kittle ventured the opinion that the dog had found the woman and thought his work was done. Others were skeptical. Tom was persuaded to make another run. The men and the dog made another five-mile circle before quitting for the day.

Tom was put to work again on Monday morning. Twice he was taken to the nun's room, and twice more he jerked his master through the back door of the school and out across the fields, only to lose the scent and run in circles.

"The trail's getting too old now, boys," the sheriff said. "He's just confused by the faint scent."

That day several people had noticed a terrible odor coming from a certain part of the swamp. Everybody was relieved when the source was found, late that afternoon: the dead and badly decomposed body of a woodchuck.

That evening Sheriff Kittle returned home to Bellaire after collecting a fee of twenty-five dollars from Father Bieniawski for the use of the dog.

The search was resumed on Tuesday under the direction of Sheriff Martin Brown. The authorities were now convinced that the missing nun would be found somewhere within a three-mile radius of the church, but hope was fading that she would be found alive.

That day, however, a farmer who lived near the swamp reported a strange occurrence. Late at night he'd heard a woman singing somewhere in the swamp. From his window he had also seen a flickering light moving slowly among the cedar trees. His story lent credence to the possibility that the nun was still alive, wandering about the swamp.

Sentries were posted that night on the roads bordering the swamp. Next morning a party of five reported to the sheriff that they too had heard a woman singing. They said the song had "floated on the night air," from somewhere back in the deep part of the swamp.

Meanwhile, the rumors were abounding

—that Sister Janina had run off with a man;

—that she had been abducted by a passion-crazed lover;

—that she had been seen boarding the train at Solon (a whistle-stop on the railroad three miles south of Cedar), wearing civilian clothing;

—that her body had been found in the church belfry;

—that she had gone to live with her brothers in Chicago.

Father Bieniawski wrote to her brothers. They replied that they hadn't seen their sister in years, not since she had entered the convent and become a nun. They offered to come and help in the search, but neither of them ever showed up.

At about this same time another letter was received from Chicago. It was addressed to the Mother Superior at Isadore (Isadore had no Mother Superior; Janina was Sister Superior). It was postmarked September 12 and bore no return address. It read as follows:

"Sister Mary who disappeared from the Convent was not abducted or murdered. She was simply tired of her job and slipped quietly away, knowing that this was the only method which could be successful. You were foolish to have raised all this hue and cry. It was a mistake which I presume you now realize, and so, for appearance's sake, gave out to the public that she was abducted. Nonsense. Let her alone. Giver her a chance. You probably won't hear from her and she won't want that you should."

The letter was signed, "A Protestant Pup." Father Bieniawski turned it over to the authorities.

Abduction was in the minds of two other people who entered the case in a bizarre way. They were Charles Norris of Traverse City and Otto Sorensen of Kingsley; both were well-known clairvoyants. They offered their services, but Father Bieniawski rejected them angrily, saying that he would forbid any such nonsense.

Nevertheless, Sorensen went into a trance and proclaimed that the missing nun was being held captive in the basement of a house near Glen Lake. He described the house as "squarish and standing on a hill." He said three men were implicated in the plot, and that one of them, a swarthy man with a bushy black beard, could be seen pacing up and down the road near the house, on the lookout for police.

There were dozens of places at Glen Lake that fit this description, but the police were now reduced to grasping at straws. Deputy Sheriff Mike Horn of Empire led a small party to Glen Lake. They found a house that seemed to best fit Sorensen's description and made a thorough search of it despite the vehement protests of its two occupants. They were the cook and chore boy in the summer residence of a Chicago man named Burke. Needless to say, no trace of Sister Janina was found there.

The blessing of the new church school by Bishop Richter took place on Sunday, September 8. A crowd of some 350 people gathered, more out of curiosity over Janina's disappearance than for the ceremonies. After the services Father Bieniawski offered a reward of $250 to anyone who found the nun or her body. Search parties were organized, but before they could set out, a torrential rain began to fall, and the operation was postponed until the next day.

Rain fell heavily on Monday, too. Sisters Angelina and Josephine unexpectedly came back from Manistee that morning. They were on hand to open school and resume classes. They gave no explanation, but presumably they'd been able to overcome their fear.

Rain spoiled the search on Tuesday, too; only a few hardy souls turned out. By this time, all hope of finding the nun alive had been abandoned. Sheriff Brown and Father Bieniawski would continue their efforts, tramping the woods and fields until heavy snow put an end to the search. Over the years they would continue to investigate every rumor, run down every possible lead; and the priest would continue to write letters to every possible source of information about the nun — all to no avail.

And so the years rolled by, and the case of the missing Isadore nun remained an unsolved mystery. Nothing was heard from her or about her. It was as if she had vanished into thin air.

Two months after her disappearance, a pair of glasses was found under the church, just a few feet inside the cellar door. Rimless and with steel bows, they were of the same particular type worn by Felician nuns. How they came to be overlooked during the first few days of the search, when half a dozen people poked about under there, has never been explained.

In October of 1910, the housekeeper's daughter Mary, and Joseph Flees, brother of the sexton, were married. Father Bieniawski officiated, and the couple went to make their home in a little town near Milwaukee. In 1913, Bieniawski was transferred to a church in Manistee, St. Joseph's parish. Mrs. Lipczynska accompanied him and stayed long enough to help get him settled in the rectory and to find a replacement. Then she went to live with her daughter near Milwaukee.

Murder Will Out

Father Bieniawski corresponded with Stella Lipczynska on a regular basis, and in 1915 he asked her to return and keep house for him. She took a ferry from Milwaukee to Frankfort and the priest picked her up in his automobile there. It had been eight years since Sister Janina had disappeared.

33

A priest by the name of Leopold Oprychalski had replaced Father Bieniawski at Holy Rosary Church in Isadore. Oprychalski's tenure as pastor there is notable for two things. First, he made plans to build a new church on the same site as the old wooden building that had been built in 1883 and was now becoming dilapidated. Second, as he was leaving for another parish early in 1918, he told his replacement that he was afraid there would be a scandal in the church because the bones of the missing nun were buried in the church cellar.

His replacement was Father Edward Podlaszewski, an ambitious man whose goal it was to carry out Oprychalski's plan to build a new church. He was a good-looking young man of medium height, slender, with dark Slavic features. His sermons in Polish were given in nervous bursts as he fidgeted behind the pulpit. He was much admired by the women of the community.

Podlaszewski was shaken by Oprychalski's warning. Bones in the basement? He pressed the older man for more information, but the priest had little to offer. He'd gotten his information from Sister Mary Antonina of the Felician House in Detroit, he said. Where she had learned it he didn't know, but it seemed to be common knowledge among the Polish sisters. Podlaszewski didn't know whether to believe the story of not. Perhaps it was just another rumor. Unable to decide what to believe, he did nothing.

But then he got a second warning. In May or June of 1918, he attended a religious gathering known as the Forty Hours Devotional. It was held in Grand Rapids and was attended by priests from all over Michigan. At the meeting he was approached by Father Lempka, who served as chaplain of the Felician Order in Detroit. Lempka questioned the young priest about his plans to build a new church at Isadore. Podlaszewski told him that the old church would be torn down and the new one built on the same spot.

Father Lempka then told him, "I heard from Bishop Kozlowski in Milwaukee that Sister Mary John, who disappeared in Isadore some years ago, was buried under the church." He said he didn't know how the bishop had gotten this information, but he understood that the body had been buried under a pile of lumber in the church cellar.

The Chaplain suggested that Father Podlaszewski secretly move the bones before the old church was torn down. Otherwise, they would surely be discovered when the new foundation was being dug.

The Chaplain said, "I'm not positive of this, but the information I received is that she was buried there by Mrs. Lipczynska."

The two priests discussed the best method of removing the bones. Lempka advised Podlaszewski to do it himself and to move the bones to the church cemetery.

Father Podlaszewski returned to Isadore more perplexed than ever. It was his nature to let things slide. Besides, he had other, more urgent things to worry about, things of a personal nature. So it was several months before he roused himself to action. Then, after swearing Jacob Flees to secrecy, the two men found the grave, dug up the bones, and reburied them in the cemetery, as has already been related.

On the day after the discovery, before the bones were moved, Father Podlaszewski took two other people into his confidence. Among the objects found in the shallow grave was a knotted robe cord. He took the cord and showed it to the two nun teachers in the parish, Sister Mary Gastold and Sister Mary Hilaria. They identified it as being of the same type as those worn by Felician nuns.

The young priest then took them to the church cellar and showed them the remains. They were satisfied that what they saw in the wooden box was all that remained of Sister Janina. They sent a letter to Mother Superior Antonina in Detroit, telling her what they had seen. Henceforth, they would include Sister Janina in their prayers for the dead. Podlaszewski told them of his plan to move the bones to the church cemetery; they said they hoped that Janina would thus be laid to rest forever.

The bones remained in the cellar until the following night. Then Flees buried them at the foot of the big wooden cross in the cemetery. He buried the box without a cover because a cover would rot in time and cave in, causing the ground above it to sink and reveal the grave. As church sexton, Jacob Flees knew about things like that. Several days later he covered the fresh grave with several wheelbarrow loads of black dirt. Later he planted flowers and shrubs to cover the bare ground.

It does not seem to have occurred to any of these people that, technically at least, they were committing a crime: obstruction of justice and compounding a felony. Perhaps, if they gave it any thought at all, they contented themselves in the belief that the church could keep its secrets.

The duties of a backwater parish priest are rigorous and often lonely, and hard work doesn't always fill the void. Successful priests find their salvation in God. Those not so successful may try to find it in liquor, still others in women. Father Podlaszewski tried the first, skipped the second, but succumbed to the third.

Soon after his arrival in Isadore he got involved in a love affair with a nineteen-year-old farmer's daughter whom he had hired as housekeeper. In the summer of 1918 he found himself an expectant father.

The girl's parents came to see him in late August. In their shame and dilemma they sought help from the only source they knew, their church. The young priest listened to their story of a daughter who refused to reveal the name of her baby's father. He offered to drive the girl to a hospital in Ann Arbor, arrange for the adoption of the baby, and to bring her home after it was born. The parents eagerly took him up on this, thinking perhaps the whole affair could be hushed up. Accordingly, in December of 1918, the priest drove the girl to Ann Arbor and left her at the hospital to have her baby. In January he returned and drove her home, the baby having been put up for adoption. For some strange reason—perhaps because he wanted to share the burden of his awful secret with someone he loved—he told her the story of the bones. (It was said later that Podlaszewski threatened the girl, and told her that if she revealed the secret, "what happened to Janina might happen to you." But this is nonsense. There is every reason to believe that the two were deeply in love.)

Some time in late January or February, the girl broke down under her parents' persistent questioning and confessed to them that Podlaszewski was the father of her child. She also told them about the bones found in the church cellar.

The parents went immediately to the church board. They denounced the priest, and Father Podlaszewski was dismissed. He was called to Detroit to stand trial before a church tribunal.

Many of his parishioners were sorry to see him go, for the gentle young man was loved by many of his people. He departed on the morning train from Cedar. A small group of people, mostly women, gathered at the station to see him off.

"He left us with tears streaming down his face," said a Cedar housewife. "He was crying unashamedly when he bade us goodbye. He asked us not to blame the girl, whom he truly loved. He said all fault in connection with their intimacy justly rested on his shoulders."

Others were not so charitable. Their attitude was summed up by one parishioner, who said, "If priests are going to practice here just what the church teaches us not to do, then the church is no good to our community."

A few went so far as to leave the church and vow never to attend services again. One man, indeed, kept that vow until the day of his death, then recanted on his deathbed and received extreme unction.

Meanwhile, the girl's father had gone to Sheriff John Kinnucan and told him the story of the bones. The sheriff immediately contacted Martin Brown, now a county judge of probate, and together they went to have a talk with Jacob Flees.

Flees readily admitted his part in the cover-up. He led the two officers to the cellar of the church and pointed to the spot where he had found the bones. Then he took them to the cemetery and showed them where the wooden box lay buried.

That night he told his wife, "The stone is off my head now."

The bones were dug up, taken to Leland and locked in a jail cell. The authorities wanted to make sure that Sister Janina wouldn't get lost again.

On Sunday, February 24, 1919, Sheriff Kinnucan took the train to Detroit for an interview with Father Podlaszewski. He and Judge Brown believed that the priest might have received a written communication from someone in the church hierarchy about the

37

burial in the church cellar. Such a letter, if it existed, would be all they'd need to break the case wide open.

Kinnucan found the young priest at St. Bonaventure Monastery awaiting his church trial. Podlaszewski was extremely nervous and upset. He told the sheriff that his information had come from a conversation with Father Lempka, who in turn had heard it from Bishop Kozlowski of Milwaukee.

He also said that one of the Felician sisters had told him of a dream she'd had. In the dream she saw the body of Sister Johns laying in a trench, then two men came and took the body and buried it in the church cemetery. This was before he and Flees had found the grave. He said he had procrastinated about hunting for the remains because he believed it to be a matter for the Felician order to investigate.

Next day, Kinnucan caught an early train and joined Martin Brown in Manistee. Brown had warrants for the arrest of Father Bieniawski and his housekeeper, Stella Lipczynska.

They found them both at the rectory of St. Joseph parish in Manistee. The two officers proceeded to question them separately. The priest was permitted to remain at the rectory, but Mrs. Lipczynska was taken to the County Home, where she was questioned with the aid of an interpreter, since she spoke little English.

Neither the priest nor the housekeeper was served with a warrant of arrest—the officers wanted to try to get a confession first. But it wasn't long before they realized that no confession would be obtained from either of them.

That afternoon a Manistee newspaper reporter interviewed Father Bieniawski.

Bieniwski said: "I do not believe that the body found under the church is that of Janina. She wore a heavy brown woolen dress. The goods would not have decayed in eleven years, to any extent. I have no idea of whose body it is."

He added that Sister Janina had no enemies he knew of. "She and my housekeeper were on good terms," he said.

"I want this murder solved," he declared. "I will go anywhere the officers want me to go to help solve it. I will spend all the money I have to solve it. I have suffered untold torture since this started. It must be settled."

He was determined, he said, "that the poor woman should not be put in jail to await trial," and that he would put up her bail with liberty bonds out of his own personal savings.

"And if that is not enough," he told the reporter, bringing out a small black money chest, "here is $500 more in gold. They may take it if they need it. She must not be put in jail."

Meanwhile, at the County Home, Mrs. Lipczynska steadfastly declared her innocence. She knew nothing about the nun's disappearance except what she had observed at the time. It was all so long ago. Why did they bother her with it? She had nothing to do with it.

Nevertheless, she was served with the warrant and placed under arrest. Kinnucan and Brown were convinced that she knew a lot more than she was telling.

The priest was not arrested. It was becoming clear to the officers that he had nothing to do with the murder. Nevertheless, the next day he went along with them and the prisoner on the train to Traverse City. He was needed as a material witness; he also wanted to help his housekeeper as much as he could.

Upon arriving in Traverse City, the party checked into the Park Place Hotel. That afternoon, Mrs. Lipczynska was interviewed by a local reporter. She seemed eager to talk. With many apologies for her broken English, she told the following story:

"I first knew the Sister was lost about six o'clock that day. Sister Angelina and Josephine came to the priest's house and said, 'Sister Mary Janina is lost. I guess nigger got her.'

"I last saw Mary Janina about twelve o'clock that day," she continued. "She was walking in the garden with a paper or something in her hand. When the two sisters came at six o'clock they asked me if I thought she might have gone picking apples by Mrs. Peplinski."

She said she went over to Mrs. Peplinski's and also to Mrs. Gatzke's, but saw nothing of Janina. She said the nuns came to the priest's house at eight o'clock. "It is so dark and lonely in the schoolhouse we can't stay there," they said.

After the return of the fishing party, they all went over to the schoolhouse and hunted, she said. The looked under every seat, behind every door. "We hunted through the basement. There wasn't a spot we didn't look into. We thought maybe she had fainted again, and died. She got sick like that sometimes."

"Did you look under the church?" the reporter asked.

"Yes, yes. We looked all over, everywhere under the church. Sister Angelina looked under the church before that."

Mrs. Lipczynska lapsed into silence, her face quivering. Then she burst out: "It was all so long ago. How can I remember all that happened? Why do they say I did it? Missis, I don't know anything about it. I think it was a tramp who did it."

Tears came to her eyes and her hands worked convulsively. "I don't know who did this," she said. "I tell you, I don't know. Sister Angelina got a vacation after that, I think in September, and went to Detroit. We heard later that both sisters had died of consumption."

Mrs. Lipczynska was described by the reporter as being a very little woman, barely five feet, two inches tall, and weighing less than 100 pounds. Her hair was thin and brown, and she had brown eyes.

That same evening she was arraigned before Justice of Peace Charles Burroughs at Greilickville, a village on Grand Traverse Bay just north of Traverse City. In the presence of her attorneys Howard L. Campbell and Thomas Smurthwaite, both of Manistee, she stood mute. Her examination was scheduled for Tuesday, March 11. Bail was set at $5,000, and she was taken to the jail at Leland, since Father Bieniawski was unable to raise that much money.

The Catholic Church, through its spokesman, bishop's administrator LeFebvre of Cadillac, pledged its full support in aiding the investigation, LeFebvre said that no effort would be spared to help solve the mystery of Sister Janina. But the police were disappointed to learn from him that Bishop Edward Kozlowski had died in Milwaukee on August 15, 1915.

February 25, the day after the arraignment, brought two interesting developments. The first was a letter addressed to the Traverse City Chief of Police, John Bracken. It read as follows:

40

Chicago, Feb. 24

Dear Sir:

We, Frank and Emil Mezek, brothers of Sister Mary Johns, who was Josephine Mezek before she entered the convent, are ready to assist you and any of the authorities in any way possible to bring light on the story.

Josephine has never been in Chicago, to our knowledge, and she never even visited in our homes before she entered the convent.

We have letters of A. Bieniawski which were received during the search for her, after her disappearance, and some a year or so later from Sister M. Nepomucene which may be of interest to you.

(signed)
Frank Mezek, 727 Stewart Ave.
and Emil Mezek, 911 W 88th
Pl., Chicago, Illinois

The second development was that Sheriff Kinnucan had gone to Milwaukee to question Mrs. Mary Flees, the housekeeper's daughter, and to consult with church authorities there. He planned afterward to go on to Chicago and call on the Mezek brothers.

Meanwhile, Judge Martin Brown had instituted a thorough search of the church cellar. A crew of men was sifting great quantities of soil in search of more bones, articles of clothing, and anything else that might throw light upon the mystery.

Brown announced the results on Friday, February 28. Along with several small bones—not yet identified—the men had turned up two small iron crucifixes, a ring, a thimble of curious design, a scapular and other pieces of cloth. Brown was particularly interested in the thimble. It was made of silver and steel, and it had a combination of sunsets and other symbols engraved on it. It might have been a gift to Sister Janina, Brown thought, and thus might help in a positive identification of the remains.

Also found was a spool of red thread wrapped up in a piece of Traverse City newspaper. The paper was dated shortly before the nun's disappearance and was stained bright red.

41

Jacob Flees, who had helped in the search, told reporters there was evidence that someone else had been digging in that area beneath the church since he and Podlaszewski had opened the grave. He said the hole was enlarged and the ground around it disturbed. He was in charge of the keys to the basement, he said, and no one was allowed to enter unless he was there. It looked as though someone must have a duplicate key.

Meanwhile, the police received a report from Detroit that seemed to cast suspicion on Father Bieniawski. Authorities there had interviewed a man named Victor Berkowski, who said he'd lived at the rectory as a ward of Father Bieniawski about a year and a half before the nun disappeared. He had stayed there for two months.

He said that at age 18 he'd come to the parish from Wisconsin, to be "orphaned out" by the priest. A farmer named Jake Mikowski had taken him in for about a month but had refused to let him attend school so the priest had taken him back and let him stay at the rectory.

"I was in Sister Janina's class during the time I went to school in Isadore," he said. "She always treated us well and we liked her. Father Bieniawski would talk to her at recess and after school and pay all his attention to her."

Berkowski said that Bieniawski would go over to the school and visit on some evenings. "I do not know whether he saw her then or not. The chore boy, Gruba, said he saw the priest kiss the sister. He told me she was playing piano when the priest came up behind her, put his hands over her eyes and kissed her."

Berkowski said he didn't know much about Lipczynska, the housekeeper. "She was a good cook. She would whistle for Gruba when she wanted him and Gruba would come running.

"But we hated the priest," Berkowski said. "One day, when I was living with another farmer, Stanislaw Zentek, he boxed my ears until they rang. That was because I wouldn't come two and a half miles to eight o'clock mass. When I went home I thought a hundred alarm clocks were ringing inside my head.

"Another time," Berkowski went on, "because one of the boys missed confession, he hit him about the head and beat him unmercifully . . . He had a terrible temper."

42

This was the first time anyone had suggested there might have been intimacies between the priest and the nun. But the police were inclined to discount the story, because it was second hand and because of Berkowski's strong feelings about the priest.

Father Bieniawski had returned to Manistee after the arraignment. A few days later, in the presence of the defense attorneys, Judge Martin Brown and newspaper reporters, he issued a strong statement. He charged that he had been framed.

"I do not want to accuse anyone specifically," he said. "But I believe that if the body found under my former church in Isadore is proven to be that of Sister Janina, it was placed there after her disappearance."

The defense attorneys, Campbell, Smurthwaite and P. T. Glassmire, all of Manistee, refused to elaborate, but said that an enemy of Father Bieniawski—whose name would be disclosed at the examination—would be blamed for the death of Sister Janina. Suspicion had been deliberately and intentionally cast upon the priest and his housekeeper, Campbell said.

A newspaper reporter described Father Bieniawski as a striking figure. "He is a man of magnificent physique, but he is not handsome. His dark eyes are small and inscrutable; his nose is flat at the bridge and slightly tipped at the end; his cheekbones high, his mouth large, his jaws square. He speaks rapidly but weighs his words well."

At this same meeting, Judge Brown produced a letter he said had been forwarded to him by Sheriff Kinnucan from Milwaukee. It was written by Mrs. Mary Flees and was addressed to her mother, Stella Lipczynska. A part of it read as follows:

> "As you have taught me to love Christ and tell the truth, so you must tell the truth about the death of Sister Janina, if you know it, and take your punishment on this earth instead of hereafter."

Attorney Glassmire accused the sheriff of a cheap trick. It was apparent to him, he said, that Kinnucan had told the daughter that her mother had made some kind of confession, and that she wrote the letter accordingly.

The examination of Stanislawa Lipczynska opened on March 28 at Leland before Justice W. C. Nelson. It had been moved to Leland, the county seat, because Justice Burroughs, since his election as Justice of the Peace, had been elected township treasurer; it was illegal to hold both offices.

The prosecution was represented by County Prosecutor C. L. Dayton and Parmius C. Gilbert, both of Traverse City; the defense by Campbell and Glassmire.

First to be called to the witness stand was Father Bieniawski. He described the events before and after Sister Janina's disappearance. Under cross examination by the defense, however, he introduced something new.

Asked when he first heard about the body under the church, he said it was in October of 1918. He was approached at that time by Bishop L. P. Krakowski of Saginaw. He said he was surprised by Krakowski's visit because he and the bishop were not on speaking terms; there was bad blood between them. He said he was downtown when the bishop called at his rectory in Manistee. Mrs. Lipcyznska told him about it when he returned.

"I wonder what he wants?" he asked her.

"I don't know," the housekeeper said. "But if you hurry you can catch him at the railroad station. He is taking the train to Isadore."

Bieniawski said he went down to the Manistee & Northeastern station and found the bishop waiting there for his train.

"He said to me, 'What are you going to do about the bones under the church?' " Bieniawski testified. "And I said, 'What bones?' and he says, 'Sister John's.' "

"I looked at him scornfully," Bieniaswki said, "and I sized him up and called him some names I would not care to repeat, and I told him to notify the officers, and that he should not judge me by himself."

"What did you make of his story?" Glassmire asked.

"I didn't believe it. I thought he was trying to provoke me. There was bad blood between us. It was an old quarrel we had."

44

"You did not believe the story?"

"No, sir."

"And you did nothing about it?"

"Nothing. I thought he was merely trying to provoke me."

Sister Mary Antonina, Mother Superior at the Felician House in Detroit, followed Bieniaswki to the stand. She said she first heard the story of the bones from Sister Mary Veronica of Milwaukee.

"She came to Detroit and told me the story," Antonina said. "She told me that Bishop Kozlowski told her. She said that the bishop didn't tell her who killed the nun, but Veronica understood she was killed in the basement of the church by a woman."

Sister Antonina also told about a trip to Isadore she'd made in 1917 in company with another Detroit nun. Together they had made a search of the church cellar but found no sign of a grave. Of the two nuns who were at Isadore when Janina disappeared, she said that Angelina died on October 16, 1914, and that she believed Josephine was dead also.

Testimony was taken from Mrs. Mary Gatzke, who in 1907 had lived across the road from the church. She said that on the day of the nun's disappearance, the housekeeper ran into her house and said that Sister Mary had gone away.

"She carried on," Mrs. Gatzke testified. "She said they would not spread the alarm until Father Bieniawski returned. She came on many occasions later and called Sister Mary vile names.

"She intimated to me," Mrs. Gatzke said, "that she was mad because when the priest brought fruit and so forth, he always gave it to the sisters. She told me that Sister Janina was no sister—that she ran away with some man. When she talked of Janina she appeared angry and would strike the air with her fists."

Next day, a Saturday, testimony was taken from the three doctors who had performed an autopsy on the remains.

Dr. G. W. Fralick said he frequently attended Janina for her illness. He said that in his examination of the skeleton he found a fracture of the skull, about one inch long. The fracture had severed an artery between the membrane and the skull, an injury that could cause death if not attended to. The fracture would certainly have rendered the victim unconscious, he said.

Drs. J. F. Slepica and E. R. Flood agreed with Fralick's findings. Flood said he had assembled the bones to determine the height of the victim, and would judge that to be between 62 and 65 inches. All were agreed that the bones were those of the woman.

The next witness, Jacob Flees, told how he and Podlaszewski had searched the church cellar and found the grave.

"What did Father Podlaszewski tell you in regard to where to find the body?" Dayton asked.

"He said he heard it was put under a lumber pile."

"What did you do?"

"I took a shovel and searched for it, and found it."

"Did you know of there being a lumber pile under the church?"

"Yes. I recollect a lumber pile being there . . . but there was no lumber pile when I searched."

"You knew where the pile was?"

"Yes, sir."

"And you dug there?"

"Yes, sir."

"What did you find?"

"I found the corpse of a person."

Flees said it took him only a few minutes to locate the grave. He found a soft spot in the northwest corner, about sixteen feet from the door, where he remembered the lumber pile had been. He dug there and found the grave. He said he and the priest entered the cellar after dark to dig up the bones. The grave was about three feet wide and three feet deep, as he remembered, and the uppermost part of the body was about eighteen inches below the surface.

After a postponement until April 10, when little new evidence was presented, Justice Nelson handed down his ruling. He said there was sufficient evidence to warrant a charge of murder, and he bound Mrs. Lipczynska over to the July term of circuit court. Because of the nature of the charge, bail was denied, and Mrs. Lipczynska was taken to the little county jail at Leland to await trial.

A reporter wrote that she looked haggard and wan as the matron led her away. Father Bieniawski hurried over and took her hands, murmuring words of comfort and encouragement.

Circuit court was scheduled to open on July 10, but shortly after the first of May, the case took a bizarre turn: the prisoner seemed to have lost her mind. She had been seen rolling about on the floor of her cell, uttering strange animal-like sounds. She was refusing all food, and had to be fed forcibly through a stomach tube.

A special hearing was called. After reviewing the condition of the prisoner, Judge Frederick W. Mayne ordered a postponement of the trial, and the accused was taken to the state psychopathic hospital at Ann Arbor for examination and treatment.

After several weeks of observation, Dr. A. M. Barrett, chief alienist at the hospital, issued a report. He found Mrs. Lipczynska's behavior puzzling at first, but concluded finally that she was shamming.

"Her behavior was unusually odd," Barrett wrote. "When alone in bed she lay rather quietly with her eyes closed. If aroused, she appeared startled, sat up in bed with eyes staring, gazing slowly around the room, not fixed on anything for any length of time. She would then put out her arms, moving them stiffly around, then with her fingers in a claw-like position she would pull her hair down over her eyes, pick at her face and then rub her hands together . . . Her facial expression during this phase was one of terror."

He said that she would reach out to the physician, trying to take his hands or pat his arm, and, if permitted, would kiss his hands or sleeve. Usually she would end these gestures with the remark in English, "Now I pray, Holy Ghost, amen, amen."

"At times she had spoken of being influenced by devils," Barrett wrote, "of snakes in her hair. These bite her head and made her forget. The devil took her prayerbook and rosary. The devil said to her, 'Jump! Jump and lock the door!' They are taking her to hell. She is afraid that people and devils are coming for her . . . Later on, however, her actions became seemingly normal."

The report concluded that Mrs. Lipczynska was mentally and physically competent to stand trial. She was returned to the Leland jail on July 28.

Next day, looking weak and pale, she stood before Judge Mayne in circuit court, charged with the murder of Sister Janina of the Isadore convent.

"Mrs. Lipczynska, how do you plead?" the judge asked her.

The housekeeper stood mute, and a plea of not guilty was entered in her behalf by attorney Howard Campbell.

Francis O. Gaffney, of Cadillac, who had replaced Thomas Smurthwaite on the defense team, immediately asked for a change of venue. His client could not get a fair trial at Leland, he argued, because of all the sensational and misleading publicity.

The judge's reply was somewhat sarcastic. "Do you want this trial to be held in Grand Rapids, Muskegon, or do you prefer Detroit, counsel?"

That afternoon he temporarily denied the motion, and bound the defendant over to the October term of court.

The Trial

The trial of The People vs Stanislawa Lipczynska opened at Leland courthouse on Monday, October 13, 1919, before an all-male jury. (Along with the right to vote, women had recently been given the right to serve on juries, but no woman had been called in this case.) It had taken the best part of two weeks to impanel a jury. During this time the defense had used 27 of its peremptory challenges, as compared to 3 of 15 for the prosecution. A total of more than 60 veniremen had been examined. The examination of prospective jurors had been conducted mainly by Parmius C. Gilbert, for the prosecution, and Frank O. Gaffney, of Cadillac, for the defense; the latter had replaced Thomas Smurthwaite on the defense team.

These two men were strikingly similar in appearance and personality, and sparks flew between them. Both were quick-tempered, wiry, intense, full of nervous energy; both nearly bald. They provided the only courtroom drama during the long, boring days of jury selection, growling and snapping at each other like feisty bull-terriers, seeming at times almost on the point of coming to blows. Gilbert accused Gaffney of stalling tactics, of trying to force a change of venue. Gaffney countered by accusing Gilbert of trying to railroad his client to prison. Their clashes amused the spectators.

As at the hearing, C. L. Dayton served on the prosecution team, while P. T. Glassmire and Howard Campbell continued to serve for the defense. Since Mrs. Lipczynska and several of the witnesses were more fluent in Polish than in English, Roman Glochewski, a Grand Rapids attorney, had been hired by the court to serve as interpreter.

A jury was secured on Thursday, October 9. It came as something of a surprise. The defense still had 3 preemptory challenges and was expected to use them. However, since the prosecution had used only 3 of its 15, the defense realized that its opponent could seat an entirely new jury if it saw fit, disposing of the already seated jurors by the challenge route.

The jury was composed almost entirely of farmers. None of them was of Polish descent. Critics of the trial point to this as evidence of a conspiracy to exclude Polish-Americans, who might have been more sympathetic to the defendant. The fact is that several men of Polish ancestry were called for jury duty; for various legitimate reasons they were disqualified, or rejected, most of them by the defense. Both the prosecution and the defense had agreed that no jurymen be drawn from the Isadore neighborhood.

The trial opened for the taking of testimony on Monday, October 13, before Judge Frederick Mayne. He was a trim little man in his early sixties, with grey hair ("grey-maned judge" would become one of the bad puns in the case) and a neat military mustache.

The crowds that had dwindled during the jury examination were now out again in full force. People had been arriving since early morning in wagons, buggies, a few new-fangled automobiles, and on foot. During the course of the trial, many farmers would bring their wives early in the morning, go back to do their chores, and then return later in the day to hear a bit of the case before supper. This trial was the most exciting thing that had ever happened in Leelanau County, and hundreds of people wanted a ring-side seat. Many were turned away. The courtroom, which occupied the upper floor of a 28 by 40 foot frame building, could accommodate only about 100.

As the prisoner was led into the courtroom by two bailiffs, the spectators searched her face for a sign of emotion. They found none: the little Polish woman was stolid and composed. She looked to be in much better condition, physically and mentally, than during the hearing, when reporters had described her as a "nervous wreck". She didn't notice her daughter, who was seated directly behind her, until Mary touched her on the shoulder. Then the two jumped to their feet and fell into each other's arms, kissing and embracing in a touching display of emotion that had some of the women spectators dabbing at their eyes with handkerchiefs.

In his opening address, Prosecutor Dayton told the court he expected to prove the following:

—that Sister Mary Janina (Josephine Mezek) was killed in the basement of the Isadore church on Friday, August 23, 1907, by Mrs. Lipczynska, the respondent;

—that the nun was going into the basement of the church to obtain some paper flowers contained there in a box, the flowers to be used for the decoration of the school, which was to be blessed;

—that the respondent struck the nun on the head with a blunt instrument, knocking her unconscious;

—that the respondent hurriedly dug a grave 18 inches deep in the basement of the church, the grave being shorter than Sister Mary;

—that the nun was placed in the grave her knees doubled up, and that, still alive, she was buried, her body being covered with earth;

—that the respondent had been jealous of the nuns and called them "priest's wives" and names unprintable;

—that the respondent had made a full confession of just how the alleged murder was committed;

—that the respondent has told how she feigned insanity since her imprisonment and that she told certain persons beforehand that she was going to feign insanity.

The prosecution also expected to show, Dayton said, that the secret of the alleged crime was known to church officials long before the body was discovered.

Father Bieniawski was the first witness for the prosecution. He retold the story of the fishing trip, and of how the whole church "family" searched the buildings and the premises until after midnight. His story of the subsequent search that lasted two weeks, of his trip to Detroit, of the use of the bloodhound, and all the other details were substantially the same as his testimony during the hearing. The priest seemed eager to talk and had to be cut short frequently by the examiner.

"Did Sister Mary ever declare her intention of leaving the convent?" he was asked.

"Absolutely not. Never!" he said.

"Was she well liked in the neighborhood?"

The priest said that she was generally well liked but that a few people had complained about her being mean to some of the children in school. Among those making complaints were Mrs. Frank Bodus and Mary Gatske.

Next morning, in plain and simple language, Jacob Flees, the sexton of Isadore church, told the gruesome tale of how he dug up the remains of Sister Mary Janina in the church basement. He said that the matter of the remains under the church was first mentioned to him by Father Podlaszewski some time in October of 1916.

One day that month (he couldn't recall the exact date) he and Podlaszewski started looking for the remains about three o'clock in the afternoon. They had dug in one soft spot in the northeast corner and found nothing. He then proceeded to probe with his shovel in another spot and the shovel struck something hard and he reached down and picked up a bone.

As he unearthed other bones, Father Podlaszewski put them in a box. The skeleton lay with its head toward the south, he said. A potato fork was used for most of the digging, as the priest thought some flesh might still be adhering to the bones. Next day he made a box two feet long and one foot deep and put the bones in it. Two nights later he buried the new box of bones in the church cemetery.

"What else did you find in the grave?"

Flees said they found a pair of shoes and some dark cloth around the corpse, "just as a person would be dressed."

Recalled by the defense, Father Bieniawski said he had met Mrs. Lipczynska in 1900 when she was visiting relatives in the Isadore

51

neighborhood. She became this housekeeper shortly after that and remained with him in that capacity until the time of her arrest — except for three years when she was living with her daughter near Milwaukee.

Asked if any outsider had access to the nuns' quarters, he said no one except a doctor who came to attend them when asked. He said Janina had asked to have the doctor call just before she disappeared. He personally asked the doctor to come, and the doctor said he would. But Bieniawski said he didn't know if the doctor had come or not.

Bieniawski said that when a doctor called, he usually rang a bell to summon the sisters, then remained in the lower part of the convent while the doctor paid his visit.

Did he mean to say that the doctor was permitted to see the nun alone in her room?

Bieniawski said he thought that one of the other two sisters was usually present, but he wasn't sure about that.

He went on to say that he had never noticed any enmity between the housekeeper and the nuns. On the contrary, she had been in the habit of carrying special items of food to them.

Under redirect examination by Dayton, the priest said that after Janina disappeared, the housekeeper had said that Janina was ungrateful considering all that had been done for her, it being the opinion among some people, including the housekeeper, that the nun had run away from the convent.

"When the old convent burned, didn't the sisters object to going to your house to live because they were afraid of Lipczynska?" Dayton asked.

"No," said the priest. "No such conversation ever took place."

Jacob Flees was recalled by the defense.

"Why didn't you call the sheriff or the prosecuting attorney when you found those bones?" Gaffney asked him.

"Because it wasn't my place to," Flees said.

"Didn't you make any effort to notify Father Bieniawski of the find?"

"No."

Father Edward Podlaszewski, very pale and nervous but anxious to tell his story, was on the stand for three hours on Tuesday afternoon. He said he had first learned of the remains under the church in April of 1918. The information, he said, came from Father Lempka in Grand Rapids. He said that after he and Flees had dug them up and while they were still lying in a box in the basement, he took one of the nuns at the convent, Sister Mary Gastold, to look at them.

In cross-examination, the defense submitted an affidavit that Podlaszewski had made to the police on May 9, 1919, in Cleveland, where he was serving in exile as assistant pastor of a small church. The defense pointed out several inconsistencies between that document and Podlaszewski's testimony in court.

For example, Gaffney pointed out, Podlaszewski had said in the affidavit that he had first heard about the bones from his predecessor, Father Oprychalski. Furthermore, in the affidavit Podlaszewski had stated that one of the nuns at the convent, Sister Leoncia, had told him there was a rumor that Sister Janina was buried under the church. Both of these incidents had happened long before his meeting with Father Lempka in Grand Rapids.

Podlaszewski explained that he regarded the first two pieces of information as mere rumor, probably without foundation in fact, while Lempka's warning had sounded like the truth. He said that Lempka told him the information came from Bishop Kozlowski in Milwaukee. That gave it considerably more authority.

Mary Flees, the housekeeper's daughter, was called next to the stand. She proved to be a difficult witness. She flatly contradicted a portion of an affidavit she had made to Sheriff Kinnucan in Milwaukee. In that testimony—repeated at the hearing—she said that her mother was working in the garden on the afternoon that Janina disappeared. She said she hadn't seen her mother between one-thirty and four o'clock that afternoon.

Now, on the stand, she said she had heard her mother going about her duties in the house during that time.

The prosecutor read that part of her testimony in the affidavit. "Now, you swore to this affidavit, didn't you?"

"Yes, I did," Mary said.

"And you swore to it again at the examination?"

"Yes."

"Then how is it that you say this now, and never said it before when you were sworn."

"Ma was in the kitchen,"Mary insisted. "I heard her."

The prosecutor pressed her for an explanation, but Mary calmly refused to acknowledge the contradiction. The difficulty was complicated by the necessity of having her testimony translated from Polish to English; Mary claimed she knew very little English.

On Wednesday afternoon, the prosecution sprung its first big surprise. Sister Mary Pius of the Milwaukee Province testified that Bishop Kozlowski had told her and Mother Superior Veronica that Mary Janina had been killed by a well-known woman in Isadore.

"State his exact words, Sister, if you can."

"Well, he said that Sister Mary Janina didn't leave the convent, but was killed by a woman on the premises; she was the woman that struck the sister on the head and buried her under the church."

"Is Bishop Kozlowski living now?"

"No," Mary Pius said. "He died about August 7, 1915."

Father Joseph Lempka, the next witness, said that he learned about the remains from the Felician sisters. That was about two years ago, he said, about the time that repairs were being considered for the Isadore church. He said he met Father Podlaszewski in the spring of 1918. They were both staying at Father Skory's for the Forty Hours Devotional.

"Did you tell him your source of information?"

"Yes, I told him it was from Bishop Kozlowski in Milwaukee. I heard it directly from Sister Superior Antonina in Detroit, in the fall of 1915. She told me her source of information."

"And who was that?"

"Sister Mary Pius of Milwaukee."

"Do you know anything more about the disappearance of Sister Mary Janina?" he was asked.

"I know nothing about how she came to her death except what I have heard," Lempka said.

The defense objected: What he had heard was not admissable. The court agreed and refused to allow it.

A horrified murmur, punctuated by the rattle of bones, filled the courtroom on Thursday morning as Drs. G. A. Fralick and J. F. Slepica assembled the alleged remains of Sister Janina on a table in front of the judge's desk. The skull was turned so that its sightless eyes were facing the defendant, less than six feet away. Except for a slight flush in her face, she remained as stoical as ever.

Four wooden boxes were entered as exhibits of evidence. One contained the bones; another the cloth and shoes; in a third were some robe cord and trinkets; the fourth held some gravel scraped from the basement grave.

Sister Mary Antonina, on the stand, broke down and wept as she was asked to identify a ring found in the grave. It was a class ring, she said, given to each of the members of a class of novitiates who took their final vows and became nuns in 1901. She herself was wearing one; she was a classmate of Sister Janina. The ring was made of silver and steel, and was engraved inside in Polish with *Jesus Moj Wezystko D. M. 25801*, which in English reads: "Jesus my all, 1901."

"Sister, you took your vows the same time as Sister Janina?" she was asked.

"Yes, sir. In the year 1901. There were twenty-two in the class and I was acquainted with all of them and it is part of my work now to know where they are."

"How many of them are living at this time?"

"Seventeen are living."

"Have you made any investigation to ascertain whether those who are living have their rings?"

"Yes, sir." Antonina explained that she had examined the whereabouts of every ring of the seventeen nuns known to be living. Four nuns had died and were buried with their rings on their fingers. Janina was missing. One nun, Sister Romona, had left the convent, but had left her ring there. Thus, all the rings were accounted for.

Antonina went on to explain that some of the original rings had been worn out. They were returned to the Superioress at the Detroit home in exchange for new ones.

55

Dr. G. R. Fralick, of Maple City, told of examining the skeleton at the Leland jail on March 1, 1919. He said the skeleton was complete except for the twelfth rib on each side and several small bones of the hands and feet. He also said the bones were dirty but in a good state of preservation.

Fralick related that he had found a one-and-half-inch-long fracture of the skull two and a half inches back of the eyes, and four and a half inches from the top of the skull. The fracture ran diagonally across the temporal bone, crossing the groove of the meningeal artery, which supplies blood to the membrane covering the brain. The fracture had severed the artery. Death would not have been immediate, but would have probably occurred within twelve hours. The blow would almost certainly have rendered the victim unconscious.

The skeleton, he said, was that of a woman not more than sixty-five inches tall and not less than sixty-two, the difference allowing for the undetermined curvature of the spine. The sex was easily determined by the shape of the pelvic bones.

Dr. J. F. Slepica, of Suttons Bay, confirmed Dr. Fralick's report. He said that the fracture, barely noticeable on the exterior of the skull, was readily apparent on the inside when the skull was sawed open.

At this point, the shoes were opened for the first time, and eleven bones of the feet were found inside.

At noon recess, a group of brown-robed Felician nuns gathered around what they believed were the remains of their missing sister and prayed. A reporter called it the most dramatic and poignant scene of the trial thus far.

An attack by the prosecution developed rapidly on Thursday afternoon. The prisoner, who up until now had shown little concern, grew visibly perturbed. For the first time, a church confession was hinted at in the testimony of Helen Strang, who had been a friend of Mrs. Lipczynska in Isadore.

Q. Now did Mrs. Lipczynska say anything to you about this case — about Sister Mary John?

A. She said, "Listen, Helen. All the people are blaming me now. I don't know nothing about the killing of Sister Janina." And I said, "Auntie," — I call her aunt, you know — "you can't blame the people. It isn't the people, it was the priest who let it out." And she asked me, "Is Father Podlaszewski in trouble at Isadore?"

I said, "Yes, that's true. It seems like the world is coming to an end."

And she said, "If the secret of the confessional is coming out, it will be the end of the world."

Sister Neopomucene, of the Detroit Province, testified that she had come to Isadore twelve years before to help in the search for the missing nun. She had talked with Mrs. Lipczynska at that time and said the housekeeper had made remarks about Janina's character.

"She said the priest was too intimate with her, and that the sister wasn't a good nun."

Mary Gatzke, who lived with her husband across the road from the church, said that Mrs. Lipczynska often called at her house. She said the defendant frequently talked about the sisters and called them names.

"What did she say?"

"She said that the priest was no priest. He was no more than a man with wives. She called Janina a slut."

"Anything else?"

"She said something worse, a worse name than that."

"Well, let's have it. What did she say?"

"She said they were whores."

"Anything else?"

"I heard her say that Janina wasn't worthy to be on holy ground, that she was no nun."

Another neighbor, Mrs. Jacob Flees, testified that she also had talked with the housekeeper shortly after the nun disappeared.

"I was at vespers," Mrs. Flees said, "and I stepped out of the church and Mrs. Lipczynska was there at the front and I heard some of the ladies say that the sisters were going away tomorrow — that was Monday. And I said, 'I suppose the Mother Superior is afraid that someone will come and steal another sister.' And Mrs. Lipczynska said that sister wasn't worthy to walk on holy ground. She said that she was such a light character that she let Father

Bieniawski and the doctor go in her cell, and they are not allowed to do this even upon their dying bed."

Next day the prosecution continued to develop its case through the testimony of several more Felician sisters. There were sixteen of the brown-robed nuns in attendance when the morning session opened.

Sister Mary Regina, of Manitowoc, Wis., testified that she began teaching in Isadore two months after the nun disappeared. One day, when she went under the church to get some artificial flowers for a Forty Hours Devotional, she found a pair of steel-rimmed glasses near the cellar door. She said she gave them to Father Bieniawski.

Sister Leonissa, who also moved to Isadore after Janina disappeared, said that Mrs. Lipczynska had told her that Janina was a no-good nun, and that it was God's blessing she disappeared when she did. She told her that Janina did not fulfill her duties and that she'd had a lot of trouble with her, saying that she was so angry with the nun at times that she could just shake her.

All this was damaging enough, to be sure, but it was not the kind of evidence on which a jury was likely to convict. On Friday afternoon, however, the state unlimbered its big guns.

It called to the stand Mary J. Tylicka, an operative of the Wilson Detective Agency of Milwaukee, who spoke fluent Polish. She testified that she had been brought to Isadore in April, 1919, by Sheriff Kinnucan. Posing as a social worker under the name of Mary Dumbrowski, she was arrested on a fake charge and placed in Mrs. Lipczynska's cell as an informant.

"Did she make a request of you?" Tylicka was asked.

"Yes, she did. On April 28 she asked me to go to Father Bieniawski and tell him to have Father Podlaszewski put out of the state. She said the Father would pay me well for my trouble."

"What else did she say?"

"She said, 'I fear him. He knows all.'"

"What did you tell her?"

"I said, 'If you want me to help you, tell me what and tell me all!' "

At this point, the defense objected vehemently. Overruled, it requested time for a conference with the defendant. Time was granted, and the three attorneys huddled around the prisoner and talked with her through an interpreter for several minutes.

Then Gaffney addressed the court: "Your honor, the prisoner states that no voluntary statements of an incriminating nature were made by her to Mrs. Tylicka, and that if such statements were made, they were obtained by fraud, the result of coercion."

Resuming its examination of Mrs. Tylicka, the prosecution asked, "Now, tell us what Mrs. Lipczynska said to you then."

"She said, 'I went to confession and confessed my sins to Father Nowak in Milwaukee. Father Nowak would not give me absolution at once. He said he first must see Bishop Kozlowski. He went away and told me to remain in the church. In a few minutes he returned and gave me absolution.' "

"Go on," the prosecution prompted.

Mrs. Tylicka continued: "She said, 'I have done my penance; my sins are forgiven. Why do they bother me? But I guess I might as well tell you. Yes, I killed Sister Janina.'

"You did?" I asked.

" 'Yes,' she said. 'I killed the sister. First I stunned her and then went out into the garden and got a spade. I dug a hole under the church, dragged the body to the hole and put it in. As I was trying to cover the head, it would always rise up. I threw two or three shovels of dirt on the head, but each time it rose up. Then I took the back side of the spade and knocked the sister three times on the head with all my might.' "

"Is this true?" I asked her.

" 'Yes,' she said. 'I have told you just as I told it to Father Nowak in Milwaukee."

"Next day what?"

"Mrs. Lipczynska asked me if I was angry with her because she confessed. I said no. Then she repeated her story."

"Now, what did she say to you the next day?"

"She said when she confessed her sins and came to the part about the crime, Father Nowak said he couldn't give her absolution right

59

away, that he had to see Bishop Kozlowski, that she should stay in the church till he returned. She said she waited fifteen or twenty minutes, or maybe a half hour—she couldn't remember exactly—but it wasn't long, she said, because it wasn't far to where the Bishop lived. He lived on Grove and Mitchell streets in Milwaukee, and the church where Father Nowak took her confession was on First and Lincoln. She said Father Nowak returned and gave her absolution. Then she left the church."

"Now, at any time did she complain about Bishop Kozlowski?"

"She said it was all because of him that this came out, the murder of the nun."

Mrs. Tylicka went on to say that the housekeeper had told her, "Pretty soon I won't be here. I'll be in a hospital or an insane asylum. I'm going to pretend to be crazy, and they must believe me. The doctors can't tell the difference because they can't see inside me."

Under cross-examination by Glassmire, the woman detective stuck firmly to her story. Wasn't it true, Glassmire asked, that Mrs. Lipczynska had been intimidated by the sheriff, that she had been subjected to a third degree, that she had been beaten into making the confession?

Not true, Mary Tylicka said. Not true at all.

Notwithstanding the vehement protests of the defense, the written and signed confession was admitted as evidence by Judge Mayne.

The state resumed its examination of Mrs. Tylicka on Saturday morning. She testified that the defendant first began to show signs of insanity on Wednesday, April 30, when they returned to the jail after lunch.

"She began scratching and yelling, throwing herself on the bed, kicking and making motions with her hands, yelling at the top of her voice," Tylicka said. "I asked her if she was sick and she said yes. So I told Mr. Kinnucan, and a short while after that the doctor came.

"Next day she began scratching and yelling again, and she would not talk to me. She would get up once in a while, roll about on the floor, then pick herself up, go back to bed and start the same commotion."

"Did she make any remark about the sheriff?"

"Yes. It was just before she took sick. She looked out the window and saw him and she changed colors. I asked her what was the matter. She shook her fist at the window and said, '*Psia krew*' — that's Polish for "dog's blood" — "You think you are smart. I am wiser than all of you. I will lead you out into the field and fool you. I am wiser than all of you.' "

Tylicka said that Mrs. Lipczynska then signed a written confession.

Over the bitter protests of the defense, the written confession was admitted as evidence by Judge Mayre.

Shortly after the conclusion of Tylicka's testimony, the state rested its case.

Attorney P. T. Glassmire made the opening statement for the defense on Monday morning. After sketching the defendant's life history and giving a detailed account of what took place from the time of her arrest to the opening of the trial, he said the defense would prove:

—that Mrs. Lipczynska suffered inhuman treatment at the Leland jail;

—that her attorneys were refused permission to see her;

—that a Milwaukee woman detective, having been put in her cell as a stool pigeon, told her lies and beat her in an attempt to obtain a confession;

—that the bones found under the church were not those of Sister Janina;

—that, tricked by the detective and the sheriff, Mrs. Lipczynska was led into a room where there was an object covered by a sheet and lying on a long table; the sheet was stripped off, revealing a human skeleton; all lights were turned off except the two candles burning by the skull; the sheriff from a darkened corner chanted in a sepulchral voice, timed with the opening and closing of the hinged jaws of the skull, "You killed me! You killed me!";

—that the defendant emerged from this ordeal a raving maniac, and had to be sent to a mental hospital;

—that more bones of the skeleton were missing than was claimed by the prosecution;

—that if indeed the nun was killed, she was not killed under the church; the body must have been moved from its original grave to the spot where it was found in the church basement.

Among the first witnesses called by the defense was Sheriff John Kinnucan, a tall, lanky, loose-jointed man. He told about hiring the detective, Mary Tylicka, in Milwaukee; that she arrived a few weeks later, was arrested on a prearranged plan and placed in the defendant's cell, and a few days later told Kinnucan of the alleged confession. He admitted that Mrs. Lipczynska's rosary and prayer book were taken from her, and admitted that Mrs. Tylicka had told him they were necessary for Catholic people to say their prayers. He said he found that the prisoner had obtained another rosary from Mrs. Tylicka and that "perhaps" he found fault. He didn't remember if the second rosary was taken from Mrs. Lipczynska.

James Anderson and his wife, in charge of the jail, and William Dalton, deputy sheriff, testified that they had refused admittance to defense attorneys Campbell and Glassmire on May 8. They said it was because the sheriff and Judge Martin Brown were away from the village and had left orders that no one from either side could see the prisoner in their absence.

Mary Tylicka denied that she told Father Koback that Sheriff Kinnucan was cruel to the prisoner. She also denied that she had held Mrs. Lipczynska on the bed after the priest's visit to the jail. She said that the prisoner had told her that she had "told Father Koback everything."

Father Koback, of St. Michael's parish in Suttons Bay, said he knew Mrs. Lipczynska and saw her in the jail at Leland on April 30 for about an hour. He said that Kinnucan had called him on the telephone and asked him to come and see the prisoner. He said that Mrs. Tylicka was giving the defendant some medicine when he entered the cell. Mrs. Tylicka then left and closed the door. But later, he said, she came rushing in, saying the sheriff wanted her to remain with the prisoner at all times. Father Koback said he protested, told the sheriff that either Mrs. Tylicka had to leave, or he

62

would. After some discussion the sheriff acquiesced.

Father Koback said that during his interview with Mrs. Lipczynska she told him Tylicka was a spy.

"Did Mrs. Tylicka, while you were there, tell you that the sheriff reprimanded her for letting Mrs. Lipczynska have her rosary?"

"Yes, sir; very severely."

"Did Mrs. Lipczynska make any statement to you whether or not she had killed Sister Mary Janina?"

"She did."

"What was that statement?"

The prosecution objected that the statement would be immaterial and self-serving, and Judge Mayne sustained the objection.

On Tuesday morning, Patrick Bowse of Traverse City, who had taken part in the search for the nun, told at great length how he had made a thorough inspection of the church basement. He said he had found no sign of anything having been dragged under there, and no sign of a grave. He had moved part of a pile of scrap lumber, but admitted, under cross-examination, that he had left most of it untouched.

Late on Tuesday afternoon came the moment everybody had been waiting for. The defense called Stanislawa Lipczynska to the stand.

The fifty-year-old little Polish woman proved to be an excellent witness. She testified in Polish in a calm deliberate tone, frequently smiling but generally showing little or no emotion. During the previous week she had sat quietly in relative ignorance of the proceedings, since she understood little English. Now, through the interpreter, she readily answered Gaffney's questions about her life, from cradle to the present.

Finally, Gaffney began to address the business at hand.

"Did you ever go to confession in Milwaukee?" he asked her.

"Yes. That's what we came to the city for."

"What was the priest's name?"

"Father Barron."

"Did you ever know a priest by the name of Nowak?"

"No, I never knew him."

Recalled to the stand on Wednesday morning, Mrs. Lipczynska explained that she had been baking bread on the day the nun disappeared. She said she didn't leave the house at all that afternoon. She said she had supper ready when the fishing party returned, but that nobody sat down to eat.

"We all went to look for Sister Janina. We had a lantern. We looked everywhere. We searched until midnight; then we ate supper."

In response to Gaffney's questions, she went on to tell of how she had been tortured in the Leland jail.

"What did this Mrs. Dumbrowski say to you while she was in jail?" Gaffney asked her.

"When Father Koback went away, she came in and licked me and pulled my hair and said she had heard what I told him, that she was a spy."

"Before Father Koback came, did this woman talk to you about the disappearance of Sister Janina?"

"Yes, she did. She would pretend to be a friend of mine. She said, 'You brave woman, I will help you out of this.' She told me that my lawyers had quit me and that Father Bieniawski was in prison for fifteen years and that my daughter was dead. I thought she was a spy the minute she came in."

"Did she try to get you to make a confession?"

"She said that Mr. Kinnucan had promised her one thousand dollars if I signed the papers, and she would give me half of it."

"What other effort did she make to get you to make a confession?"

"She says she knows from sisters and Mr. Brown and Mr. Kinnucan that I killed Sister Janina."

"Did this Mrs. Dumbrowski ask you if you wanted to see Sister Janina?"

"Never."

"Did Mr. Kinnucan ask you that?"

"Yes."

"What did you say?"

"I said yes. I thought Sister Janina came to life again."

(The prosecution made a note of this: how did she know Sister Janina was dead?)

"Now, what happened that night when they asked if you wanted to see Sister Janina?"

"I remember it was in the evening. I was ready to go to bed when Mr. Kinnucan came in. We went through a little room and Mr. Kinnucan opened the door and pushed me in there. I didn't see anything except some bones and two candles. I don't remember what they laid on because when Mr. Kinnucan hollered I got scared and couldn't see."

"Did you see the skull?"

"Yes. He had it on strings like threads and he came to me and was opening and shutting it and he tried to force it in my mouth."

"Was anything said to you while you were in there?"

"He was always hollering something, but I did not understand."

"When you got done in that room, where did you go?"

"He put me in some kind of box up above. Right there where the bones were. I don't remember how long I was in that box."

"Do you remember what happened the next day?"

"I just remember that I was so sore and sick and it seemed like I was seeing double. I could hardly get over to Brown's for dinner."

"Did you at any time tell Mrs. Dumbrowski that she should go to Father Bieniawski and tell him to have Father Podlaszewski put out of the country, and that he would pay her well for her trouble?"

"It is not so," said Mrs. Lipczynska. "That is a lie."

Following the noon recess, testimony was taken from several medical men, including Drs. Slepica and Fralick for the prosecution, and pathologist Dr. Ludwig Hoekton of Chicago for the defense. They were in disagreement as to the cause of death. Slepica and Fralick testified that death was due to a fracture of the skull and internal bleeding; Dr. Hoekton argued that the fracture was made after death. The jury seemed bored with the obscure medical terms and technicalities. Their interest picked up when Mrs. Lipczynska was recalled to the stand.

"Did you make a confession as Mrs. Tylicka says you did?" Gaffney asked her.

"No, it is not the truth. That is a lie."

She said that Mrs. Tylicka came to her one day with a piece of paper and wanted her to sign it.

"The first piece of paper had nothing on it," she said. "The next piece of paper there was Judge Brown on it. She tried to get me to sign the paper on Saturday afternoon. On Sunday and Monday she got hold of my hand and wanted to write with my hand. She had written something on the paper and she was wanting me to sign somewhere at the bottom."

"Did she tell you what the writing was?"

"She says she had to go with that writing to the bishop to remove these three priests, and if I would not sign, the bishop would not believe me."

"What did she do when you refused to sign?"

"She began to choke me. And she had a black robe on and she said, 'If you do not sign, I'll fix you. I will put you in jail for all of your life."

"Did you tell this woman you were going to pretend to be going crazy?"

"Never."

"Now, there has been some testimony that you made motions as though you were playing a violin and acted queerly in other ways. Do you have any recollection of that?"

"No, never. I do not remember of that at all."

Gaffney paused for several seconds. Then he said, "I want you to say now, Mrs. Lipczynska, whether you killed Sister May John or not."

"No."

"Do you know anything about how or why she disappeared?"

"When she disappeared I know. The people said that someone took her away, and the sisters said so."

"Do you know yourself how she disappeared?"

"The day she disappeared I know."

The state called Dr. A. N. Barrett, head of the Psychopathic Hospital in Ann Arbor as a rebuttal witness. He said the defendant had been under observation at the hospital from May 17 to July 28.

"From your observation, did you think she was insane?"

"I did not think she was insane," Dr. Barrett said. "Her actions were those of a person feigning insanity."

On that same afternoon, the defense sought to introduce a document from the birth and death records of the Vital Statistics Division in Lansing. The prosecution wanted to know what their reason was.

Glassmire explained, "We expect to identify Dr. Fralick's handwriting. We expect to prove that he is the author of the 'Protestant Pup' letter."

Attorney Gilbert objected: "Introduction of this letter has nothing to do with the case. They are attempting to try the doctor and not the respondent in this case. I know of no law to uphold it."

The court ruled that the defense was permitted to set forth, as counter proof, that the deceased came to his or her death by other than the means set forth in the charge. The testimony would be permitted, he said.

But, after examining the 'Protestant Pup' letter, the judge excused the jury and made the following statement to the defense attorneys.

"Gentlemen, I want to say that this anonymous communication, of which the defendant evidently knows nothing, may do her defense real harm if the assertion that Dr. Fralick is the author is disproved. If the evidence shows that he is not the author, the jury's impression may be distinctly detrimental to the defendant."

The attorneys for the defense asked for time for a conference. Then Gaffney addressed the court:

"On account of developments of this case," he said, "we have decided to withdraw the introduction of the letter, and we ask that the court so instruct the jury."

Upon the return of the jury, Judge Mayne told them they must put the matter out of their minds, as it had never happened.

After more medical testimony on Thursday morning — much of it repetitious — the prosecution called Mrs. Lipczynska to the stand for cross-examination.

Under questioning by Parm Gilbert she denied that she had ever said anyting bad about Sister Janina. She said she liked the nun.

"Often she was good to me because she taught my daughter, and everything she asked me I gave her and did for her."

Gilbert questioned her about the torture episode in the jail.

"Did Mrs. Anderson stay with you every night?"

"I remember one night she wasn't there."

"When was that?"

"At the time that woman tortured me she wasn't there."

"Was that the night of the day that Father Koback was there?"

"Yes."

"Well, what happened that night?"

"They left me alone in the jail; locked me in there. It was dark and I was calling for Mrs. Anderson because I was awful thirsty. Afterwards, Mr. Kinnucan came and got the skeleton's head, and he was ramming her head close to my face. The woman came afterwards. She took a dipper and was striking me on the head with it. It was the spy who did that."

At this point, the housekeeper for the first time lost her composure; she broke into tears.

After a pause, Gilbert said, "And Mr. Kinnucan was there, was he?"

"He came himself, with that head. He was opening it up—he came and rammed in front of my face, and opened it and shut it. When I opened my eyes I got awfully scared of him."

"Did you get up in a higher place to sleep, up overhead?"

The witness again broke into tears. "I laid in that bed—"

"But did you climb up or did he put you up in the higher box you told about?"

Mrs. Lipczynska continued to cry, sobbing into her handkerchief. After several moments she said, "I remember that there was one day he took me and put me in the box. It was the day he brought me over when the two candles were lighted. But I can't remember all. I can't remember what day it was."

Gilbert persisted. "Where was that box?"

"It was in the place, in the room where he had the bones. It was some higher than the floor and a kind of box."

"Was it so you could lie down in it?"

"I don't remember. I just remember that he put me in a box. I didn't know where it was."

"Did you stay up there?"

"I don't know, " said the witness, crying again. "But I was in my room afterwards, when I came to."

Gilbert tried a new tack. "Did you tell Mr. Kinnucan that you wanted to see Sister Janina?"

"No. Mr. Kinnucan came over and asked me if I wouldn't like to see Sister Janina. I told him I would."

"Did you tell him you thought she had come alive again?"

"Yes. I thought she was alive again."

"Then you knew she was dead, didn't you?" Gilbert said.

"I didn't know. I didn't know nothing," Mrs. Lipczynska said.

The trial was now nearing an end. On Friday morning, the prosecution introduced several rebuttal witnesses. Mrs. Anderson, matron at the jail, was questioned about Mrs. Lipczynska's alleged ordeal.

"Were you there that evening when something was said or occurred about showing this lady the bones in the jail?"

"I was there."

"Tell us what happened."

"After supper, on Saturday night, Mr. Kinnucan took her in the back room and then locked the door. I was in my room and there is a doorway between that room and mine. The door was open and I could see the people in there and hear them," Mrs. Anderson said.

"Tell us what was said and done as you saw and heard it."

"Mr. Kinnucan asked her if she recognized the bones and she said no. She said, 'What is it? What is that?' He said, 'Why, it is only bones.' Then he said, 'If you do not know, go back to your room.' So she did."

"Now, you heard the statement here that Mr. Kinnucan took this skull and ran it up in front of her face and worked the jaws of it and tried to crowd it down her throat. What do you say to that?"

"I saw nothing of that kind while I was there," Mrs. Anderson said. "After she went back to her room with Mrs. Tylicka I heard them talking in a sociable way. I heard them laugh and giggle as on other occasions."

James Anderson, the jailer, corroborated his wife's testimony.

"They went into the cell where the bones were," he said. "I went to the door of the cell and looked through the window. The electric light was on; there was no other light. All I seen was some bones lying in that box I had taken in there. He asked her if she knew whose bones they were, and she said no. Then she said, 'What is it, what is it?' That is all he could get out of her. She didn't pick up or handle any of the bones, and neither did Mr. Kinnucan."

"Tell us whether the sheriff had those bones rigged up with a string so he could work the jaws of the skull, and whether he presented that to Mrs. Lipczynska and then said, 'You killed me! You killed me!'"

"I didn't see or hear anything like that, nor that he took this woman and threw her into a box, nor anything of the kind. He didn't touch her or lay hands on her."

Sister Mary Pius, of Milwaukee, testified that she knew Father Nowak. She said he lived in Milwaukee several years and she was positive he was there in 1914 and in the early part of 1915.

Martin Brown testified that Mrs. Lipczynska came to breakfast as usual at his home on the morning after the alleged torture. He said he had a talk with her then.

"Now, what was her condition at that time?"

"That morning at the breakfast table she said that Mr. Kinnucan showed her some bones last night and said they were Sister Janina's. There was nothing unusual or peculiar about her talk that I could observe."

The defense rested its case early Friday afternoon, and the prosecution followed suit. Final arguments were made by each of the five attorneys, and after receiving detailed instructions from Judge Mayne, the jury retired at eight o'clock that evening to consider its verdict.

Juries in those days usually deliberated straight through the night. It was more or less taken for granted that a jury should be able to resolve its differences and arrive at a verdict in a matter of hours, not days. This, indeed, was the case in most jury trials of that time.

It was true in this one, too. At four o'clock the next morning, the jury sent word that it had reached a verdict. An hour later, the court having assembled, Judge Mayne asked the foreman for the verdict.

"We find the prisoner guilty of murder in the first degree," he said solemnly.

Mrs. Lipczynska had watched the faces of the jurors closely. Now she shot an urgent glance of inquiry at Attorney Campbell. He hurried to her side.

"I no understand," she said faintly.

"They say you killed Sister Janina," he told her gently.

She shook her head. "I no kill Sister Janina," she said. Her stolid, Indianlike features showed no emotion.

Later it was learned that six ballots had been taken. The first was nine to three for conviction. The second stood at ten to two, and for four hours it had remained at eleven to one — until the final vote was taken.

Judge Mayne denied an appeal by the defense for postponement and pronounced sentence a few hours later.

"It is the sentence of this court, Stanislawa Lipczynska, that you are sentenced to the Detroit House of Correction, at hard labor, for the rest of your natural life."

It was the first life sentence Judge Mayne had ever given in his twenty years on the bench.

Mrs. Lipczynska remained stoical. Not a flicker of emotion crossed her face. Father Bieniawski came up and offered his hand. She took it eagerly, and he murmured some words of consolation in Polish. Then he turned and left the courtroom. He would never cease to believe in the housekeeper's innocence nor relax his efforts to obtain her release.

The priest's sister Susan embraced the prisoner and kissed her.

Then came the parting of mother and daughter. They stood for a moment in anguish, then fell into each other's arms. The mother covered her daughter's face with kisses. The daughter sobbed a last goodbye. Outside, the wind howled in a tempest, and a cold, driving rain beat against the windows.

Mrs. Lipczynska was taken to prison the following Monday. She served seven years as a model prisoner, and on New Year's day, 1927, she was pardoned by Governor Alex J. Groesbeck in one of his final official acts.

In an interview with the *Detroit Free Press* at the time of her release, Edward Denniston, superintendent of the Detroit House of

Correction, said, "I have always believed that Stella (Mrs. Lipczynska) was innocent of the crime for which she was committed. I have seen many prisoners come and go here. But I have never seen one go who I thought was more deserving of executive clemency than Stella."

Strangely enough, upon her release Mrs. Lipczynska went to work for the Felician order of nuns in Milwaukee. She spent her last years at the home of her daughter near that city, and died at the age of 92.

Afterword

Was Stanislawa Lipczynska guilty as charged? Did she kill Sister Mary Janina and bury her body in the church cellar? A jury of her peers thought so; the verdict was unanimous. So did the State Supreme Court. After a thorough review of the case, the Court handed down a carefully reasoned opinion that Mrs. Lipczynska had been given a fair trial, that she had been adequately represented by counsel, that they saw no reason to meddle with the verdict.

Yet some doubt remains. There were others besides Father Bieniawski and Warden Denniston who believed her to be innocent. There was some conflicting evidence at the trial, some loose ends never gathered up, some anomalies never satisfactorily explained. One wonders how closely detective Tylicka stuck to the facts. It seems likely that at least part of the housekeeper's story of her torture in jail, both mental and physical, may have been true—such third degree methods were common in those days. The impression comes down over the years that this was a very shrewd little Polish lady. But did she have the imagination to invent such a scene as the talking skull between two candles?

And what about the spectacles? Why weren't they discovered by any of the half dozen people who poked around under the church soon after the nun's disappearance? Why was it weeks before they were found?

One thing seems certain. Without the confession (which she

repudiated in court) she would not have been convicted. But that, of course, doesn't disprove her guilt.

It has been suggested that the killer was an outsider who hated the nun, knocked on the convent door and lured her on some pretext to the church basement. Some have a different theory. They suggest that Sister Mary was pregnant and arranged with Dr. Fralick to pick her up in his buggy that afternoon somewhere between the church and the swamp. After a bungled operation for abortion, she was buried under the church. (The defense, by innuendo at the trial, suggested that Dr. Fralick was the author of the "Protestant Pup" letter.)

Another variation is this: The nun decided to leave her vocation. She waited in the swamp for a friend who never showed up. Heat, darkness, fear drove her over the edge. Finally, she crawled into a barn and died. The farmer belonged to an anti-Catholic group who sought to embarrass the church by burying her in the cellar.

But the law of parsimony, in logic, cautions against considering any more causes or forces than are needed to explain an event. The simplest explanation that fits all the facts is that Mrs. Lipczynska killed the nun. All the other theories have one glaring deficiency: There isn't a scrap of evidence to support them.

THE BEARDED BANDIT MURDER

They called him the "whiskered train robber," a man of mystery. Heavily armed, extremely dangerous, approach with caution — that's how the "wanted" posters read. Whereabouts unknown.

John Freeman Smalley and his gang robbed trains and banks for more than a decade, but he was so cool and clever about it that even though he never wore a disguise, the police didn't discover his true identity until after he died in a shoot-out in 1895.

Smalley was a very tough hombre. Born in Brinton in Michigan's Isabella County he spent his early years knocking about in the lumber camps along the Muskegon River. There he built a reputation as an awesome fighter and an excellent marksman. Nobody in the camps dared tackle him, a friend said. But sometime around the early 1880s Smalley decided there were easier ways of making a living than cutting down trees.

At the age of forty, in the prime of his life, Smalley weighed 180 pounds and stood five feet, eight inches tall. He wore a full beard and reddish-tinged mustache. Barrel-chested, powerful and quick, he had a bulging forehead, small blue eyes, a large hawk nose and a

75

square jaw with good teeth. In the winter and summer he wore a dark sack overcoat and a soft black slouch hat. Beneath the coat and around his waist he carried a cartridge belt with two double-action pistols in the holsters. The side pockets of his coat had been removed so that he could draw both guns through the slots with lightning speed.

Smalley was shrewd enough to stage his holdups a long way from home, sometimes as far away as Oklahoma and Nebraska. Afterward the gang would return to Michigan and scatter, lying low until the next job. That way they were all able to stay at least one jump ahead of the law.

The closest Smalley ever came to getting caught was in 1893 when he and his gang held up a train in Kendalville, Ind. A few days later Smalley showed up at the American House hotel in Cadillac with a well-filled valise. Hotel-keeper Orrin Dunham, who also served as county sheriff, didn't like his looks and arrested him on suspicion.

An inspection of Smalley's valise revealed eight revolvers and $1,700 in cash. Dunham, who knew about the train robbery, wired the railroad authorities in Indiana. After having heard nothing for two weeks, however, he had to release his prisoner for lack of evidence after fining him $17 for carrying concealed weapons. Until the shoot-out in 1895, that was Smalley's only serious brush with the law.

But all good things come to an end, and Smalley's luck began to run out on the night of August 20, 1895, when he and his men robbed the Chicago & West Michigan passenger train near Fennville, Mich. That was getting a little too close to home.

The men halted the train by throwing oak ties across the tracks and swinging a lantern. Then the job turned into a real fiasco. One man held up the engineer and fireman, while Smalley and the others raced back to the baggage car. Conductor E. E. Rice and the baggageman locked themselves in, but the bandits blew off the side door and dynamited the safe—it was empty. The gang wanted to rob the passengers (who were desperately trying to hide their valuables) but Smalley said no, they'd already spent too much time. So the desperados fled into the night, firing a few shots at the cars and cursing their luck because they'd held up the wrong train.

The total take was less than $50 in cash and three watches belonging to members of the crew. Smalley had lifted the conductor's watch but returned it when Rice protested it wasn't worth much and that he needed it on his job. Smalley stuffed it back in Rice's vest pocket, saying, "We don't want this junk. We're after money."

"This is a pretty tough business to be in, pardner," Rice remarked.

"Yes, and dangerous, too," Smalley said. "But we've got to have money."

That was on a Monday night. Two nights later, at ten forty-five at the Bridge Street station in Grand Rapids, two men bought tickets to Reed City on the Grand Rapids & Indiana railroad. One was heavily bearded, the other younger and smooth-faced. The older man wore a dark coat and soft slouch hat, and carried a brown satchel. Ticket agent C. H. Shirley thought he recognized the older man as the Fennville train robber, whose description had already been circulated among railroad men. He telephoned the police and alerted a fellow agent at a railroad junction north of town. Four city detectives jumped aboard a streetcar and headed for the junction.

They were waiting there when the train pulled in around eleven o'clock. The detectives boarded, each entering a different coach. One of them was George Powers, fifty-two, a big man with a drooping gunfighter mustache. A Civil War hero, even among his fellow officers Powers was known to be a man without fear.

The train was already in motion again when Powers spotted Smalley and his companion in the smoking car. He approached them and said to the bearded man:

"Where did you get on?"

"Bridge Street," Smalley said.

"Where's your partner?"

"Right here," said Smalley, pointing to the young man seated across the aisle.

Powers snatched up Smalley's brown satchel and then reached for the emergency-brake line overhead. In one smooth unhurried motion Smalley stood up, drew a pistol from his coat pocket and shot Powers in the face. The detective fell back, mortally wounded.

As the train ground to a halt, the two gunmen ran down the aisle and out the open door into the night. Powers died at Butterworth Hospital four hours later with a bullet in his brain.

The cold-blooded killing stirred up a tremendous hue and cry. Next morning the whole countryside was swarming with armed men. It was believed that the fugitives were headed for Sparta and Muskegon, and for the next two days teams of detectives and posses of farmers armed with shotguns, rifles and even pitchforks combed that area.

But Smalley had given them the slip. He had started out that way but then doubled back, crossing the GR&I railroad tracks north of Mill Creek and striking out across country to the northeast. What happened to his companion is not known, but Smalley himself turned up the next afternoon in Evart, 60 airline miles north of Grand Rapids.

He was seen there at three-thirty by an old acquaintance, William Stevens, who also spoke with him. Smalley asked Stevens how far it was to Clare, and when Stevens told him it was twenty-five miles, he said, "My God, I've got to be there tonight!"

But this may have been a ruse because Smalley spent Friday night not in Clare but at the home of a friend named Reynolds in Brinton. Next morning he walked to Farwell and caught the Toledo & Ann Arbor train for McBain, arriving there around three o'clock in the afternoon.

Home to John Smalley was any one of a dozen tough towns in Clare and Isabella counties, where he had many friends and relatives. Two years previous he had taken up residence of a sort at McBain in Missaukee County. His "wife," Cora Brown, lived there with her mother and brother. Smalley didn't spend much time there; he'd drop in once in a while for a few days.

Some people called Cora Brown "the Black Diamond," a nickname she obtained like this: In the late 1800s whole tent cities of blueberry pickers used to spring up along northern Michigan rivers during the season. For many of these people—small farm families, out-of-work loggers, and Indians—picking blueberries was their only means of making a little money.

One such encampment on the Muskegon River was known as "Diamond City." Cora Brown, a lady of easy virtue, peddled her favors there. For identification she had a black diamond patch sewn onto her tent flap. Smalley married, or at least "took up" with her, in 1893.

In McBain that Saturday afternoon Smalley headed for the nearest saloon for some quick refreshment. He left a package with the bartender; later it was found to contain only a shirt drenched with sweat. Then he went to see the Browns.

News of Powers' murder had by this time reached McBain, and people there suspected that John Smalley was the killer. He had been seen, and recognized, getting off the train. Ex-sherrif Gillis McBain, now a banker, was notified.

McBain had no stomach for going up against the outlaw alone. He telephoned the cities of Clare and Cadillac for help, but both sheriffs there were out of town. Finally, Deputy Sheriff Bert Spofford of Cadillac offered to come. He hired a fast rig and reached McBain shortly before dark.

The two men organized a posse. All armed with Winchester rifles, they quietly surrounded the Brown house. It was dark now, and John Smalley, sitting near the open front door, was plainly visible in the yellow lamplight. Others in the room were Cora and her mother, her brother Chip, a friend of the family named Mahlon Malcolm, and a neighbor girl named Nellie Carter. Clearly, they were expecting no trouble.

McBain and Spofford approached the open door with rifles ready. When they were within a few feet of the house McBain cried, "Put your hands up, Smalley!"

Smalley jumped to his feet, kicked the door shut and reached for his guns. McBain and Spofford poured a fusillade of shots through the door.

Inside, there was pandemonium. Women screamed, men shouted, somebody doused the light. All came running out the back door, Chip yelling "Fire!" — all except Smalley, that is.

The house now was as dark and silent as a grave. The door had been shot off its hinges, but it was too dark to see anything inside. The posse waited uneasily, calling out from time to time for Smalley to surrender. But not a sound came from the dark house. Was Smalley dead, wounded, or simply playing possum? Nobody had nerve enough to go inside and find out.

After a while one of the women was persuaded to come back. McBain asked her to go inside, light a lamp and look around. "If he's still alive," he told her, "tell him to come out with his hands up. Otherwise, we'll riddle the building."

Not surprisingly, the woman told him to go to hell.

Finally, after an hour had passed, one of the men offered to hold a lantern at the door to light up the room. McBain and another man followed him to the doorway, guns ready. Peering inside they saw what looked like a body at the far end of the room. They entered then and found Smalley lying across the threshold of the kitchen door. He was stone-dead. He had been hit by two bullets, one entering his left arm and passing through his body, the other lodged in his neck.

Still in their holsters were Smalley's self-cocking, .44 caliber Smith & Wesson pistols, their fluted barrels nine inches long. Smalley hadn't had time to fire a shot. The guns were later displayed in the show window of a jewelry store in Grand Rapids; the riddled door was on public view at a museum.

For a time it appeared that Smalley might cheat the law even in death. Several witnesses—including ticket agent Shirley and the GR&I conductor—identified him as the man who had killed Powers. But presently an affadavit was received from Brinton signed by fifty people who swore that Smalley had been there when Powers was shot. The City Attorney scoffed at the document; the people of Brinton were known as a tough, lawless bunch, he said. But the newspapers gave the story a big play, suggesting that the law had blundered.

Then a Grand Rapids man named Emmett Deitrich came forward. He was superintendent of the Veneer Works. He told the police he had seen and talked with John Smalley in Grand Rapids on the night of the murder. He said he'd known Smalley for fifteen years, their friendship going back to the days he had worked with Smalley in the lumber camps on the Muskegon River.

Deitrich said he chanced to meet Smalley near the Bridge Street Station as he was going home from work. Smalley had greeted him, "Hello, Reddy," calling Deitrich by his lumber camp nickname.

"Hello, Free," Deitrich had said, and they shook hands.

They had stood chatting for several minutes about old times, then parted. Deitrich said that at first he hadn't connected Smalley with the Powers murder. He said he had always known Smalley as "Freeman," and was therefore slow to make the connection.

Smalley was buried at McBain. Cora Brown initially refused to pay for his funeral, but finally relented. She drew the line, however, at buying him a tombstone. The grave is still unmarked—though old-timers at McBain will point out its location for the inquisitive stranger.

And so, in obscurity lies John Freeman Smalley, the bearded bandit, last of the old-time train robbers.

WHO KILLED ADAM
BELLINGER?

The old Bellinger farm lies halfway between Cedar and Maple City in Leelanau County. It is an aimless cluster of ramshackle wooden buildings, innocent of paint, in a hollow off County Road 616. No one has lived there in years, and the place looks it — all the buildings are in a terminal state of disrepair. The bleak, squarish two-story house leans fifteen degrees east, and has been propped up with long cedar poles. Remove them, and the house would likely collapse instantly in a cloud of dust.

In 1931 only three members of the Bellinger family were still living on the homestead farm: Orval and his wife, Katherine, and one son, Adam, a tall, goodlooking boy of nineteen whom everybody called Happy because he always wore a smile. The oldest daughter, Grace, was married to Donald Pelky, a rural mail carrier, and lived nearby. The other daughter, Selma (called Sally) — a pretty girl of 18 — lived with the Pelkys. Both girls were at odds with their parents, and in particular with their father, who was said to be a cold disciplinarian.

It was rumored too that there were bad feelings between father and son—something about a .32-caliber gun Adam allegedly "borrowed" or stole from a neighboring farmer. To make it unanimous, Donald Pelky, too, was on bad terms with his father-in-law.

On April 19, 1931, a Saturday, all four of these young people went to a dance at a tavern in Cedar. In company with the Pelkys, Adam escorted a former schoolmate, Evelyn Lewis. Evelyn lived now in Grand Rapids and had come up for a visit with her aunt and uncle, who lived near Maple City.

Adam and his girl, with the Pelkys, arrived at the dance around nine o'clock, and stayed until it was over, about twelve-thirty. They then drove to the Bellinger farm for a round of home brew. Both Adam and Donald Pelky were moderately intoxicated; they had been drinking beer all evening. "They were pretty drunk," a witness testified later, "but not so bad you couldn't reason with them." The two girls were comparatively sober; they had drunk very little.

It was after one o'clock when they arrived at the farm. The house in the hollow was dark; Adam's parents had gone to bed early. The young people went inside and Adam lighted a kerosene lamp in the parlor. Then he stepped into the downstairs bedroom and asked his father to come out and join the party. His father replied that he wasn't feeling well and didn't want to get up. So Adam got two bottles of beer from the icebox (the girls said they didn't want any) and they sat talking and drinking for perhaps half an hour in the yellow lamplight.

It was around one-thirty when they decided to leave. Evelyn said she mustn't stay out too late; her aunt and uncle would be worried. Pelky and the two girls went out to the car, but Adam lingered in the house after blowing out the lamp. At Grace's suggestion Evelyn went back into the dark house to see what was keeping him. She fumbled her way through the kitchen and found him in the parlor, standing quietly in the dark.

"Come on, Happy," she urged him, taking his arm. "We're all waiting for you."

She was still coaxing and tugging at his arm when there was a flash in the dark and a sharp explosion. The flash illuminated Adam's face for an instant—or rather, as Evelyn said later, just his nose. Grace who had followed Evelyn as far as the parlor door, also saw the flash and heard the shot.

Adam fell heavily to the floor. The two girls ran screaming from the house.

"Something terrible's happened," Evelyn screamed at Pelky, who leaped from the car and ran into the house.

He found a strange tableau in the parlor. Adam was lying on the floor with his head in his mother's lap. His father stood nearby holding a lighted lamp. Both parents were in their nightclothes. Mrs. Bellinger told Pelky to fetch a doctor. "Hurry!" she said. "Please hurry!"

Donald turned and ran from the house. He jumped into the car with the girls and drove at breakneck speed to Cedar. There they roused Frank Schramski, owner of the Cedar Tavern. Schramski telephoned Dr. L. R. Way in Traverse City. Then the tavern owner and a friend, John Otto, followed the young people back to the Bellinger farm. They all went inside but after a few moments Schramski and Grace Pelky emerged supporting Evelyn Lewis between them. The girl was hysterical.

"It wouldn't be so bad if I hadn't seen him do it!" she cried again and again.

The doctor from Traverse City arrived half an hour later. He examined the body, questioned the parents and the young people briefly, then drove back to Traverse City. There was nothing he could do, he said. The boy was dead; the rest was up to the authorities. One thing greatly troubled him. Although death was caused by a gunshot wound in the head, he could not find a gun anywhere in the room.

Early in the morning County Sheriff Walter Steimel and two coroners, Fred Murphy and Ralph Kernkamp, having been alerted by Frank Schramski, arrived at the Bellinger farm to make a preliminary examination. What they found was both startling and mystifying.

The boy had been shot through the head, the bullet entering at the center of the forehead and exiting at the base of the skull. The sheriff found a .32-caliber casing under a table in the parlor. He also found a hole in the ceiling where the bullet must have lodged. But the bullet was missing and so was the gun. He couldn't find one anywhere on the premises.

Most puzzling of all were the strange marks on the boy's forehead. Just above the bullet hole was a Y-shaped cut about two inches long. It looked as if it had been made with a knife or a razor blade. But neither the boy's father or mother could explain it, nor could any of the others. They all denied any knowledge of how it got there.

The sheriff and the coroners decided it must have been made by Dr. Way in the course of his examination. But for what reason they couldn't imagine. They'd just have to wait for his testimony at the inquest.

The inquest was held in the nearby town of Suttons Bay on Monday morning. A coroner's jury of six local citizens, together with witnesses and officials, gathered at one end of a small basketball floor over Send's Barbershop.

The first witness, Dr. Way, astonished the authorities by saying he didn't now who made the strange marks on the boy's forehead. Certainly he had not done so, he said. Beyond ascertaining that the boy was dead, he had not touched the body.

Grace Pelky, a pert brunette not at all intimidated by the situation, told about following Evelyn into the house. From the kitchen she saw the flash in the parlor and heard what sounded to her like the slamming of the cellar door. She turned and ran out of the house, with Evelyn right behind her.

"You didn't hear the report of a gun?" Coroner Kernkamp asked.

"It didn't sound like a gun," she said. "I didn't know. I thought maybe my father and him had trouble." There were bad feelings between the father and all the kids, she said. She and her sister Sally never went home except to see their brother Adam.

The coroner pressed for information about the gun, but Grace denied any knowledge of it.

Maybe Evelyn had carried it outside and tossed it from the car as they drove to Cedar, Kernkamp suggested.

Not possible, Grace said. Evelyn had sat in the back seat and cried all the way. The car windows were not opened at any time.

"When you went back in the room, where was the gun lying?"

"There wasn't any gun."

Adam's father, a round-faced greying man of fifty-eight, also disclaimed any knowledge of the gun.

"Did you hear the report of a gun?" Kernkamp asked.

"I couldn't tell it was a gun," Orval said. "It sounded just like a crash. It sounded like something hit the stove pretty hard. The stove iron and shaker are out there and it sounded like those irons dropping."

He said his wife was the first to reach Adam's side and that Pelky was there when he came from the bedroom. But there was no gun. "I didn't see any gun," he said flatly. "I didn't look for a gun. I didn't dream of such a thing as a gun." He said his son owned a .22 rifle and that was all.

Mrs. Bellinger told the same story. She said she heard a crash and thought Adam had tripped.

"You leaped from the bed and ran into the living room just because you thought he had tripped?" she was asked.

"That's right," she said.

"Did you see a gun?"

"No, I didn't look for a gun."

The next witness, Evelyn Lewis, a small dark-haired girl, nervously twisted a handkerchief in her hands. She told about going into the house to get Adam. She was pleading with him and tugging his arm when she saw the flash, heard the explosion, and Adam fell to the floor.

"What did you do with the gun?" Kernkamp asked her.

"I didn't see a gun," she replied softly.

Dr. Murphy interrupted to say that she had told him on Sunday that she saw a small dark gun in Adam's hand. The girl insisted she had told him no such thing. "I beg your pardon, but I didn't," she said.

"You don't need to beg my pardon, sister," the doctor said testily. "You not only said you saw a gun in his hand, but when I asked you if it was a bright gun you said, 'No, it was a dark gun!' " The girl denied it.

Kernkamp unwrapped a small black .32 automatic and held it up. "Is this the gun?" he asked her.

The ruse failed. "I don't know," Evelyn said calmly. "I didn't see a gun."

Donald Pelky, the next witness, threw little light on the mystery.

"Grace went inside when they didn't come out," he testified.

"Evelyn had been gone about two minutes. She'd just got inside when she came running out again and Evelyn was right behind her. Evelyn was screaming, "Something happened!' "

"Did you hear any noises?"

"Yes, some kind of explosion."

"There was no question about its being a gun?"

"It was a gun of some kind."

Pelky said that Mrs. Bellinger was kneeling beside her son and Mr. Bellinger was there with a lamp when he came in. "Mrs. Bellinger told me to get a doctor. I turned and ran out. I didn't get into the room at all."

Kernkamp brought up the question of suicide.

"He had a good disposition," Pelky said. "I liked him. He was never quarrelsome."

"Did he ever talk about doing away with himself?"

"Not that I know of."

None of the witnesses had any knowledge, they said, of how the strange marks got on Adam's forehead.

James B. Hendryx, author of outdoor adventure stories, was the next witness. He had a home near Suttons Bay and had been asked by Dr. Kernkamp to join the investigation as a ballistics expert. A colorful man with handlebar "gunfighter" mustache, he produced an exhibit of animal skins which he had used to determine the amount of powder burns from a .32 pistol at a various range. No powder burns had been found on young Bellinger's face.

Hendryx said the bullet must have been fired at an angle of thirty-five to forty degrees, suggesting that Adam was not standing erect as Evelyn had testified. Moreover, he said, no matter how far Adam was able to hold the gun from his head, the shot would have made noticeable powder marks on his flesh.

It took the jury only twenty minutes to reach a verdict. Death was the result of a gunshot wound inflicted "by an unknown person," they said. This was murder, not suicide.

The Michigan State Police entered the case on Tuesday. Ace homicide detective Neil Black was sent from Lansing to take charge of the investigation. Two troopers spent the day at the Bellinger farm in a fruitless search for the missing weapon. Orval Bellinger was arrested and grilled at the police post in Traverse City. In

Gestapo fashion Evelyn Lewis was awakened by two troopers at midnight and lodged in the Leland jail for questioning.

This heavy-handedness produced no dividends. Orval continued to insist he knew nothing about the gun. "Boys, if I knew where the gun is I'd tell you," he insisted. Eveyln was released to her parents later that morning. They had taken the train from Grand Rapids as soon as they heard the news.

"I didn't kill that boy!" she cried out to her mother. "I didn't kill him!"

Her mother assured her she knew she didn't.

The first real break in the case came on Thursday morning. Donald Pelky went to the police and volunteered some interesting information. He told them that just after the inquest he had told his father-in-law, "Why don't you produce that gun?"

He said the old man told him the gun was where nobody would ever find it. "My boy wasn't a criminal when he was alive and they aren't going to make a criminal out of him after he is dead," Pelky quoted the old man as saying.

The police now redoubled their efforts to get the truth out of Orval Bellinger. Late that afternoon he broke down and admitted he had hidden the gun. He led them to its hiding place on an old stump about a hundred yards back of the house. The gun was covered with leaves.

Bellinger said he had found the gun, a .32 Savage automatic, on a sawdust pile near the barn early Sunday morning. The pile was about 60 yards from the house — too far from the driveway for anyone to have tossed it from a car.

The police examined the gun for fingerprints but found none. Not satisfied with Bellinger's story, they continued to question him.

The truth came out the next day. Bellinger admitted he had found the gun on the parlor floor and thrown it outside. He said he saw the gun beside his son's body when he first came from the bedroom. He picked up the gun, walked through the kitchen and out the back door. He threw the gun as far as he could toward the barn. Later he hid it in the barn, and, after the inquest, on the stump.

That resolved the mystery of the missing gun, but there were many other unanswered questions. Who killed Adam Bellinger? Was it murder or suicide?

On Saturday morning County Prosecutor James Fitzpatrick astounded almost everybody by saying the case was closed. He announced to a group of newsmen in Traverse City that both Orval Bellinger and Evelyn Lewis were now considered free from all suspicion.

"The police have checked every story, every detail," said the young prosecutor. "They report to me that this fellow committed suicide. It's kind of hard to take but it's the truth."

Detective Black called the case the most popular in his experience. "We started this investigation in the absence of any material evidence to support a theory of suicide. There was no weapon to be found and there were other bizarre facts, including the marks on the boy's head. Now we believe, after investigating every detail, that the boy shot himself, just as Evelyn said he did. There is nothing about Evelyn's character that can be questioned. Her reputation is immaculate.

"She said if we took her to prison, she could not tell a different story," he continued. "We had nothing to support the theory that the boy's father killed him. The girl was there. She knew what happened. I am convinced she was telling the truth."

So ended the Adam Bellinger case.

Yet, in the minds of many people, the mystery still remains. Who killed Adam Bellinger? Did he die by his own hand? What about the strange trajectory of the bullet? Why were there no powder burns on his face? Who made those marks on his forehead? Were they a crude attempt by some member of the family to make it look like an accident?

Now, as memories fade, old theories persist. Some suggest Adam was killed by a bullet fired through an open window in the parlor. In the dark room, either by accident or design, the bullet struck him in the exact center of his forehead. But, by whom? And why?

Others, including at least one of the investigating state policemen, believe Adam was killed accidentally in a scuffle over the gun.

But the family scoffs at these theories.

And there the matter rests.

Death Battle at Rattle run

Gideon Browning's sister and her husband, and their family at Adair.

Newspaper photo of the interior of the little church at Rattle Run, scene of the murder.

The Dying Sparlings at Ubly

John Wesley Sparling.

Carrie Sparling.

Peter Sparling.

Albert Sparling.

Dr. Robert A. MacGregor

Scyrel Sparling.

The Mystery of the Missing Nun

Holy Rosary church at Isadore as it looked at the time of the murder. The addition at the rear was built in 1901.

Scenes and Figures in Nun Mystery Case · at Leland

Top, left—Leelanau county courthouse where Mrs. Stanislawa Lypczynski is being tried on a charge of murdering Sister Mary Janina, a nun, at St. Isadore's convent. Bottom, left—The jury in the case (left to right): John Westcott, Glen Arbor; Joseph Bussey, Leland; Benjamin Wilsey, Cleveland township; George Shalda, Cleveland township; John Young, Empire; William Challender, Sutton's Bay; C. H. Treat, Empire; Welby Ray, Glen Arbor; John Bright, Kasson; Herbert Lindley, Bingham; John Shorter, Kasson; George Eckardt, Cleveland township. At right—Mrs. Lypczynski and Fr. Andrew Bienowski, pastor of the Isadore church at the time of Sister Mary Janina's disappearance, and for whom Mrs. Lypczynski was housekeeper.

From the *Grand Rapids Press* at the time of the trial.

The housekeeper Stanislawa
Lipczynska.

Defense attorney Francis Owen
Gaffney.

The little jail at Leland where Mrs. Lipczynska was held before and during her trial.
It was used as a historical museum for several years; now a county storage
building.

The nun's body was reburied at the foot of this metal crucifix, which replaced the original wooden cross on the same spot.

1978 aerial photo of the church buildings at Isadore: Holy Rosary church convent and school. The large building at the rear of the church is the new headquarters and home for the priest.

The Bearded
Bandit Murder

**Grand Rapids police
detective George W.
Powers.**

Who Killed
Adam Bellinger?

**The old Bellinger farm
between Maple City and
Cedar in Leelanau County,
1980.**

Murder in Manistee

George Vanderpool.   Herbert Field.

The Bank of Manistee. Was Field murdered here?

A plan of the bank
building.

The Mad Bomber of Bath

Andrew P. Kehoe, the mad bomber of Bath.

The Ground Glass Murder Case

Rodolphus Sanderson.

Mary Butterfield Sanderson.

The "Perfect Murder" Case

R. Irving Latimore.

Robert F. Latimer.

Mary Latimer.

Invitation to a Hanging

Newspaper photo of Anthony Chebatoris.

The Kicking Horse Murder

Stephen Carroll.

Stephen Carroll with baskets of apples in his Model T. pickup.

IN COLD BLOOD — 1883

The brutal murders that wiped out the Clutter family on a farm in western Kansas one night in November 1959 — told by Truman Capote in his great crime classic, *In Cold Blood* — were foreshadowed three quarters of a century earlier by similar crimes in southern Michigan. Like their Kansas counterparts, four people on a farm near Jackson were gunned to death one night in November 1883.

The Crouch farm a few miles west of Jackson was one of the largest in the county, and Jacob D. Crouch, its owner, was one of the county's richest men. His estate was valued at $90,000 (the equivalent of a million dollars today). He also owned 300,000 acres in Texas, worth $80,000 more.

Crouch had been a widower for 24 years. He had three sons and two daughters, four of them living but none still at home. At 73 he was as powerful and robust as most men of 50. Like Herb Clutter in Kansas, it was rumored that he kept large sums of money in the house.

On November 22, 1883, six people spent the night at the big

91

Crouch farmhouse. They were its owner and his two servants, housekeeper Mrs. Julia Reese and choreboy George Boles, a negro lad of seventeen; also Crouch's daughter Eunice and her husband Henry D. White, here for a short visit. The sixth was a young man from Pennsylvania, Moses Polley, who had arrived the previous day to buy cattle. Polley had formerly worked for Crouch and had lived at the farm. Boles had a room upstairs. Mrs. Reese slept in a little bedroom at the rear of the house, off the kitchen. Crouch and his guests occupied the three other bedrooms on the ground floor.

All retired early; first the servants, then Crouch and his guests. They had chatted for an hour or two in the parlor after supper, drinking sweet cider. Rain began to fall around ten o'clock and by midnight a storm was raging, with thunder and lightning and howling winds: a perfect night for murder.

The choreboy was awakened shortly after midnight by sharp explosive sounds that had nothing to do with the storm. They went on for almost a minute. Badly frightened, he got up and crept into a small painted pine box at the foot of his bed, lowering the cover down over himself. (Later, police and newspaper reporters marveled that he was able to get into such a small space.) There, shaking with fear and cold, he stayed until he heard the clock downstairs strike seven. That was his usual time in the winter to get up and tend the fires.

He went downstairs — with some trepidation, one imagines — and, finding his master and the guests dead in their beds, ran out to sound the alarm. The housekeeper seems to have slept through it all. She told police she hadn't heard any unusual sounds during the night. And she didn't wake up until the neighbors, roused by George Boles, began to flock around the house.

It was found that all the victims except one had apparently died in their sleep. The exception was Mrs. White, who must have awakened and tried to defend herself. She had been shot five times, twice in the upper arm, once each in the neck, breast and head. An autopsy revealed that she was eight months pregnant.

Her husband had been shot in the neck and the head; another bullet had creased his skull and ledged in the wall behind the bed.

Crouch had been killed instantly by a bullet in the brain. Moses Polley had received two fatal wounds: one in the head and one through the heart.

Since at least eleven shots had been fired, the police at first believed that two killers were involved. But then they found the spot where the executioner had paused to reload, scattering cartridge casings on the floor. Ballistic tests showed that all the bullets had been fired from the same gun, a .38-caliber pistol. The police also found a set of footprints in the mud at the southeast corner of the house, suggesting that the killer had had an accomplice who had stood watch outside.

In any case, he'd had no trouble getting inside. There were three doors: One at the front of the house and two at the side. None of them had serviceable locks. Indeed, neighbors said that the house was never locked.

First to enter the house that morning was a neighbor couple named Hatch. They told police they had noticed a strong smell of chloroform in the rooms. So, for a time the police theorized that the victims had been anesthetized before being shot. Another theory was that they'd been drugged by something put in the cider. But the leftover cider was analyzed and nothing suspicious was found in it. And no one besides the Hatches had smelled chloroform in the house that morning.

Although robbery seemed the likeliest motive, the authorities soon had to rule it out. Contrary to rumor, Crouch never kept large sums of money in the house. Nor was Moses Polley carrying any appreciable amount of cash on his person. (It had been suggested that hoodlums in town might have seen him flashing a roll of bills and followed him to the Crouch farm.) Moreover, the killer had left untouched Henry White's hundred dollars in cash on the windowsill and Mrs. White's forty-five dollars and a handful of valuable jewelry on a commode in their bedroom.

What then — revenge? The police rounded up two likely suspects and grilled them. One was George Boles' brother, John, whom Crouch had discharged a few days previously. He was said to have made threats against his former employer. The other was a man named Elder, who had been caught stealing from Crouch and sent to prison in Ionia. He too had threatened revenge, and was now at liberty, having served his three-year term. But both men proved to have unassailable alibis and were cleared of suspicion.

The police had now reached a dead end. They had no additional suspects and no solid clues. They had to admit that all they had to go on concerning the killer who had snuffed out four lives as cooly and methodically as a butcher slaughtering pigs or chickens were probabilities. He probably knew the family and their habits. He was probably familiar with the layout of the house.

In contrast to the scarcity of clues, the authorities were beseiged by amateur detectives and cranks offering advice on how to go about catching the murderer. One man suggested that Eunice White's eyeballs be examined microscopically "because the image of her killer must be imprinted on the retinas."

The first break in the case came on February 2, 1884 — though the authorities didn't realize it at the time. On this day Jacob Crouch's youngest daughter, Susan, died of natural causes. Some twenty years earlier she had married against her father's wishes Daniel S. Holcomb, a farmer who lived nearby. He was a rough, profane sort of fellow whom her father detested. Her mother died a year or so later, leaving her father with a months-old baby boy. And Susan, to please her father, offered to take the child and raise him. The boy, Judd Crouch, grew up to be a weak, spindly young man with a club foot who idolized and tried to emulate his foster father and hated his real father, Jacob Crouch.

Susan had been ailing for some time before the murders, and she took the death of her father and sister very hard. What the police didn't know was that she was also exceedingly worried that her husband and younger brother might have had something to do with the murders. They had been questioned at length by the police and cleared, at least temporarily — even though the police learned that Holcomb had recently taken out a $1,000 insurance policy on his father-in-law's life.

Three days after Susan Holcomb's death, however, something happened that caused the police to take another hard look at the members of the Holcomb household. One of them, a hired hand named James S. Foy, tried to kill the editor of the *Union City Register*.

Foy was a weak-minded drunkard given to sudden violent rages.

On February 5 he went by train to nearby Union City with a .32-caliber pistol in his pocket. He intended (as he told a friend) to "settle his hash" for printing a story casting suspicion on him and Dan Holcomb for the Crouch murders. But he mistook another man, Elmer Shuler, for editor J. D. Easton, and gunned him down on the street.

Shuler, a deputy postmaster, eventually recovered. But Foy shot and killed himself in the kitchen of the Crouch farmhouse the next morning when a deputy sheriff from Jackson arrived to take him into custody for the attack on Shuler. Foy had been staying there with Judd Crouch since the day after the murders.

Three days later there was another attempted murder in connection with the Crouch case, and people began to wonder if the violence was ever going to end. Galen Brown, a private detective, had been poking around the Crouch farm one day in the hope of collecting the $5,000 reward ($3,000 had been offered by the sheriff; $2,000 by Eunice White's brother Byron). He was accosted by two men in an open buggy that night while walking along a lonely country road. The driver pulled up and asked in a friendly way if he was detective Brown. When he said yes, the other — a smaller man — leaned down, thrust a pistol at Brown's body and fired, saying, "Take that, God damn you!"

The bullet passed through Brown's chest three inches above the heart and lodged behind his shoulder blade. He staggered to the nearest farmhouse for help, and he also recovered from his wound. Next morning he told the sheriff that, although he hadn't gotten a very good look at their faces in the dark, he was sure the two men were Dan Holcomb and Judd Crouch.

Meanwhile, the sheriff had obtained new evidence. A servant girl, Ella Shannon, had started working at the Holcomb house five days after the murders, replacing an older woman who had quit at the time. Ella told the sheriff that she had discovered some bloody clothing — pants, shirts and underwear — behind a wooden chest in Judd Crouch's bedroom. Soon after that, she said, the clothing disappeared.

On the basis of this and other evidence, Judd Crouch and Daniel Holcomb were arrested on March 2 and charged with the Crouch murders. They took their detention calmly. Judd's older brother,

Captain Byron Crouch, declared his belief in their innocence. The Captain had come from his home in Texas shortly after the murders. He was described by one reporter as a "tall, lean man with a slight tan and a grip of iron."

The hearing opened in a courtroom in Jackson on March 6. The police had already questioned all the members of the Holcomb household not once but several times. On the witness stand they told substantially the same stories as when questioned earlier.

Seven people were living in the Holcomb house at the time of the murders. In addition to the Holcombs and Judd Crouch, there were three hired hands: James Foy, Fred Lounsberry, seventeen, and Charley Andrews, thirteen; also the servant woman Nettie Synder. The Holcombs and Synder slept in bedrooms on the lower floor; Judd and Andrews slept together in one upstairs bedroom, Foy and Lounsberry in another.

They had all gone to bed about nine o'clock. Around midnight Judd and Foy got up to put the cat out. A little later, Holcomb said, he got up and went outside to secure a barn door that had been left open: it was banging in the wind. Neither Andrews nor Lounsberry could remember when their bed partners came back to bed because they had slept soundly until morning.

The distance across open fields from the Holcomb house to the Crouch farm was about a mile and a half. Thus it was possible, argued the prosecution, that all three men — Holcomb, Crouch and Foy — could have gone to the Crouch place, committed the murders and returned in less than an hour. The defense of course scoffed at the notion.

Another witness, the private detective Galen Brown, testified that Foy had told him that he and Holcomb knew who committed the murders. According to Brown, Foy had said that three men were responsible. One killed the Whites; another killed Crouch and Polley. Foy said that Polley was shot when he poked his head out the bedroom door; and was then carried back to bed. One man, Foy waited outside while the killers went about their business.

Curiously, Foy told much the same story to another man, a stranger he met on the train to Union City, who so testified.

Ella Shannon took the witness stand in tears. She said she'd been struck by a man as she was entering the courthouse. She described him as short and thick-set, with squinty eyes. Her story about the bloody clothing was flatly contradicted by Nettie Synder, who said she had cleaned Judd's bedroom on the day after the murders and had found nothing of the kind.

A farmer in the neighborhood testified about finding two sets of tracks in a field between the Crouch and Holcomb farms. He followed the footprints for some distance, then lost them on harder ground. He was sure that one set belonged to Judd Crouch, because the right footprint, made by Judd's deformed foot, was deeper than the other.

George Boles was an excellent witness—in some ways helpful to the defense. He said without apparent resentment that everybody called him "coon" or "coonie."—"Coon, coon, get on my grey horse and go tell the neighbors that they are all murdered here," a farmer named Hitchens had told him that morning. He said that Susan Holcomb, upon learning of the murders, cried, "Oh, no! It can't be true!" and burst into tears. He said that Holcomb, too, had tears in his eyes. "Was Polley there too?" he said Holcomb asked him.

Nevertheless, the jury found that there was sufficient evidence to hold both men for trial on charges of murder. Later, the State decided to try them separately.

Holcomb was first. His trial opened in circuit court in Jackson on November 11, 1884, and dragged on for almost eight weeks. Many more witnesses were called than had testified at the hearing, but little new evidence was produced. In the end, it took the jury only three hours to find the defendant not guilty. Judd Crouch was never brought to trial.

Afterward, Holcomb declared there was never any case against him—"only what the God damn newspapers made," he said.

"It must have been tramps, after all," Captain Crouch said.

But hardly anybody really believed that, probably not even the captain. In any case—unlike their counterparts in Kansas almost a century later—the mystery of the Crouch murders remains unsolved to this day.

MURDER IN MANISTEE

The rough-and-tumble lumber town of Manistee in 1869 could take in stride a killing or two among barroom brawlers and thieves, but when both of the town's bankers became involved in a mysterious murder case, respectable people were shocked beyond belief.

The two young men, Herbert Field, twenty-one, and George Vanderpool, about thirty, had opened Manistee's first bank in 1868. Neither man knew much about banking, but nobody else in town did, either, so they filled a need and their business prospered. Both were newcomers to Manistee, as indeed were most people in the town. Fed by the boom in pine lumber, the town had burgeoned from around 500 people to nearly 5,000 in less than ten years.

A strange fate had brought these two men together for their rendezvous with death.

Vanderpool came to Manistee from New York state by way of Muskegon, where he had worked for several business firms, except for three years' service in the Civil War. In Muskegon he had acquired a reputation as a good businessman — so sober, industrious and reliable that his friends were willing to back him in the new banking venture. In keeping with his solid reputation, he had taken a wife before leaving Muskegon.

Field was more of a rover. At thirteen he ran away from home in Lewiston, Maine, for an unsuccessful attempt to join the Union army in Washington, then went to sea. He jumped ship and was jailed in Valparaiso, signed aboard a navy vessel which was wrecked in the Baltic, and spent some time in England before returning home. Later he made a voyage to the Caribbean in search of guano.

His adventures caught the attention of a wealthy spinster of fifty-five, Miss Rachel Hill, who made him her protégé. She offered to pay his way through college or to set him up in the business of his choosing. After several false starts, this odd couple landed in Manistee in 1868 as "aunt and nephew," looking for a business opportunity.

After a brief acquaintance, the two young men — who had taken an instant liking to each other — formed a partnership and opened their doors as "Field & Vanderpool, Bankers." As capital, Vanderpool put up about $2,500, mostly borrowed from Muskegon friends; Field, $7,000 of Miss Hill's money. It was thought that Vanderpool's greater business experience made up for the financial disparity.

The firm occupied half of the ground floor of a two-story frame building on River Street. The other half was occupied by a shoe store and a lawyer's office. An eccentric dentist, Dr. Jackson B. Wilcox, had offices on the second floor. They were reached by an outside staircase on the west side of the building; another flight of stairs led to a small dock at the river's edge.

The banking room was long and narrow, about twelve feet by fifty. It was divided into three parts by a counter with a frosted glass screen a dozen feet back from the door and a curtain strung on wire. The space behind the counter was used as an office. It had a desk, a safe, a lounge against one wall and a stove at the rear.

Despite their short acquaintance and differences in temperament the two men soon became close friends. It was Field's habit to drop in on the newlywed Vanderpools nearly every day. Just before his death Field made a gift of his little black-and-tan terrier to Mrs.

Vanderpool. (Field's other, much larger dog stood guard at the bank at night.)

By June of 1869 the firm had made a profit of $3,000 — a tidy sum in those days — and Field took a vacation trip to visit his family and friends in Maine. When he returned, he offered to buy Vanderpool out. The latter refused and countered with an offer to find a replacement partner for Field. But Field rejected the offer, and they agreed to go on as before.

But when Vanderpool in turn took a vacation in July and August, visiting friends in Wisconsin, Field wrote him he didn't like Manistee and wanted out of the business. Apparently he was growing restless under the constraints of the partnership.

Upon his return, Vanderpool found things in a mess — books unbalanced and important papers gone astray. He also found an apparent shortage of $1,700 in the books, but Field nonchalantly assured him it must be somewhere in the business. During Vanderpool's absence, Field on an almost daily basis had begun to withdraw his investment, depositing the money in a safe at the Willard & Hall drugstore down the street.

Despite these difficulties the two men seem to have remained on friendly terms right up to the end. They drew up and signed a notice of dissolution of the partnership, and Vanderpool paid Field the remaining $800 of his investment.

That was on Saturday, September 4. They met again by chance early Sunday morning. Vanderpool asked Field to meet him at the bank after breakfast, and Field agreed.

For what happened there on that Sunday morning we have only Vanderpool's word: Field wasn't seen alive after that.

According to Vanderpool, they met at the bank around ten o'clock. After a brief discussion of a few items overlooked the day before, Field proposed they give each other a receipt in full. They made out the papers and then went next door to the shoe shop, where a group of idlers was discussing Swedenborgianism. They asked two of them, A. A. Smith and William D. Ramsdell, to sign the papers as witnesses. After this was done, the two men returned to the bank.

Vanderpool said he started for home, then tarried awhile to fill the spittoon with fresh water; he had intended to give the place a thorough cleaning on Monday. Field meanwhile had begun to play with the little black-and-tan dog, tossing him in the air to make him growl. Vanderpool protested in a joking way, saying he wouldn't see his dog abused. But Field continued to horse around, making passes at Vanderpool with the growling dog.

Just then, somebody banged on the front door and called out to them to stop the racket or he'd call the sheriff—it was Sunday and they ought to be ashamed of themselves. The voice belonged to William Ramsdell, on his way home from the shoe store. He had tried the door and found it locked, then peered through a crack in the blind but couldn't see anyone inside.

There was no reply but the commotion ceased abruptly and Ramsdell went on his way. After a few minutes, however, Field started tossing the dog in the air again and catching it. Then he missed one catch, and the two partners began to chase the little dog around the room, knocking down chairs and other objects. If true (remember, we have only Vanderpool's word for this), it must have been a slapstick comedy spectacle—especially when Vanderpool, who was suffering from the "summer complaint", had an unfortunate accident, soiling his trousers and vest. Field obligingly loaned him clean underwear and a pair of pants from a trunk he had stored in the back room. Vanderpool threw his ruined clothing into the stove, intending to burn it the next day.

Vanderpool said he then went home, taking the little dog with him. He left Field stretched out on the couch, reading. Field had said he had some letters to write before he left. That was the last time he saw his partner, Vanderpool said.

That may have been the last time anyone saw Field alive. At the trial, the defense produced three witnesses who testified they saw him that afternoon, but they may have been mistaken about the hour or even the day.

Rachel Hill was the first to notice Field's absence. Early the next morning she sent a messenger to Vanderpool saying Field had been missing all night. Vanderpool interrupted his cleaning chores at the bank to call on her. He tried to reassure her by saying that Field had probably gone off on a little trip and would be back soon. But she wouldn't listen. She was sure something dreadful had happened to him.

Back at the bank Vanderpool resumed his cleaning, which he'd begun at six that morning. He took up the carpet (with some difficulty because he couldn't find the lathing hatchet to remove the tacks), then scrubbed the floor and sluiced it down with buckets of water. The floor was slightly tilted, and the water ran to the back and out a trap door over the river.

Vanderpool left in place the parts of the carpet that were under the desk, stove and safe; he cut around them and pulled up the rest. He also removed a large spot where the watchdog had been tied nights because, he said, it was disgustingly dirty. This he burned in the stove. Also consigned to the flames were his soiled trousers and vest.

People had been dropping in all day, and the news of Field's disappearance soon spread all over town. Most of his friends were inclined to agree with Vanderpool that he'd gone off somewhere — Vanderpool said Field had spoken about going to sea again.

But when Tuesday's boat brought no word from him there was a growing feeling of alarm. Miss Hill went to the authorities and voiced her suspicions. County Sheriff Charles Secor and three justices of the peace set a quiet watch on Vanderpool and the bank.

Next morning, after Vanderpool had done more before-breakfast cleaning, these men called on him at home and escorted him to the bank. They were joined there by three bookkeepers who made an audit of the books and found that two entries of $400 and $700 — representing payments to Field — had been changed to $1,400 and $1,700.

The law officers also made some significant discoveries. In addition to the partially burned clothing and carpet in the stove, they found what appeared to be blood spots on the remaining carpet. There were stains on the bare floor and when some of the matchboarding was taken up, they found that blood had seeped through the cracks. At the trial, a professor of forensic medicine testified that it was human blood.

Vanderpool explained that both he and Field — and the dog, too — had had nosebleeds. But he couldn't account for the false entries in the books, and they were never satisfactorily explained.

103

Vanderpool was taken into custody that noon. Sheriff Secor, who still believed him innocent, went home with Vanderpool and had dinner, then took him to jail. There he was allowed considerable liberty for the next few days.

A large party of volunteers combed the river and the surrounding country for days without finding any trace of Field. People began to think again that he'd run off somewhere.

But on Friday, September 17, a man walking the beach in Frankfort, twenty-eight miles north of Manistee, found a body lying on the sand. It was clad in a black vest and trousers, and a rope was tied around the waist. There were rust stains on the shirt, and it appeared that the body had been weighted down and submerged.

The body was positively identified as that of Herbert Field. His dentist recognized the teeth, and a letter addressed to "Herbert F—" was found in one of the pockets. The cause of death was obvious. There were two mortal wounds in the head, one at the back and one near the top of the skull. Apparently the assassin had struck Field two powerful blows from behind with something like a hammer—the lathing hatchet that Vanderpool said he couldn't find could have done it. A coroner's jury found that Field had been killed by George Vanderpool on September 5 at the bank building.

Feeling ran high against the accused, and there was talk of a lynching. Two of Vanderpool's acts brought him deeper under suspicion. He had hidden some gold coins in his woodshed before being taken to jail. When these were found by the sheriff, Vanderpool said he'd placed them there for his wife. Later he fabricated a letter ostensibly written by two illiterate sailors, confessing to Field's murder, which was found before it could be smuggled out of jail.

Vanderpool said he was sorry. Though completely innocent, he said he knew his situation was desperate, calling for desperate measures. Naturally, the authorities thought otherwise.

Though Vanderpool had no witness to support his story of what had happened at the bank on Sunday morning, he had an iron-clad alibi for his whereabouts from Sunday noon until Monday morning—except for one short period between 9:30 and 10:55 on Sunday night.

During that time, Vanderpool said, he'd gone out to get some medicine for his illness but found that all the stores were closed. He went from place to place and finally got some medicine at Dr. Fisher's. He then went home to bed, and his wife said he stayed there until morning.

Vanderpool's trial for murder opened in Manistee on February 1, 1870. The prosecution, led by Thomas B. Church of Grand Rapids, charged that he killed Herbert Field with a lathing hatchet at the bank around noon on September 5, and that he weighted the body, towed it to the mouth of the river and sunk it in Lake Michigan.

Among the prosecution's witnesses were two men who said they'd seen a rowboat on the river that evening. One said he noticed a white boat lying at the dock below the bank at about nine-thirty; a man in a light-colored suit was sitting in it. The other, a fisherman who lived on the north side of the river, saw a white boat with a single oarsman around ten o'clock. When he stumbled and made a noise, the boat stopped, then crossed to the south side and continued on down the river.

The defense contended that Vanderpool was innocent for obvious reasons. One, Field was seen alive Sunday afternoon. Two, the weighted body couldn't have drifted twenty-eight miles; it must have been disposed of farther north, and Vanderpool had had no time to do that. Three, nobody but a madman or an idiot would have displayed himself in Field's trousers that afternoon. Four, it hadn't been shown that Vanderpool had access to a boat. And finally, there wasn't enough blood at the bank to show that a man had been killed there with a hatchet.

The defense in closing speculated that Field had been picked up that evening by a "rough sailor acquaintance" who had come secretly to Manistee. The two men rowed down the river and out on the lake. They were carried far north by the wind and currents. Field was killed, robbed and dumped overboard. The "rough" sailor was picked up by a passing steamer.

There wasn't a shred of evidence to support this tale, and after deliberating only six hours the jury rendered a verdict of "guilty of murder in the first degree." Vanderpool was sentenced to life at Jackson prison.

Almost immediately Vanderpool's friends began to petition for a new trial and to collect money for his defense. And in July of 1870 Judge Ramsdell set aside the verdict and ordered a new trial. He said the case had troubled him. He felt that guilt had not been proven beyond a reasonable doubt.

The second trial, held in Kalamazoo in October, resulted in a hung jury: seven for conviction and five against.

A third trial, at Hastings in Berry County, was held in August of 1871. The defense astonishingly introduced some testimony in support of its earlier reconstruction of the crime. William E. Smith, master of the schooner *Crawford*, said that on September 15, he'd picked up a man adrift in a white rowboat 12 miles offshore of Manistee. This person, who called himself Jacob, refused to be put ashore anywhere along Lake Michigan. He behaved very mysteriously, clutching a small bundle he wouldn't let out of his sight. Margaret Anderson, cook aboard the *Crawford*, said she caught the stranger examining a big roll of money which he promptly hid away. The stranger jumped off the ship as it was docking in Detroit and was later seen boarding the Windsor ferry.

Whether this had any effect on the jury is not known. But after six hours they brought in a verdict of not guilty, and Vanderpool was again a free man. It is said that the verdict so angered the people of Manistee that they refused to reimburse Barry County for court costs, and the matter was unsettled for years.

Life wasn't kind to Vanderpool in later years. He and his wife remained together, but as a traveling shoe salesman he wandered from place to place and lived in poverty for the rest of his life. Maybe the people of Manistee could find some consolation—and poetic justice—in that.

Field's "aunt," stayed on in Manistee and became a recluse. She was found in bed one winter day in 1873 by her physician, Dr. Lathrop S. Ellis. Summoned by a neighbor, who had seen no smoke from the chimney nor any other sign of life, Dr. Ellis found the door locked and had to climb through a window. He found the cause of death to be an overdose of morphine. She had been using that drug as a painkiller for neuralgia. In a note found at her bedside she wrote that she was tired of life.

THE MAD BOMBER
OF BATH

One of the most hideous crimes ever committed in America took place on May 18, 1927, just two days before Charles Lindbergh made his historic flight across the Atlantic Ocean. It happened in the little village of Bath, Mich., population about three hundred, eight miles north of Lansing, and it brought tragedy and heartbreak to almost everyone in town.

Andrew Kehoe, a small and not very successful farmer near Bath, had a grudge against the world in general and the local school board in particular. As treasurer of the board he regarded himself as a watchdog over the public funds. For years he had fought to hold the line on school expenses and taxes. This often brought him in conflict with other board members who weren't averse to raising money for necessary school improvements. To them, Andy's tight-fistedness seemed arbitrary and unreasonable.

The big fight came when the board proposed building a new schoolhouse. Andy fought against it tooth and nail. Outnumbered on the board, he took his case to the townspeople. For weeks before the election he would buttonhole people on the street and urge them to vote against the proposal, arguing that the district didn't need a new school building, that the old was plenty good enough, that it would be a waste of the taxpayers' money.

Some people agreed with him, but not nearly enough. When the votes were counted, Andy wound up on the losing side. By a wide margin the voters had passed a special levy on property owners of $40 per thousand dollars of assessed valuation to raise money for the new school. Andy's tax bite came to $400 per year, no trifling sum in those days.

Andy was bitter over the defeat; he took it personally. Somehow he felt cheated, that life had shortchanged him, and now these spendthrifts on the school board were raising his taxes and bleeding him white. His grudge against the board and the school superintendent kept growing until it became an obsession. It was always there: a dark and brooding shadow on his mind. It poisoned his appetite, ruined his sleep and blighted his hopes for the future. It swelled to such proportions that finally it had to explode.

It was true that life hadn't been kind to Andrew Kehoe. After a promising start with a college degree (at Michigan State) and a good job as an electrician, things had seemed to go downhill for him from there. At fifty, he was a crabbed, crotchety little man with an invalid wife and no children, an unprofitable farm, and a big mortgage that the bank had threatened to foreclose on. The school tax had ruined him, he said. That school should never have been built.

In the fall of 1926 Kehoe went to Lansing and bought 500 pounds of surplus World War I dynamite at the State Farm Agency. A farm neighbor who accompanied him wasn't surprised at the nature of the purchase and only mildly so at the size of it. The fact was that Kehoe was known around Bath as the "dynamite farmer." His neighbors on nearby farms were accustomed to hearing blasts from the Kehoe farm. It seemed that he was forever blowing up stumps and rocks on his place.

But Kehoe had another purpose for this explosive and other dynamite he purchased around this time. All during the winter of 1926–27 he made surreptitious trips at night to the basement of the new school. There he placed caches of dynamite under the whole school building, hiding them in the crawl space under the basement floor, between the joists of the basement ceiling and behind the wall panels. No one saw him do this and the explosives were never discovered until it was too late. As school electrician and treasurer of the board, Kehoe had keys to the building and could come and go as he pleased without exciting suspicion.

By the middle of May 1927, the job was finished. All the charges were wired together and hooked up to a makeshift detonator consisting of an old alarm clock and two "hot shot" batteries. On the night of May 17, Kehoe made his last trip to the school basement. He set the alarm clock to detonate the charges at nine forty-five the next morning. Meanwhile, he had been planting explosives in his own house and outbuildings.

On Monday of that week, one of the grade school teachers had called him up and asked permission to use a particular grove on the Kehoe farm for a class picnic.

"When is your picnic?" Kehoe had asked her.

"On Thursday afternoon, May 19," she told him.

"Well," he said, "if you're planning a picnic you'd better hold it right away."

He didn't elaborate and she didn't ask; she put his rather strange answer down to his well-known eccentricity.

At nine o'clock on Wednesday morning, May 18, school attendance was down from a normal 340 to about 260 students, mostly in the lower grades. This was commencement week and most of the high school students were scheduled to take examinations and weren't due to arrive until ten. Early that morning, the school janitor and another member of the school board had gone down to the basement to check on the furnace, but found nothing amiss.

At precisely 9:45, a tremendous explosion rocked the two-story brick school building. The entire north wing rose in the air and then slammed back down on its foundations, crushing scores of students and teachers under tons of twisted wood, steel, concrete and bricks. The blast broke windows and rattled dishes all over town. It was heard and felt as far as six miles away.

After the fallout had subsided there were a few moments of stunned silence — even the birds were hushed. Then the air began to fill with the screams and moans of the victims trapped under the debris. The whole town rushed to the scene. Frantic mothers and fathers clawed among the ruins for their children, often displaying superhuman strength in lifting and moving aside massive chunks of the debris.

They were soon joined by state police, firemen and volunteers from Lansing and other nearby communities. The search through the wreckage continued all through the day and with searchlights on into the night.

The seriously injured were rushed to hospitals in Lansing. The dead were laid out in rows on the school lawn and covered with blankets. Anguished scenes of grief-stricken parents lifting aside the covering to identify their dead children were repeated many times.

Of the approximately 150 students in the north end of the building, ranging in age from seven to fourteen, thirty-seven were killed outright or died of their injuries; ninety-five were injured, some very seriously; and the rest miraculously escaped with only minor cuts and bruises: a few were blown clear through the windows. The death of one twenty-two-year-old teacher (two others were seriously injured) brought the total to thirty-nine.

Later it was discovered that, although charges had been placed under the entire building and wired for detonation, only those under the north wing of the school had exploded. A defect in the wiring or the equipment had saved at least a hundred lives.

Meanwhile, back at the farm, Kehoe dynamited his house at about the same time as the school blast, wrecking the building and setting it afire. A neighbor driving by with his three teenage sons, stopped to offer assistance. They saw Kehoe standing near his barn, watching the flames.

"Boys," Kehoe told them as they came running up, "you're my friends. You'd better get out of here and go to the school."

Driving off, they heard other explosions from the Kehoe farm.

Kehoe himself got into his car and drove to town. He parked at the curb in front of the school and for several minutes sat and watched people milling about the wreckage. One of them was Emory E. Huyck, the school superintendent, who had already distinguished himself by carrying several children out of the ruins.

Kehoe caught his eye and beckoned him over to the car. As he approached, Kehoe got out, and the two men stood talking

110

together for several moments. Then Kehoe reached into the car, took out a .32-caliber rifle and fired a bullet into a keg of dynamite in the rear seat.

The explosion blew the automobile and the two men literally to pieces. Also killed in the blast were two men standing nearby. One was the Bath postmaster, Glenn Smith, who lost his legs and died on the spot in his wife's arms; the other was Smith's father-in-law, Nelson McFarren. The Mad Bomber had claimed his last four victims.

Somebody remembered that Kehoe had mailed a package the day before in a cardboard box that had apparently been used to pack dynamite. The addressee was Clyde B. Smith, an insurance agent in East Lansing, who had provided Kehoe's bond as school treasurer. The police traced it and found that the package had been sent by mistake to Laingsburg, Mich. They retrieved it and took it in a bomb-proof container to State Police Headquarters in Lansing, where it was opened gingerly by bomb-disposal experts. Instead of dynamite they found that the box contained a complete set of books of account—one for each year that Kehoe had served as school board treasurer. An accompanying note, signed by Kehoe, said that he was "leaving the school board" and hereby turning over the books to his bondsman.

Meanwhile, the police had been looking for Kehoe's wife, Nellie. It was believed that she was in a hospital in Lansing, but a check of the hospitals there and in other southern Michigan communities drew a blank. So the police went out to check at the Kehoe farm, half afraid of what they might find.

The house and other farm buildings were completely destroyed by the dynamite and fire, and there was no sign of a body in the ashes. It was discovered, finally, some twenty rods from the house, lying on a milk cart in the charred ruins of a small shed. Kehoe had wheeled his wife's body out there and had piled her valuables— silver, jewelry and other things—around her in a heap. Then he had set the shed afire.

The body was burned beyond recognition, but an autopsy revealed that her skull was crushed. Kehoe had killed her with a blow to the head, probably (let's give him the benefit of the doubt) while she was sleeping or at least unaware of her peril.

111

The police and other people who visited the farm that day were puzzled by a sign that Kehoe had painted and hung on a fence near the road. They interpreted it in different ways. It said: "Criminals are made, not born."

At an inquest held a few days later, the jury delivered the dubious and in any case irrelevant judgement that Kehoe was sane when he committed his crimes.

The Mad Bomber was buried in St. Johns, Mich., on Friday, May 20. His sister had made the necessary funeral arrangements. But she wasn't there to see him off, nor was any other relative or friend — only a single gravedigger to fill in the hole after a truck had delivered the remains in a plain wooden coffin, and maybe the Prince of Darkness to make sure he found his way to the right place.

People didn't want to remember Andrew Kehoe. They wanted to forget him as quickly as possible.

THE GROUND GLASS MURDER CASE

When old Rodolphus Sanderson married Mary Butterfield, people called it an outrage. Mr. Sanderson, in his eighties, was one of Battle Creek's most highly respected citizens. The girl, young enough at twenty-eight to be his granddaughter, was nothing but a hussy from Detroit, a gold-digger after the old man's money, they said. Sanderson's first wife and daughter, dead these many years, must be turning in their graves. Poor Mr. Sanderson, they said. It was a scandal—nothing good would come of it.

So people weren't altogether surprised when, exactly two months later, on September 6, 1898, the old man died under what some people chose to call suspicious circumstances. Among them were the first Mrs. Sanderson's brothers, Jasper and Onyx Adams (the names of many of the people in this case are astonishingly Dickensian), who stood to gain a considerable share of the estate if Sanderson died single.

Although the old man's physician, Dr. Wattles, called it a stroke, the brothers began to hint darkly of foul play. The rumor spread through the community, until finally it reached the ears of the

113

authorities, who took a sharp look and then called for exhumation of the body and an autopsy. This led to the following scene, straight out of Edgar Allan Poe or William Faulkner.

Oakhill Cemetery in Battle Creek near the hour of midnight, October 12, 1898. A group of men are gathered around an open grave. They include Justice Lewis, Sheriff Stone, Prosecuting Attorney Lockton, Drs. Wattles, Pitcher and Miller, undertaker Walter Keet, a couple of hackmen and several others. All have been sworn to secrecy.

A reporter for the *Battle Creek Journal* tells the story:

"It was a solemn, somber scene, the sexton working slowly and steadily at his task of exhuming the body, which had been placed in what was supposed to be its last resting place. The dim light of the lantern shed its flickering glimmer upon the pale faces of the spectators, and the only sound that broke the stillness was the thud of the earth as it fell upon the large canvass that had been spread beside the grave, and the solemn hoot of an owl which sounded through the city of the dead."

The *Journal* reporter wasn't there. He got his story second hand, and one wonders about that owl. Imaginary or not, it was the perfect touch—no writer with an appreciation for the macabre could have failed to put it in.

"The moments seemed hours as the work progressed in the awful stillness, but finally the gruesome task was completed and all that was earthly of this good old man was taken from the grave . . . The casket was in good condition, and it was borne to an old barn between Walter Keet's residence and the old Davis property on South Avenue. The doors were closed and a watch was kept outside to prevent interruption. The spectators gathered in a circle to watch the coroner, Dr. Miller, and Drs. Wattles and Pitcher at the task of dissecting the body. The brain, stomach, intestines, kidneys and heart were removed and taken by Dr. Pitcher to Ann Arbor to be examined by experts.

"When the coffin was opened it was found that Mr. Sanderson looked as natural as he did the day he was buried, the embalmer's fluid having done its work perfectly, but as soon as the remains were exposed to the air the stench was terrible, and some of the spectators had to leave the barn and throw up their suppers."

So much for the exhumation and autopsy. The reporter goes on to describe the latter at some length, but the details are best left to the imagination.

A few days later, Dr. Albert B. Prescott, professor of chemistry at the University of Michigan, made his report. In his examination of the vital organs, he said he found six pieces of glass in the stomach and intestines. The largest was about three thirty-seconds of an inch in diameter, the smallest about one-twentieth. He also found arsenic and mercury in sufficient quantities to cause death, but he believed these elements were a residue of the embalming fluid.

On the strength of this and other evidence, Mary Butterfield Sanderson was arrested on a charge of murder.

Rodolphus Sanderson was born of prosperous farmer parents in Milton, Vermont, in 1818. Starting out at eighteen as clerk in the village drygoods store, he became a successful merchant, married the daughter of a prominent Vermont lawyer, and served two terms in the State Legislature. He moved his family to Michigan in 1853, settling on a farm near Newton, a now-vanished hamlet in Calhoun County, roughly equidistant from Battle Creek and Marshall. The Sandersons had no children of their own, but had adopted a baby girl; she died on the Michigan farm in her teens.

Pursuing his interest in politics, Sanderson was elected to the Michigan legislature in 1865, and again in 1873. After his wife's death in 1874, he moved to Battle Creek (but still kept the farm) and bought a fine house at 194 East Main Street. There, as alderman of the Fourth Ward and a director at the bank, he soon became a distinguished citizen, much sought after for his expert advice in business and money matters. He was wealthy and wise, but also lonely, ailing and vulnerable.

Sanderson was eighty and in failing health when he met Mary Butterfield. They were introduced on the street by a mutual friend in the spring of 1898. Mary was in town visiting her sister. She was a trained nurse, having worked in hospitals in Minneapolis, Ann Arbor, and most recently in Detroit.

From the very beginning, Sanderson seems to have been captivated by Mary's wit and charm. So much so, in fact, that after a few more meetings, accidental and then by design, he proposed marriage, pointing out the mutual benefits of such an alliance. Mary demurred, and went back to work at Harper Hospital in Detroit. Sanderson pursued, (if that's the right word to describe an octogenarian courtship), first by letter and then in person, and finally he persuaded the lady to say yes.

They were married in Windsor, Ontario, on July 6, 1898. There is no record of a honeymoon. Whatever the old man's hopes or aspirations, with Mary the union was strictly a business proposition, quid pro quo and no hanky panky. The old man in his twilight years would benefit from her companionship and expert nursing care, while she would share in the amenities of his wealth. She so testified at the trial.

She said the minister who married them had noted the disparity in their ages, and Sanderson told him, "Yes, she is making a great sacrifice but she will be amply rewarded." She also said that Sanderson had told her he couldn't live for more than a year or two, and that when he died she would come into a very large sum of money.

Shortly after the newlyweds returned to Battle Creek, Mary sent for a friend of hers in Detroit, Marie Robertson, Canadian born and about Mary's age, to come and take a job as her personal maid. Mary had met Marie while working at Harper Hospital, where Robertson was a maid, and the two had become close friends. Mary picked up her friend at the railroad depot in a hack and, while driving back to the Sanderson residence, talked about the old man and his money.

"He's got scads of it," she told her friend. "He owns a beautiful farm and he has mortgages all over town."

But Marie soon found that life in the Sanderson household was far from tranquil. The old man was already complaining about his wife's extravagance. She was driving him to ruin buying expensive dresses and jewelry. He couldn't stand it, he said.

Mary, on the other hand, was complaining that Sanderson was a mean old man who hated to part with a nickel. "It's getting so I can hardly tolerate him at my table," she told Marie. "Think of winter coming on and being shut up inside these four walls with him."

The old man grew progressively worse as the days went by. He slept in a downstairs room, while his wife had a bedroom upstairs. Often she would be called down during the night to take care of him. He complained of partial paralysis and general debility. During the last week of his illness, Mary hired a male nurse to help take care of him. Finally, one night he cried out, "Mary! Mary!" and when she reached him he was dead.

Shortly after his death the two women had a violent quarrel. Marie left the house for good, and went to Sanderson's brother-in-law, Jasper Adams, with a dreadful story. She told him how Mary had killed her husband by feeding him ground glass over a period of weeks. Rumors of foul play had already been flying; this gave them substance.

Mary's trial for murder opened in Battle Creek on December 6, 1889. The state's chief witness was Marie Robertson; in fact, its whole case depended almost entirely on her testimony. Although a reporter described her as "looking not too bright as she nervously twisted her hands," she proved to be a good witness.

She said that three weeks after her arrival, Mrs. Sanderson began to entertain male visitors. One fellow came at least three times a week and stayed in her room overnight. Marie said she carried beer and cake up to them. The visitor left early in the morning by the back stairs, and Marie locked the door after him.

Marie said that Mrs. Sanderson kept late hours and sometimes was gone from the house all night. On one occasion, she said, Mary told her she was "out riding in a hack and had a jag on." Later, she told her husband that if he asked the neighbors about what she did when she was gone, "she would make it mighty hot for him." Another time she told Marie, "Look at the time. Only ten o'clock. I ought to be out getting a jag on. I'm not used to this kind of life."

Marie also quoted her as saying, "I did not marry him for love, but for money. I kept company with a young doctor and I would have married him long ago if he had money."

Twice, Marie said, Mary mentioned poison. "The old man is dying anyway and I will give him something to hurry it along." She would feed him ground glass. She said she knew of women who fed it to their husbands, and it couldn't be detected in a post mortem.

One morning, Marie said, Mrs. Sanderson "took an old newspaper and went out in the yard, where she gathered some old bottles and broke them with a hammer. Then she went down in the cellar and ground the broken glass in an old spice mill."

Next morning, Mrs. Sanderson told Marie to make some porridge. "She spooned out the porridge in a saucer, then sprinkled a teaspoon of ground glass on it, then another layer of porridge," Marie testified. "She did this every morning for two weeks."

Marie said that at first the old man showed no ill effects of his ground-glass diet, and Mrs. Sanderson complained to her, "The old fool is getting fat on it. Can you imagine that?"

But soon he began to fail, and presently took to his bed. She said she persuaded Mrs. Sanderson to call in a doctor, for appearances' sake at least. She said she felt sorry for the old man. A week or so before he died, she helped him outside to the backyard. She said he pointed out a certain tree. "I'm just like that tree," he told her. "It's been dying ever since my poor wife died."

"Why didn't you go to the police?" the prosecutor asked her.

"I don't know," she said. Then, pressed for a better answer, she said she was afraid of Mrs. Sanderson.

At this point, the witness broke into tears and had to be excused.

"She'll be worse off than that when I get through with her," defense attorney W. A. Crosby said grimly.

But next day on the stand Marie proved more than a match for Mr. Crosby. She stuck resolutely to her story. So the defense attorney, unable to punch any holes in it, sought to discredit the witness by attacking her character and reputation.

Wasn't it true, he asked, that as a domestic servant in Windsor she'd been dismissed by several employers for drinking and for theft? Absolutely not, Marie said. Did she have a drinking habit? Never drank anything but a little beer. Was that why it made her so intoxicated when she did drink it? "That would make a good story to tell the Hottentots in Africa," Marie said scornfully, winning that round, too.

The state introduced only a few more witnesses before resting its case. They included Dr. Albert Prescott of Ann Arbor, who declined to say whether or not the ground glass found in the old man's stomach could have been the cause of his death. "I'm a toxicologist, a chemist," he said. "I haven't practiced medicine for

118

years." Other doctors, however, testified that the glass could indeed have caused death.

The defense wasted no time in putting on its own star witness, Mary Butterfield Sanderson. In her own defense she proved to be as good a witness as her former friend. On the opening day of her testimony she appeared in court in a stylish black dress and a large black velvet hat with an ostrich plume. According to a reporter, she was "striking in appearance" and looked "beautiful and interesting." She was escorted into the courtroom by a constable at one side and her father at the other. Henry Butterfield had come from Mary's hometown, Baraboo, Wis., to be with her at the trial.

On the witness stand she seemed cool and collected. Only her constant toying with a large silver bracelet on her left wrist and frequent adjustments to her hat betrayed her nervousness.

Flatly she denied Marie Robertson's accusations. They were nothing but a pack of lies, she said, prompted by jealousy and spite. She said she had faithfully kept her part of the bargain, had given her late husband the best of care and made his last days as comfortable as possible. Under cross examination, she parried insinuations that she had been fired from hospital jobs in Ann Arbor and Minneapolis for drinking and other improper conduct. She was scornful in her denunciations of Jasper and Onyx Adams. They wanted to grab all of Mr. Sanderson's estate, she said. It was an impressive performance.

Among other witnesses for the defense were two neighbor ladies who said they'd visited the house during Mr. Sanderson's illness and saw nothing amiss. Two doctors testified that, in their opinion, the ground glass needn't have caused death. And Dr. Wattles stuck to his diagnosis that death resulted from a stroke of apoplexy.

Finally, after two weeks of testimony, the trial came to a close. At eight o'clock in the evening of December 23, the jury retired to deliberate a verdict.

The trial, which had been covered by newspapers all over the Midwest, brought forth some curious responses.

Shortly after the trial began, a professor at a Detroit medical college and three of his students conducted some experiments on dogs. One of them was fed powdered glass; a second, pulverized glass; and a third, glass ground in a coffee mill. At the end of a week all dogs were hale and hearty—one of them had gained two pounds. One of the students was so firmly convinced that ground glass was harmless to the human body that he wrote the prosecuting attorney and offered to place himself in his hands for a week, during which time he would eat ground glass mixed with his food.

A Dr. Miller of Chicago, on the other hand, wrote that his dog had died after eating ground glass for six days.

A woman from Galesburg, Mich., wrote the *Detroit Free Press* that her sister, Mrs. Clarence Thrasher, chewed chimney lamps and similar material with impunity.

Another woman wrote that her brother, a professional glass-eater, would be glad to put on a demonstration in court. Unfortunately, he was travelling somewhere in the West, but she believed he could be found, possibly in Iowa. None of the offers was accepted.

The courtroom was filled to capacity when, at twelve o'clock, after only four hours of deliberation, the jury announced it had reached a verdict. The judge warned the spectators that he would tolerate no demonstrations, but when the foreman said, "Not guilty," the courtroom rang with shouts and cheers. Mrs. Sanderson fell weeping with joy into the arms of her father, as people pressed forward to congratulate her and shake her hand. Later it was learned that the first ballot had been eleven to one for acquittal, and three hours later the lone holdout changed his mind.

It seems that the verdict was generally anticipated by the public, and even those who believed her guilty could not see enough in the evidence to convict her. There were some—Jasper and Onyx Adams, of course, included—who called it a gross miscarriage of justice. They pointed to one hard, incontrovertible fact, and it remains a mystery to this day:

The ground glass. If Mary was innocent, how did that ground glass get into the old man's stomach?

THE "PERFECT MURDER" CASE

Back in the days when Benjamin Harrison was president of the United States and well-dressed men wore shirts with detachable collars and cuffs, there lived in Jackson, Michigan, a young man who planned to commit the "perfect" murder. His name was R. Irving Latimer, and he was the twenty-four-old son of a well-to-do Jackson druggist. (The "R" stood for Robert, but everybody had always called him Irving because Robert was also the name of his father, who had died two years previously — in 1887 — under "mysterious" circumstances.)

Latimer wasn't simple minded; quite the contrary. He understood that murder is a serious business, something not to be undertaken lightly. But he had little respect for authority and believed he could easily outwit the police.

Latimer was known to almost everybody in town and was considered a pleasant and attractive young man. But there was something about him — perhaps in the slightly disdainful curl of his sensuous mouth and the tilt of his patrician nose — that turned people off. He had few close friends. Lately he had ruined his reputation among "respectable" citizens by escorting a prostitute to a dance at the exclusive East End Club. And there had been other similar incidents involving drink and loose women.

Latimer was fond of loose women. At least twice a month he went to Detroit and spent a night or two in one of the fancy cathouses there.

The fact was that since his father's death Irving had been living very high off the hog. He was deeply in debt, hounded by his creditors, face-to-face with bankruptcy. With several thousand dollars from his father's estate, and a big loan from his fifty-three-year-old mother, Mary Latimer, Irving had bought a small drugstore, intending to make a career of it as his father had done. But instead of tending to business, he squandered the profits, plundered the till, and was left with not even enough money to pay the interest on his loans, let alone restock the shelves.

Lately he had hung a mirror at the back of the store so he could spot creditors coming in the front door and duck out the rear. Facing ruin, he had now come up with a plan to recoup his fortunes. Irving was nothing if not resourceful.

Murder was naturally repugnant to a well-bred young man like Latimer. Even more repugnant was the fact that the intended victim was his own mother. They were on pleasant terms, but it was unavoidable — his mother's demise was the only possible solution to his problems. Although he had borrowed and spent most of her money (without her knowing of his desperate circumstances), she still owned two valuable houses (the one she lived in and the one next door), and as her sole heir he could sell them, pay off his debts and start a new life.

He labored over his plan for six months, trying to foresee every possible contingency. Three months back, he had left home and began sleeping in a room at the back of the drugstore. To friends who chided him about leaving his mother alone at night he said she fully approved of the arrangement. He said it was for economy's sake. His chief clerk, who had been sleeping there, had left him for a better job in Detroit. Instead of replacing him Latimer had assumed the duty of guarding the store at night. Besides, he had left all his clothes and personal things in his room at home, and he continued to take breakfast there with his mother every morning.

And so, on Thursday, January 24, 1889, his plans were complete, and the time had come to execute them.

Yesterday he had walked a few doors down the street to the sheriff's offices and telephoned a friend in Detroit. Making sure that the conversation was overheard, he told him he was planning to attend a funeral there the next day. And now, Friday morning, he sent his junior clerk to the same place to telephone for a hack to take him to the Michigan Central depot.

At one o'clock that afternoon he caught the "fast train" to Detroit, wearing a suit, overcoat and derby hat, and carrying a small valise. The valise contained a Smith & Wesson .32-caliber revolver, a black ulster and a dark cloth cap. Around five o'clock he checked in at the Griswold House in Detroit. He wasn't known there, but he signed his own name to the register, and the clerk handed him the key to room 42.

After supper he left the hotel and took a hack to a certain house on Gratiot Street, where he spent an hour or so upstairs with one of the "ladies."

Returning to the hotel at nine o'clock he entered by the front door, got his key from the clerk, and went back out the front door. A few minutes later he reentered the hotel by a side door — the Ladies Entrance — and went up to his room. Fifteen minutes later he left the hotel by the side door, wearing the ulster and the dark cloth cap pulled down over his eyes.

He then walked to the depot, twenty minutes away, carrying the valise, which was empty now, except for the pistol. He bought a ticket to Ann Arbor on the ten thirty train, changed trains there and boarded a sleeping car destined for Grand Rapids. He told the conductor, who had sold him the ticket, that he planned to go on to Grand Rapids if, as expected, a friend met him at the Jackson depot.

Arriving in Jackson about one o'clock in the morning he walked the half mile to his mother's house, no doubt taking care to use dimly lighted, unfrequented streets along the way. The night was cold and dark, with patches of ice on the sidewalks. Without incident he arrived at the house on First Street a little before two. He knew that his mother was alone in the house except for the old family dog, which he knew wouldn't make a fuss.

With his house key Latimer let himself in through the side door, the Wilkins Street entrance. He found a small kerosene lamp in the kitchen and lighted it. After taking off his shoes he climbed the stairs to his mother's bedroom, pistol in hand.

No need to linger over the gory details: Latimer entered his mother's bedroom in his stocking feet, approached the bed where she lay fast asleep, and shot her in the head. But in the dim light he aimed too low. The bullet tore through her cheek and upper jaw, and lodged in her neck.

She leaped to her feet and staggered toward the window on First Street, as if to raise it and cry for help. Latimer followed close behind and shot her again in the neck, the bullet ranging downward and lodging in the muscles below her shoulder blade. As she fell Latimer pressed a large handkerchief over her nose and mouth, to stifle any outcry. As he did so, his mother's teeth clamped spasmodically down on his right thumb, cutting it to the bone. Later an autopsy showed that neither bullet would necessarily have been fatal. Mrs. Latimer had probably strangled to death on her own blood.

Did she recognize her assailant during those frightful moments? There is no way of knowing, but mercifully, probably not.

To make it look like burglary Latimer opened drawers in the bedroom and emptied their contents on the floor. He took his mother's jewel case into his own bedroom and pocketed most of the jewelry. Downstairs he broke the lock on the cellar door with a spade and left it open. (The outside door to the cellar was never kept locked.) His thumb was still bleeding and he left a trail of blood wherever he went.

Now there is a gap of two or three hours when Latimer's movements were never determined. There was a train to Detroit at 6:10 a.m., but he couldn't afford to be seen waiting at the depot. He may have passed the time at the house or possibly at the drugstore.

In any case he caught the train, obtained his ticket and a Pullman berth from the conductor, and lay down fully dressed to rest for a couple of hours. In western Detroit he got off the train on the opposite side of the depot and took a trolley downtown to the hotel, arriving there about nine thirty.

After breakfast he went to a drugstore and had his injured

thumb treated and bandaged. A message was waiting for him when he returned to the hotel. It was from a clerk he knew at another Detroit drugstore, and is said merely: "Your mother is dead." At the drugstore, the clerk confirmed the message but could give Latimer no details. The telephone call, he said, had come from one of the clerks at Latimer's drugstore.

After a leisurely meal at a nearby restaurant Latimer checked out of the hotel and rode to the depot to catch the "fast train" to Jackson.

At the railroad station he encountered a nasty shock. He ran into an old friend, Lou Burch, editor of the *Detroit Sunday Sun*, who said he'd been looking for him all over town and asked him where he had spent the night.

"At the Griswold House," Latimer replied.

"But there must be some mistake," Burch said. "The clerks at the hotel and the chambermaid told me your room was unoccupied all night."

Latimer made no reply. A few minutes later he complained of a raging headache.

Two friends met Latimer at the Jackson depot and drove him to the house on First Street. It was full of people: policemen, detectives, coroners and other law officials. City Prosecutor James A. Parkinson, who knew the young man, gently drew Latimer aside and filled him in on the terrible details.

His mother's body, Parkinson said, had been discovered by Emily Burrows, a widow who lived in Mrs. Latimer's house next door. Familiar with her neighbor's habits and concerned about her health, she got worried when she saw that the windowshades were still drawn and there was no sign of life at the Latimer house at nine-thirty that morning.

Mrs. Burrows went over to the house and tried the front door; it was locked. As she stood there she was joined by a painter, Harry Nichols, who had been papering in the house during the past two days and had more work to do. They tried the side door and found it locked, too. Finally they gained entrance by the cellar door. Mrs. Burrows went upstairs and found the body.

Parkinson urged Latimer to tell him everything he knew that might shed light on the awful crime. "I've known you for years,

125

Irving," he said, "and I want to clear you of any suspicion, for I believe you are innocent."

Innocent he was, Latimer replied, but he didn't know anything at all about the crime, and right now he had a terrible headache. At no time that afternoon did he express a desire to see his mother's body, which was still lying on the bedroom floor upstairs.

Irving spent the night at the home of a friend, passing the evening hours there playing cards and reading. Although he still complained of a severe headache, his appetite was good.

The next morning he was summoned downtown to Parkinson's office, where the following conversation took place:

Parkinson: "We are making some progress, Irving. We think we have found the murderer of your mother. The man who did the vile deed came from Detroit that night."

Latimer: "Ye-es."

Parkinson: "The murderer left Detroit on the 10:30 train, came to Jackson, murdered your mother and returned to Detroit on a train leaving here at 6:10, and he got off that train in west Detroit."

Irving: "Ye-e-s."

Parkinson: "Irving, that man was yourself. We have the proofs. Now what have you to say?"

Irving: "Only this. I stayed all night at the Griswold House."

But Irving was hooked and he must have known it. It had taken the police less than thirty-six hours to crack the case. Far from committing the perfect murder, Latimer had dropped clues all over the place.

Parkinson pointed them out at Latimer's trial for murder in April. First, he had used the sheriff's telephone to make calls, even though he had a telephone of his own at the drugstore. Second, in trying to disguise himself at the hotel on Friday night, he had actually attracted attention: the night clerk and the porter recognized him and thought his actions suspicious. Third, he should have bought a through ticket from Detroit to Jackson instead of changing trains in Ann Arbor. Both the porter and the conductor on that car remembered him, and identified him later in a lineup. Fourth, the curious behavior of the family dog. It had not barked in the night because it knew Latimer.

126

The list of blunders went on and on. He had been recognized by three conductors and a porter on the 6:10 train to Detroit. They all thought it strange that anyone would want a sleeping berth at that hour of the morning, and the porter saw him leaving the train surreptitiously in west Detroit.

And the hotel chambermaid who had entered his room at nine o'clock Saturday morning found the bed undisturbed and nothing to show that anyone had slept there. Moreover, he had failed to provide himself with a change of clothing; blood stains were found on his coat and trousers, and his socks were soaked with it. He had left Jackson with detachable cuffs on his shirt, but returned on Saturday without them.

The family doctor, Charles H. Lewis, remembered seeing the Smith & Wesson revolver on Latimer's desk when he dropped in one evening at the drugstore. Latimer asked him "not to tell the boys about it, as he didn't want them to know." The gun was never found.

On the witness stand Latimer told a tangled story. Actually, he said, he had gone to Detroit to meet a girl named Trixie. He had missed her at the appointed place on Woodward Avenue, and then, thinking she might have taken the train to Jackson, he followed her, getting off at each station along the way to look for her. The police made a serious effort to locate her, but "Trixie" was never found.

The story was so disingenuous it was almost comical. Nobody believed a word of it, including the jurors, who took just fifteen minutes to find Latimer guilty of murder in the first degree. He was sentenced to life imprisonment in Jackson penitentiary.

Our story should end here, but it doesn't. Latimer had more tricks up his sleeve. In prison he soon made friends with most of the guards and the inmates, including millionaire lumberman, Charlie Wright, who had murdered two sheriff's deputies in Aral in northwest lower Michigan in 1889. Soon he was made a trusty and put in charge of the prison dispensary, where he had the privilege of ordering special drugs from outside the building.

At midnight on March 26, 1893, he poisoned two friendly prison guards by lacing their lemonade with a mixture of prussic acid and nitroglycerine, and escaped into the night. He was captured by farmers the next evening, walking the New York Central tracks near Jerome, a small town twenty miles south of Jackson. He was wearing only a thin prison coat and worn-out boots and was suffering from the cold. Once again Latimer had botched his plans.

Told of the death of one of the guards (the other recovered), he expressed grief at the loss of a dear friend. He hadn't meant to kill him, he said, only to "knock him out while I made my escape." Evidently, he said, the mixture had been too strong.

Latimer soon restored himself to favor with the prison guards, who apparently believed his story. In the mid-1920s Latimer was proud of his position and privileges as "senior con," and criticized the younger inmates, who, he said, weren't in the same class with the old boys. Later, when the prison was moved to a new location, he protested having to leave his comfortable cell with its books and plants and flowers. Considered harmless, he was given a job as watchman at the deserted prison. Finally, after serving forty-six years in prison, Latimer was released in 1935. Picked up several times later for vagrancy, he was committed to a state home for the indigent, and died there in 1946.

Latimer never admitted his guilt — few convicted murderers ever do. But he was proven guilty of matricide beyond the shadow of a doubt, and one can't help wondering if maybe he was guilty of patricide, too. His father, Robert F. Latimer, died under very "mysterious" circumstances indeed.

The elder Latimer was a member of the drug firm, Weeks, Latimer & Co., where son Irving also worked as a clerk. At fifty-five he was in apparent good health. But on October 21, 1887, he complained of not feeling well and walked home from the drugstore accompanied part way by Dr. Charles Lewis. At home he sat down in an easy chair and read a newspaper for a while, then suddenly began to cough and vomit. He complained of feeling cold and numb. His wife summoned Dr. Lewis, who did for him all he could, but Latimer died half an hour later. Dr. Lewis said that his death was caused by "paralysis of the heart."

Did Irving poison his father? Who knows? Maybe it was a heart attack. Or maybe Irving, for all his bungling, did commit *one* perfect murder after all.

MURDER IN A BALLOON

Ballooning originated in France in the latter half of the eighteenth century. The sport quickly crossed the Atlantic, and the first part of the nineteenth century produced a whole flock of American balloonists who didn't really know what they were doing. Many were injured, some were killed, a few simply disappeared.

One of the most reckless and flamboyant of American balloonists was "Professor" Washington Harrison Donaldson. An account of his exploits and misadventures (which later he wrote himself) reads like a script for a Harold Lloyd movie or *The Perils of Pauline*. Born in Philadelphia in 1840, Donaldson had already gone through several careers before he took up ballooning. A man of great strength and agility, he had been a magician, knife thrower (using his brother as target), ventriloquist, acrobat, and tightrope-walker. In 1862, he crossed Pennsylvania's Schuylkill River on a 1,200-foot-long tightrope and then capped the performance with a ninety-foot leap into the river.

Donaldson made his first balloon ascent in Reading, Pa., on

129

August 30, 1871. When his balloon failed to rise he pitched all his ballast overboard. Later, coming to rest on a rooftop nearby he jettisoned everything else, including rope, grapnel and even some of his clothing. After a quarter-mile flight the balloon began a rapid descent and Donaldson hit the ground like a rock. Miraculously, he escaped serious injury.

For the next four years Donaldson went blithely from disaster to disaster, leading a charmed life. In Chicago, where Donaldson charged that the "citizens never feel satisfied until they kill someone," he flew over the city in a paper balloon. It caught fire and Donaldson came down in Lake Michigan.

In 1873, he teamed up with veteran balloonist John Wise — later known as the "father" of American ballooning — for a flight across the Atlantic Ocean. That was aborted when the gas bag tore open and collapsed. But a month later, Donaldson took off for Europe from Brooklyn in a smaller balloon with two newspapermen. Like Corrigan, though, they went the wrong way and landed in what later became known as the borscht belt in the Catskills. Donaldson and one companion leaped fifteen feet to the ground. The other newsman was carried a few miles farther north but landed safely in a tree.

In 1874, Donaldson was hired by P. T. Barnum to make publicity flights for his travelling Hippodrome shows. And in Chicago, in the following year, Donaldson's long streak of phenomenal good luck finally ran out.

The Hippodrome arrived in Chicago in July and pitched its huge tents on the waterfront in Dearborn Park, now the site of the Chicago Public Library. With great fanfare Donaldson announced that he would make a death-defying flight across Lake Michigan. He offered to take one passenger.

Of the hundreds who applied, he chose a twenty-three-year-old reporter for the Chicago *Evening News*, Newton S. Grimwood. Grimwood had never been aloft, but he was eager for adventure. In some notes for a news story he wrote the following:

UP IN A BALLOON

From the earliest days of my childhood I have always had a presentiment that some time, sooner or later, I was bound to rise.

130

. . . In accordance with my presentiment I have risen, as it were, "on a point of order." Like a great many politicians I rise by means of gas.

Whatever his merits as a humorist, Grimwood was a pleasant and agreeable young man. He was too poor to own a timepiece, but his girl let him take her small gold pocket watch as a good luck charm and token of her love.

On the afternoon of July 15, a great crowd gathered to witness the balloon launching. And promptly at four-thirty the big yellow balloon called "Barnum" rose smoothly from its moorings. The two aeronauts waved gaily and the crowd broke into cheers. After rising to a height of half a mile, the balloon began to drift slowly to the northeast on a gentle offshore breeze. The weather was fine and clear, and the yellow gas bag was visible from downtown Chicago for at least an hour.

But that night a great storm raged over the eastern part of the lake. And the next day, when nothing was heard from the aeronauts, many people feared the worst. A spokesman for the Hippodrome said they were hopeful that the missing men would soon turn up. Both were wearing life belts and both were good swimmers. It seemed reasonable to suppose that they had made it to shore in Michigan or had been picked up by a passing ship.

Next day, the captain of a schooner called the *Little Guide*, docked in Chicago and reported sighting a balloon at seven o'clock on the evening of the launch. He said the balloon was flying so low that the basket occasionally dipped into the water. He said he launched a boat to render assistance, but that the balloon rose suddenly and was blown out of sight before his men could reach it. Visibility was so poor, he said, that he and his men couldn't make out whether the basket was occupied or not.

Another ship reported seeing dimly a balloon in the storm later that night. They couldn't see the men, but they heard their cries.

Captain Furlong, skipper of steam barge *New Era*, reported seeing a life preserver with the strap pulled floating about fifty miles northeast of Chicago. He hadn't heard about the balloon flight and didn't stop to pick it up.

A floating body was sighted by the crew of a lumber barge about

131

forty miles west of Grand Haven, Michigan, but no effort was made to take it aboard. Later, it was picked up by another vessel and identified as that of a German sailor washed overboard from a lake steamer.

On July 30, a Detroit newspaper reported that Donaldson had been found alive. A report from Kalamazoo stated that a section crew of the Kalamazoo & South Haven Railroad had found him injured and exhausted, wandering along the tracks between South Haven and Saugatuck. The report said that medical aid was being rushed to him from Grand Haven. No mention was made of Grimwood.

The report proved to be false, just another rumor.

The next day a man walking the beach of Chicago's South Side found a message in a bottle. Dated July 26, 2:00 a.m. (the morning after the launch), it read: "We cannot stay up more than an hour longer, as the gas is rapidly escaping." It was signed "N.S.G.", Grimwood's initials.

Another bottle message was found on the beach near Port Hope, Michigan. The message read: "Over Lake Michigan on the evening starting. About thirty miles from Chicago and about 3,000 feet high. A gale is coming up from the northeast. The balloon is getting out of order, gas escaping fast. Can't remain up much longer. Will surely land in lake. Fearful storm." It was signed "Donaldson."

Both messages were thought to be hoaxes.

On August 4, the *New York Times* reported that Donaldson had been seen alive in Michigan:

"The latest sensation comes from Algonac, Mich., in the form of a letter from J. H. Stanwood, who emphatically declares that he saw Donaldson in that village last Friday. He says, 'Donaldson has no mustache, but the scar on his cheek rendered recognition an easy matter.' "

The *Times* went on to say that while many people believed that Donaldson and his companion were lost, there were others who claimed it was an ingenious advertising trick and that the two aeronauts would make an appearance soon. It wouldn't be the first time, the *Times* said, that Donaldson had pulled a trick like that for publicity purposes.

But on August 17, a mailman walking the beach near Stony

Creek north of Whitehall, Mich., found the body of Newton Grimwood half buried in the sand. The body was clad only in trousers and there was a life preserver tied around its waist.

It was positively identified as Grimwood. A letter addressed to him was found in one of the pockets, as well as other papers including the notes quoted earlier. Also found on the body was his girl's little gold watch. The crystal was missing and the watch had stopped at 11:20.

Farther down the beach searchers found a small canvas bag of the kind that Donaldson used for sand ballast. They also found a few tattered pieces of oil cloth similar to the material that the balloon was made of. But there was no sign of Professor Donaldson, nor any clue about what had happened to him.

The Hippodrome people said they deeply regretted Grimwood's death, but continued to hope that Donaldson would eventually be found "somewhere in the pineries of Michigan." It was pointed out that Donaldson was a very resourceful man and that there were "plenty of edible roots and berries to live on in the woods at this time of year."

Meanwhile, rumors began circulating — especially in Michigan — that Donaldson had murdered his companion by throwing him out of the basket in the storm. The allegation was printed first in a Detroit paper and it spread rapidly to other newspapers in the Midwest. But the *Chicago Evening Journal* scoffed at the story, and so did Donaldson's many friends.

John Wise, the balloonist who had teamed with Donaldson for the aborted attempt over the Atlantic, declared that his fellow sportsman was incapable of such a crime. He pointed out that the story was absurd on the face of it. Relieving the balloon of Grimwood's weight would have served to carry it no more than a mile or two farther, he said. Yet the story continued to gain credence, and police were alerted to be on the lookout for the "Professor."

Then, on August 25, Donaldson was found alive, but gravely injured, in the wilds of Canada. A fishing party travelling up the Ottawa River in western Quebec found a dying man alone in a remote trapper's shack near Lac Des Quinze. The man was dying of gangrene as a result of several untreated broken bones. Before he died he told the fishermen that he was Donaldson, and gave the following account of what happened on that fearful night over Lake Michigan:

Donaldson said that the balloon, buffetted and battered by the storm, lost great quantities of gas. No longer able to carry the weight of both men, it sank lower and lower over the water. Suddenly, he said, Grimwood drew a pistol and demanded that Donaldson jump overboard. Donaldson !unged for the weapon, he said, and the two men locked in a violent struggle. Grimwood lost his balance and plunged to his death, Donaldson claimed.

The dying man expired soon after telling his story. The fishermen buried him at the wilderness site. Weeks later, the fishing party brought out papers and other effects that seemed to confirm that the man was really Donaldson.

Did Washington Harrison Donaldson murder Newton Grimwood on that night over Lake Michigan? Some people were skeptical, many of Donaldson's friends included. But John Wise believed that the man was really Donaldson. He wrote a pamphlet based on the papers that were found at the death site. His theory was that Grimwood jumped voluntarily to lighten the load. But, of course, he had no proof.

(Ironically, John Wise lost his life under almost identical circumstances four years later. On a flight over Lake Michigan at age seventy-one, he was lost and blown away. Neither he nor his companion on the flight were ever seen again.)

Lac Des Quinze is about five hundred airline miles north-northeast of Chicago. It seems incredible that Donaldson could have made a flight of such length in a crippled balloon.

But with Washington Harrison Donaldson almost nothing is beyond belief. The "Professor" was an incredible man.

INVITATION TO A
HANGING

At the close of the five-day-long trial the lawyer for the accused pleaded for mercy: "Don't make a mistake and have this death on your conscience for the rest of your life." The prosecutor asked death for a "brutal ruthless killer . . . sly sneaking human beast." Then, with the prosecutor's final demand, "This man must die!" ringing in their ears, the jury retired to begin their deliberations.

That didn't take long. After only seven hours and seven ballots they were back in the jury box, and the foreman stood up and began to read the verdict: "We find the defendant guilty as charged, with the recommendation of the death penalty—" He stopped as the judge raised his hand. The phrasing was incorrect, the judge told him. He asked the foreman to take a pencil and copy the correct wording in the jury room. The jury returned in a few minutes, and the foreman stood up again. "We find the defendant guilty as charged and direct that he be punished by death."

All eyes now turned to the prisoner. His face was impassive. It showed no change of expression except that after the second pronouncement of his fate his jaws began to work a little faster on his wad of chewing gum. He was a slight young man with dark hair and dark, deep-set, brooding eyes — handsome in a rugged Clark Gable sort of way. He had a firm chin with a cleft in it and thick protruding ears and high cheekbones, and now there was just the faintest suggestion of a smile in the way his mouth turned up at the corners. He was dressed in baggy brown trousers, a dark shirt and brown shoes. His wrists and ankles were in chains, which clanked when he moved. He didn't look like a criminal, which is only to say that most criminals don't look like criminals. His name was Anthony Chebatoris, and his case was unique. If he died at the hands of the State, his would be the first such execution in Michigan in 108 years.

Tony Chebatoris was born in Poland in 1899 and came to this country with his parents as a small boy. The family settled in Pittsburgh, where his father got a job in the steel mills. Chebatoris went to school and got as far as the fifth grade. Then he dropped out and drifted into a life of petty crime; stealing fruit and candy, robbing pushcarts and vending machines, snatching purses. He came to Detroit as a youth and married in March of 1920. The couple set up housekeeping in Hamtramck, a predominantly Polish community on the east side of the city. That summer he was arrested and convicted of armed robbery. He was already in Jackson Prison, serving a seven-and-a-half to fifteen-year term when his daughter was born in September.

Released in 1926 on parole, he was returned to Jackson the following year as a parole violator after stealing a car in Louisville. In 1928 he was involved in an escape plot with John Gracey, another young Hamtramck hoodlum. As punishment both men were transferred to the maximum-security state prison in Marquette. Chebatoris was freed in November, 1935, on the expiration of his sentence. Gracey was released a few months later.

In the summer of 1937 the two ex-convicts got together in Hamtramck and devised a plan to rob the Chemical State Savings Bank in Midland. Their target was the $150,000 weekly payroll of the Dow Chemical Company.

On Wednesday morning, September 29, the two men drove to Midland in a stolen car. They parked a short distance from the

136

bank entrance and then entered the building a little after eleven-thirty. Chebatoris, wearing a short jacket, carried a rifle; Gracey had a sawed-off shotgun under his long overcoat. Bank president Clarence H. Macomber, a dignified-looking man of sixty-five with white hair and a goatee, was standing in front of his office in the lobby, talking with his daughter, Claire, who was also employed at the bank.

Gracey approached the elderly man and without saying a word stuck the shotgun into his ribs. Macomber turned and wrestled with the gunman, and both fell to the floor, whereupon Chebatoris shot the bank president in the shoulder. Another bank official, cashier Paul D. Bywater, was standing nearby. He came to his boss's assistance, and Chebatoris shot him in the back. All this happened in less than two minutes. Then the gunmen, apparently unnerved by the resistance and the shooting, turned and fled.

The two men jumped into their car with Chebatoris behind the wheel. He was backing up to get clear of the car parked ahead when a shot fired from above wounded Gracey in the leg.

The shot was fired by dentist Frank L. Hardy, who had offices above the bank. Dr. Hardy, along with several other men whose business places commanded the bank entrance, had been deputized in 1932, when the arrest of a gunman revealed plans to rob the bank. They formed a kind of vigilante committee and took rifles to their offices to guard against such raids on the bank. Over the years their plans were mostly forgotten, but Dr. Hardy still kept a loaded rifle in his office. He was a veteran deer hunter and a crack shot.

Hearing a commotion in the street below, Hardy looked out his window and saw the two men with guns running toward their car. He grabbed his rifle, poked the barrel through the screen and fired into the right front seat as the car backed up, wounding Gracey. He fired a second shot as the car sped forward, hitting Chebatoris in the arm. The bandits' car went out of control and crashed into a car parked in front of a garage and filling station across the street. Gracey tumbled out and crumpled to the pavement. His partner came around and helped him to his feet. Then the two men started across the street. They were in the middle of it when Chebatoris spotted a man in uniform. Apparently taking him for a police officer and the source of the hostile fire, Chebatoris swung the rifle

137

on him and shot from the hip. The man in uniform went down with a bullet in the abdomen. He was a Bay City truck driver, an innocent bystander.

Just then another car came around the corner. It was driven by a young woman who had a child on the seat beside her. The two men made for the car. Chebatoris grabbed the right side of it and the car stopped after going a few yards. Chebatoris got in and the woman and child fled frantically from the left. Gracey came up on the driver's side. He had his foot on the running board and was about to enter when Dr. Hardy shot again. Gracey flinched and reeled as though he had been hit. Then he started running down the street in a hopping kind of motion. A red truck was coming across the bridge ahead. As it neared Gracey, Hardy fired his final shot. The distance was a good two hundred yards, but the bullet tore off the back of Gracey's head, and he fell dead.

Chebaroris, meanwhile, abandoned the car and his rifle and went running down the street on the opposite side from Gracey. He was collared and wrestled to the ground by Midland County Sheriff Ira M. Smith, who held him down with a knee on the bandit's head, awaiting assistance. A man came running up and kicked Chebatoris in the face. The sheriff cursed the man and ordered him away, but Chebatoris said, "Let him kill me. I deserve it."

The gunman, who had suffered only a flesh wound, was taken to the Midland County jail and charged with assault with a deadly weapon. Both the bank president and the cashier recovered from their bullet wounds, but the truck driver died a few days later, and the charge against Chebatoris was changed to murder.

Robbing banks during the Great Depression years was a crowded profession. The banks had the money, and a lot of desperate men were willing to risk their lives to get at it. Many were successful. In Michigan alone there had been twelve "successful" (the robbers got away with the money) bank robberies since the first of January, 1937.

In response to the wave of bank robberies around the country Congress passed the National Bank Robbery Act in 1934. Among its provisions was one that made applicable the death penalty for killing during the robbery or attempted robbery of a federal bank. Since the Midland Chemical Bank was a repository for federal

138

funds, Chebatoris technically could be tried in federal court under the act.

John C. Lehr, U.S. district attorney for eastern Michigan, was quick to seize the opportunity to enact the new law. As a congressman in 1934, Lehr had helped to draft the act. He now demanded jurisdiction in the case and told reporters he would press for the death penalty. Armed with a warrant from a federal judge he took custody of the prisoner and had him transported to the county jail in Bay City to await trial for murder. Chebatoris would be the first suspect to be tried under the provisions of the new bank robbery act.

He was brought to trial before Federal Judge Arthur J. Tuttle in Bay City on Monday, October 25, 1937. The judge, a completely bald, heavy-jowled man of 65, read the charges and explained the possible consequences.

"My God, Judge," Chebatoris said. "Can't you make it second-degree murder?"

The jury was composed of seven women and five men, the women mostly housewives, the men mostly small farmers. During the jury selection process all of them had assured Prosecutor Lehr that they had no prejudice against the death penalty. The judge explained that they had a choice of three verdicts: not guilty, guilty as charged, and guilty with the direction of the death penalty.

During the five-day trial the prosecution called thirty-four witnesses. The defense called none, and Chebatoris did not take the stand. At half past eight on Friday night Ora Akin, a Houghton Lake hotel proprietor, stood up and delivered the dread verdict: Death was mandatory—Chebatoris must die for his crime. That night in his cell the prisoner slashed his wrists and throat with a rusty razor blade. But the wounds were not serious and he was discovered before he lost much blood. He was taken to a hospital, patched up and placed under around-the-clock observation. The authorities were determined that he wasn't going to cheat the hangman that way.

Michigan abolished the death penalty for murder in 1846, the first state in the Union to do so. It was assumed that Chebatoris would be taken to another state for execution. But there was a

139

loophole in the Michigan law, and U.S. District Attorney Lehr found it.

Under Michigan's revised code of laws, adopted May 18, 1846, the death penalty for murder was abolished and the maximum sentence was set at solitary confinement and hard labor for life. But the code left in place the death penalty for high treason. Nobody in Michigan had ever been convicted of treason—the law was a holdover from colonial times. Nevertheless, it remained on the books.

Lehr argued that since Michigan permitted capital punishment for treason, Chebatoris could be executed legally in the state. His view prevailed in Federal Court, and on November 30, 1937, Chebatoris was brought before Judge Tuttle for sentencing. Asked if he had anything to say before sentence was passed, Chebatoris said nothing, eyes downcast. One of the U.S. marshalls nudged him in the back but still he remained silent, eyes on the floor. The judge then passed sentence: "I sentence you to be hanged until dead within the walls of the Federal Detention Farm at Milan, Michigan."

The ruling produced a storm of protest. The only time that a white man had been legally executed in Michigan's history occurred on September 24, 1830, seven years before Michigan became a state. Stephen Simmons, an innkeeper in Wayne, had killed his wife in a drunken rage. Simmons was tried in Detroit before three Territorial judges.

The execution was carried out in a circus-like atmosphere, a huge crowd overflowing a grandstand set up before the gallows in Library Square. But spectators who came to jeer remained to weep. Simmons, a huge man, made a stirring plea for mercy at the foot of the gallows. He confessed his faults, blamed liquor for his crime, and ended up by singing a hymn of repentance.

After the hanging the crowd broke into a fury. It demolished the gallows and tore up the whipping post in the jailhouse yard. Agitation against both corporal and capital punishment became so intense that the state banished both forms of punishment sixteen years later. One murderer, sentenced to die shortly before the law went into effect, escaped the gallows on that account.

Most Michigan people, a hundred years later, were still strongly opposed to capital punishment. One of its strongest opponents was

Governor Frank Murphy. He appealed to President Roosevelt to
have the Chebatoris execution moved to another state. He said,
"The people of Michigan have a revulsion against the death penalty." Roosevelt said he'd see what he could do. He referred the
matter to Attorney General Homer Cummings, who ruled that the
execution must take place at dawn on July 8, 1938, as scheduled.

The Federal Detention Farm in Milan is a cluster of dingy old
prison cells and dormitories, surrounded by a 30-foot-high brick
wall. It lies on a two-hundred-acre plot amidst a great expanse of
rich farmland that is flat as a table. Its function is to hold short-
term prisoners and those awaiting trial in Federal courts in Michigan. Built in 1933, it was thus fairly new when Tony Chebatoris was
brought there in December of 1937. He had a little more than six
months to live.

In most respects Chebatoris was a model prisoner. He read con-
stantly, mostly books on atheism, socialism, communism and history. He had represented himself to the prison authorities as a
communist and an atheist. The prison warden, a good Catholic
named Ryan, was shocked. A bank robber was one thing, but a
communist! Nevertheless, he supplied Chebatoris with the books
he asked for.

Only a few times did the prisoner become agitated. He defaced
and tore down some religious pictures on the walls of his cell, and
when the prison chaplain came to see him, he turned him away,
saying, "You can't do anything for me." It was the same when a
group of nuns tried to visit him in his cell. He drove them away
with abusive language. Otherwise he was calm and philosophical
about his fate. Death was inevitable for all men, he said. In his case
the only difference was that he knew when it was going to happen.

The prison imported a professional hangman to do the job. He
was Phil Hanna, of Epworth, Ill., a wizened, mild-mannered little
old man whom one newspaper described as a "country gentleman."
He and his assistant arrived several days before the hanging to
supervise the construction of the gallows. It was built in a corner of
one of the unused wings of the prison, within earshot of the con-
demned man consisting of a wooden platform about eighteen feet
high covered with a canvas tent which was open at the front. Che-

141

batoris could hear the hammering of nails and other sounds of construction, and he began to pace his cell nervously, until another prisoner was placed in the cell "to quiet him."

Not one person had visited Chebatoris during the many weeks he spent in jail in Bay City. Nor had he received a single letter. But now, as the time approached, there were visits from several members of his family. His married daughter came to visit several times, and on the day before the execution he was visited by his wife, Catherine, and two brothers and a sister. One brother came all the way from California to see him. It was the first and only time his wife came to visit.

Meanwhile, Governor Murphy and others continued their efforts to obtain clemency — or, at the very least, to have the execution transferred to another state. A ruling finally came down from the assistant attorney general: If Judge Tuttle decided it could be moved to another state, the Department of Justice would not object. Having thus been passed the buck, that worthy man rose to the occasion. In a lengthy statement Tuttle declared he had "neither the power nor the inclination" to change anything, and he praised the prosecutor and the jury for their "courage and wisdom" in directing that the crime be punished by death.

To Chebatoris, of course, the point was moot. What difference did it make to him if they killed him here or in some other place? "I'm only half a man now," he told his court-appointed lawyer on the eve of execution. "The Government might as well finish me off." He disdained ordering any special food for his "last supper," and ate heartily of the regular prison fare. He protested vehemently when Warden Ryan urged that a priest accompany him on his walk to the gallows, but finally gave in out of weariness or indifference.

It was five o'clock the next morning when they came for him — the warden, a United States marshall, a prison guard and the priest. Sunrise was due at 5:06. Time to go, the warden told him, and Chebatoris nodded calmly. He was seated on his cot, already dressed in a white shirt, dark trousers and brown shoes that looked quite new. He rose when they entered and submitted quietly while the guard handcuffed his wrists. Then he followed them out the door without a word.

They descended a flight of stairs, then started down a long corridor that led to the improvised execution chamber. The warden and U.S. marshall John Barc led the way. They were followed by the priest, who was chanting prayers, then by Chebatoris with the guard at his shoulder, ready to help if need be. But the prisoner needed no help. He walked down the corridor with a steady and unfaltering stride. Only his eyes betrayed him — they darted nervously from side to side. Once he appeared to stumble, but observers attributed his misstep to the fact that his wrists were manacled in front of him, throwing him off balance.

The witnesses — all twenty-five of them — were waiting in a large anteroom off the corridor. After the procession passed by, they fell in behind. They had all been searched for concealed weapons and cameras. Most were there because they wanted to be — a clergyman, three newspapermen, several policemen, lawyers and private citizens. An execution is like a party or a wedding: invitations are necessary but nobody has to accept. There was no sound except the shuffling of feet. The first rays of sunlight were breaking over the prison walls. A passing freight train rumbled in the distance, its lonely whistle sounding somehow like a cry for help.

Chebatoris and the official party climbed the thirteen steps to the gallows platform. Waiting there was Phil Hanna and his assistant. Also there was Midland County Sheriff, Ira M. Smith, who had volunteered to spring the trap.

"Is this Hanna?" Chebatoris asked.

"Yes, sir," said the little man, then guided him into position over the trap so that he faced the witnesses standing below in front of the platform.

"Are you nervous about the rope?" Chebatoris asked.

"I'm here to give you as quick and painless a death as I can," Hanna replied.

"Then I know it will be a good job," Chebatoris said. He was smiling a little (some called it a sneer), but his lips trembled.

Nothing more was said. Two guards strapped his arms at the elbows and his legs at the knees. Hanna's assistant slipped the sateen hood over his head and made it secure. Hanna followed with the noose, adjusting it carefully. Then he made a sign to Sheriff Smith, who lunged forward on the iron lever, springing the trap. The clash of metal coincided with the thud of the body at the end of the rope. The priest continued to intone prayers. The body made a half turn from right to left and then was still. The time was 5:08.

A pit had been dug under the platform and the body reached into it to the knees. At 5:20 three doctors examined the body and pronounced it dead. The heart had continued to beat strongly for several minutes but now it was still. The rope was unfastened at the top and dropped through the trap door. Two guards loaded the body onto a waiting hospital cot.

"Now he can have a Christian burial," the priest said.

"This is a blot on Michigan's record as a civilized state," Governor Murphys aid.

"It was the first time I ever saw a hanging," Sheriff Smith said. "I felt a little solemn, but I've believed in capital punishment since one of my deputies was killed by a burglar in 1935."

One newspaper pointed out that the hanging of Tony Chebatoris established three "firsts":

First execution in Michigan in 108 years.

First under the death clause of the National Bank Robbery Act.

First in the nation in which the death penalty was ever directed by a jury.

Fiscal-minded U.S. Marshall John Barc pointed out that the execution was surprisingly inexpensive. Total expenses were $205.56, he said. Of that sum $25 went to Sheriff Smith and $124 to defray the expenses of hangman Phil Hanna and his assistant. The cost of materials for the scaffold and its housing came to $56.56, Barc said. Everything was very tidy and cost-effective: only $205.56 to snuff out a life.

Chebatoris was buried secretly in Marble Park Cemetery in Milan by some of his relatives. He had been the first and only man or woman to be put to death in Michigan in its entire history as a state.

THE KICKING HORSE
MURDER CASE

When Old Mission Peninsula farmer Stephen Carroll failed to come in from the barn for breakfast on time, his wife, Mary, began to worry. Her husband was a very punctual man, as regular as clockwork in his habits, and it wasn't like him to be late for meals. Then, too, the dog had been acting strangely, whining and fussing at the kitchen window, looking out toward the barn.

After waiting a few more minutes she decided to go out and see what was keeping him. She had a queer feeling that something was wrong.

What she found fully justified her fears. Her husband was lying on the stable floor, at the open end of one of the horse stalls. His head was battered and bloody, and there was no sign of life. Overcome with horror, she ran back to the house to summon the neighbors for help.

In that year of 1921, the Stephen Carroll farm lay near the middle of the long, narrow tongue of land that separates the two arms of Grand Traverse Bay. Its thirty-five acres, more or less, were bisected by Island View Road, and the house and barn stood

145

on the north side of the road, as they do today. The middle-aged Carrolls — he fifty-two, she forty-seven — were comparative newly-weds; they'd been married for only twelve years. They were child-less, but Mrs. Carroll had an eighteen-year-old son, Jesse Brad-dock, by her first husband. He lived on the farm during that summer but stayed in Traverse City during the school year. He was considered to be a rather "wild" young man: lately he'd gotten into several minor scrapes with the law. Nevertheless, he was popular with his fellow students, who liked and admired him.

On Friday, May 6, the night before Carroll's death, the couple went to bed, in their separate bedrooms, around nine-thirty. Mrs. Carroll awoke the next morning at five-thirty and heard her hus-band getting ready to go out and attend to the chores. She got up a few minutes later and prepared breakfast, which was ready at the usual time, six o'clock. Twenty minutes later she went out to the barn and found him dead.

Stephen's brother and next door neighbor, Andrew Carroll, was first to be telephoned by Mrs. Carroll, and was first on the scene. He found his brother's body as it was discovered by Mrs. Carroll, lying on its face with the head about three inches from the stall partition. A shovel lay beside the body, the blade pointing toward the head. The horse Queen stood quietly in her stall, munching hay.

Andrew Carroll was soon joined by Alfred McManus and other close neighbors, who helped carry the body outside. Andrew observed that rigor mortis had already set in: the arms were rigid and the body was difficult to move. Also called to the scene was Dr. F. G. Swartz of Traverse City, who arrived at the farm about an hour later.

Arriving there at about that same time, eight o'clock, was Car-roll's stepson, Jesse Braddock. He explained that he had started out from town on foot the previous evening and had slept most of the night in a grove of pines along the shore road called Peninsula Drive.

Dr. Swartz examined the body closely. The only wounds he found were several scalp lacerations and one massive fracture, about four inches long above the left eye, that had crushed the skull.

On the face of it, it seemed clear that this was a tragic accident,

146

that Stephen Carroll had been kicked to death by his horse Queen. The only problem with that was that Queen was a gentle horse. She was known to have kicked only once or twice before, and then only under provocative circumstances.

But among those who were at the scene, few had any doubts at all, including Dr. Swartz, who thought the cause of death too obvious to call for the services of a coroner. Only one man, apparently, had a suspicion that this might be more than met the eye. That was another neighbor, John Lyon, who knew something the others didn't.

On the night before Carroll was killed Mrs. Carroll came to the Lyon house seeking a ride to town the next morning. While there she spoke of a recent evening when Jesse and his stepfather had had a quarrel over the family car. She said that Jesse came to the farm with the understanding that he could use the car that evening, but that his stepfather locked the garage door and refused permission.

Jesse protested, Mrs. Carroll told the Lyons, that he had paid $15 for some repairs to the car and thought it only fair that he should be able to use it. During the ensuing quarrel, she said, her husband told Jesse, "Get off the place and stay off it!" Whereupon, she said, Jesse told his stepfather that he would "get even if it took a hundred years."

Lyon gave this information to the authorities a few days later, and he testified to it at a coroner's inquest held on Tuesday of the following week.

Soon after this disclosure Deputy Sheriff David R. Campbell questioned Jesse closely about his movements on the evening of May 6. Under his interrogation Jesse told a different story.

He said that, instead of his walking out part way to the farm on that Friday evening, two of his friends, Claude Kistler and Olin Wilcox, drove him out as far as the Swedish church on Peninsula Drive at the foot of Island View Road. From there he said he walked to the Carroll farm, but it was late when he got there and the house was dark. He said he went to the barn and made a bed on some blankets near the horse stall.

Before going to sleep, he said he toyed with the idea of "getting even" by advancing the spark on the Carroll automobile so that it would "kick" his stepfather when he cranked the motor, but that he thought such punishment would be too severe.

147

When he awoke about two-thirty, he said, he got up, tickled and pinched the horse until it kicked and then left the barn taking a course south over the fields to the Gray crossroad and thence to the shore. He said he walked south along the bay shore about two miles, then lay down under some trees and went to sleep. He said that a passing auto awoke him the next morning.

Why had he lied in the first place, Campbell wanted to know.

Because he wanted to protect his friend Claude Kistler, Braddock explained. Kistler had taken the car without his father's permission.

Both Kistler and Wilcox testified at the inquest. They told about dropping Braddock off at the Swedish church about ten o'clock the night of May 6, and that Braddock gave Kistler a dollar to pay for the gasoline. Both also testified that, two days later, Braddock asked them not to tell anyone about it.

On the basis of this and other circumstantial evidence, Braddock was arrested on a charge of murder and bound over to the June term of Circuit Court without bail. People marveled that he took his arrest with the same composure he had exhibited during the three days of inquest proceedings. The young man seemed to be a very cool customer.

Braddock's trial opened before Judge Frederick W. Mayne at the courthouse in Traverse City on Monday, June 20. Appearing for the prosecution were County Prosecutor John O. Duncan and John W. Patchin; for the defense, Fred Pratt and Parm C. Gilbert.

Witnesses called for testimony were by and large the same ones who testified at the inquest, and there were few surprises. Notable among the latter was the testimony of Harry Weaver, a Traverse City undertaker, who said he found blood on one of Queen's hind feet. He was contradicted, however, by Alfred McManus, who said he examined the horse and found no blood.

As is sometimes the case in murder trials, medical testimony as to the cause of death was also evenly divided. Dr. Swartz stuck firmly to his belief that Carroll came to his death from a kick by the horse. Coroner E. B. Minor, who had expressed doubt on that score in his testimony at the inquest, now admitted under cross-examination that it was entirely possible. But expert witness Dr.

J. S. McCotter, a bone specialist from the University of Michigan, believed otherwise.

"Having in mind the position of the body and the nature of the wounds, do you think the wounds on the skull of Stephen Carroll could have been made by the kick of a horse?" Prosecutor Duncan asked him.

The Professor hunched forward. "The wound over the right frontal might have been," he answered. "But with the body lying so close to the stall partition I cannot conceive how the blow on the top and at the back of the head could have been received."

"In the position in which the body lay, do you think the frontal wound was made by the kick of a horse?"

"With my limited experience with horses — no."

Upon cross-examination, however, Parm Gilbert got him to admit that he could not say absolutely, positively, that the wounds on the head were not made by the kick of a horse.

Other witnesses testified to having seen Jesse Braddock on the shore road on the morning of May 7. John Buchan said he was on his way to Traverse City about seven-thirty that morning when he met Jesse about two miles from the Carroll farm, walking toward home. He said he told Jesse that his stepfather had been hurt, whereupon Braddock started on a trot for the Carroll farm.

George Lyon said that he too met Braddock on the road early that morning. He said that Jesse was headed toward the Carroll farm and told him he had slept all night in the pines.

And Elizabeth Buchan, relative and neighbor of John, testified that Braddock came to her home very early in the morning, looking for a ride to town. He asked for a clean handkerchief and she gave him one.

On Monday, June 27, the prosecution — over the bitter protests of defense counsel — introduced into evidence a possible murder weapon. John Buchan took the stand and testified that on June 13, while searching the neighborhood with other Peninsula Township farmers for some weapon that might show that Stephen Carroll had been murdered, he found a stone of about three inches in diameter tied up in a handkerchief.

He said he found this makeshift weapon lying in a ditch near the August Nelson farm, along the route that Braddock supposedly had taken on the morning Carroll was found dead. The cloth and stone were wrapped in a bloody newspaper, he said, a sheet from the *Traverse City Record Eagle*. On the stand, Buchan demonstrated to the jury how the rock was tied in the handkerchief to make a heavy weapon, with the ends of the cloth for handles.

These materials had been turned over to the forensic laboratory in Ann Arbor for analysis. One of the witnesses on Wednesday morning was Dr. H. W. Emmerson, chemist at the University of Michigan, who made the analysis.

He had found no blood on the handkerchief, he said, but he did find some on the newspaper, and his tests showed that it was human blood. (The question of blood type naturally arises, but in 1921 the science of blood typing was still in its infancy.)

All this was characterized by the defense attorneys as so much idle speculation. They asked that all testimony concerning the so-called murder weapon be stricken from the record as having no connection with the case, but Judge Mayne ruled that it might stand at least temporarily.

For the defense, Mary Carroll denied that she told Alfred Lyon that her son had said he "would get his stepfather if it took a hundred years." She added that soon after the quarrel, when she met her son in town, Jesse told her he hadn't heard his stepfather's remark about him getting off and staying off the place. She said he told her he was planning to return to the farm for the summer.

Other defense witnesses were schoolboys Ben Samuelson, New Lowing and Max Needham, who said they had slept outdoors with the defendant on many occasions.

Charles Lyon, who had formerly owned the horse Queen, testified that although he considered her a gentle animal, she did kick at him once while he was cleaning her. And neighbor Carl Ahlstrom said that he had warned Stephen about the horse just a few days before his death.

The defense rested its case at noon on Friday, July 1. Judge Mayne charged the jury when court convened that afternoon, and they retired at two-thirty.

Just two hours later the jury announced that it had reached a verdict. As the jurors filed into the hushed courtroom, it seemed significant that their faces looked calm and untroubled.

Foreman Gardner Heager rose in the jury box and delivered the verdict: "Not guilty," he said.

The defendant broke into tears of joy. The jurors filed out of the box and one by one offered him their congratulations. As he left the courthouse with his mother, a crowd of his school friends met him at the door, singing "Hail, hail, the gang's all here." They formed an impromptu snake dance behind him and followed him downtown.

It seems obvious, from a reading of the evidence and considering how quickly the jury reached its verdict, that the prosecution failed utterly to prove its case. Indeed, it appears that they really had no case at all. The evidence was purely circumstantial (which is not to say that circumstantial evidence isn't just as good as direct evidence if there's enough of it) and prosecution was unable to link Braddock with the alleged murder weapon.

In any event, the ordeal of standing trial for murder didn't discourage Braddock from further escapades and brushes with the law. A short time later, he was caught stealing gasoline from a pump in town one night and took a few pellets of birdshot in the face.

In our system of common law — which is different from that of France and some other European countries — a defendant is presumed to be innocent until he is proven guilty, and the burden of proof is on the plaintiff. This is a seemingly simple but very profound concept, implying, among other things, that it is better to let a hundred guilty go free than to convict one innocent man.

This is not to imply that Braddock was guilty. A jury acquitted him, and the presumption of his innocence before the law still stands.

But people are entitled to their own opinions, and a great many Peninsula people — including most relatives and friends of the family — believed that Jesse Braddock was guilty, that he literally "got away with murder." To those among them who also believed in divine retribution and liked to see things tied up in neat packages, it may have seemed "fated" that the young man should come to an untimely and horrific end.

In 1930, as a fugitive from the law, Jesse jumped or fell to his death from a hotel window in Wisconsin. Some say he was pushed.

MURDER AT THE SAWMILL

All through the sultry dog days of early August the rumors had been flying like a fire in dry grass: trouble was brewing at the Otter Creek Mill. Something about a dispute over taxes. Something about Charley Wright's threat to fill the Sheriff full of holes if he tried to interfere with the operation of the mill.

Now, on a hot Saturday in August 1889, the trouble seemed to be coming to a head.

A giant of a man, 6-feet 6-inches and heavy, stood at the foot of a pile of logs, waving a paper at the men on top. He was Deputy Sheriff Neil Marshall—reputedly the biggest man in Benzie County—who had been sent by Sheriff Case to take possession of the logs in the name of the law.

The lumberjacks on the log pile looked down at the big man, who was threatening them with arrest if they rolled the logs into the creek. Then they looked at another man who was sitting on a log, some fifty feet from the rollway, with a hunting rifle in his lap. He was mill-owner C.T. Wright, burly and barrel-chested, with a brown mustache and a high domed forehead deeply tanned from the sun and wind. Shortly before, Wright had warned the Deputy: "Don't interfere with my men or I'll drop you."

The men on the pile sent a log rolling down, then another. The

Aral 1889.

big man scrambled for safety out of the way. He had a pistol in his hip pocket but did not take it out. He looked over at Wright, and for several moments the two men eyed each other. Then the Deputy turned away.

Marshall was no fool. Outnumbered and outgunned, he decided that this was one of those "he-who-fights-and-runs-away" kinds of situations and that he'd best fall back on Sheriff Case at Benzonia for reassurance and reinforcement. In robust health and no doubt feeling that a crisis had been averted at least for the time being, he would have been astonished to know that his life was drawing swiftly to an end. The remainder of it could now be measured in minutes.

Let us take a moment to go back in time and explore the reasons behind the trouble at Aral, site of the Otter Creek Mill. The reasons were political and complex.

The little town of Aral, which no longer exists, lay on the shore of Lake Michigan in the north-west corner of Benzie County, Michigan, between Frankfort and Empire. The sawmill had been built in 1882, and the town had grown up around it—all of it, that is, except early-settler Robert Bancroft's house and general store. In 1886 the town consisted of no more than a few houses, the mill buildings, a post office, and an Indian camp a quarter mile to the south.

In 1886, C.T. Wright leased the mill from its owner, one Dr. O'Leary of Detroit, who owned most of the land in Lake Township. Wright had lived most of his life in Racine, Wisconsin, where his brother had a prosperous lumber business. It was said that in his youth Wright had carried mail on horseback for several hundred miles in the Arizona and New Mexico Territories.

By 1886 most of the big pine timber had been logged off; under Wright's capable management the mill turned out shingle bolts, fence posts, railroad ties, and hardwood for furniture and flooring. (The Otter Creek site was said to have the finest stand of black cherry in the State.) At the time of the trouble, Wright employed 200 men; some at the mill, some in the woods cutting timber and tan bark, others as teamsters hauling the logs.

Wright was an attractive and aggressive young man in his late thirties. He was well liked by his men, and he treated them with kindness and consideration. One of them was Herman Bayne, who in 1937 at the age of 85, recalled: "On stormy days you would see him on the corner when the teams came in with loads of logs, saying, 'Boys, put your teams in the barn. Your time goes on.'"

But Wright had a streak of violence, too, and it came out especially when he had been drinking. He had been arrested several times for assault and battery; once for carving up a man's face with a knife. The Benzie County Prosecuting Attorney, George Covell, said later: "For years Wright was the source of half the legal business in the County, and in nine cases out of ten he was the defendant."

Wright's grievance with the County was that he had been taxed unfairly and out of all proportion. The Otter Creek Lumber Company was a Wisconsin corporation; Wright claimed that his lumber barge, *Seymour*, had been taxed in Racine, and then again by Benzie County. Moreover, because he was said to be a wealthy man (he was not), he was taxed at a higher rate than other lumbermen in the area. He had brought suit against the County the previous year, but had lost—the County officials having been unable to find that he had paid taxes on the barge in Wisconsin.

Sheriff A.B. Case had then attached logs amounting to 250,000 board feet, for unpaid taxes of $900 in round figures. Wright had begged the Sheriff to attach the sawn lumber rather than the logs, because his lease of the mill was soon to expire and without logs to saw the mill would have to shut down. The Sheriff refused and on August 5th had deputized Neil Marshall, of Honor, and Dr. Frank Thurber, Lake Township Supervisor, to keep an eye on the logs.

This, then, was the situation on that fateful day of August 10, 1889.

On his way back to Benzonia Deputy Marshall stopped at Bancroft's store, and there he met Dr. Thurber, who was returning from a house call, carrying his little black bag. A small man, Thurber wasn't exactly the kind of reinforcement Marshall was looking for; but the Doctor was one of the most popular men in the County, and highly respected. In addition to his medical practice and his job as supervisor, he also taught school: altogether, a man of parts. (It was he who gave the town its name, after the Sea in Russia, when several other names, including Bancroft and Otter Creek, were turned down by the postal authorities as having duplicates in other parts of the country.) Thurber and Marshall were of about the same age, early forties; Thurber the father of two; Marshall of four, all daughters.

Marshall told Thurber what had happened and together—apparently with some advice from Bancroft—they hatched a new strategy. They would outflank Charley Wright by an approach to the mill from the rear; there they would deputize the head sawyer, and if he refused to stop sawing logs, they would arrest him. (One wonders how they figured to make it stick, since most of the mill hands were loyal to their boss.) So together they started down the road to the mill. It was about 2:30 in the afternoon.

Meanwhile, Charley Wright (who had been hitting the bottle all morning and walking the streets with a loaded rifle, declaring he would roll the logs over dead men, if necessary) had returned to the mill and was chatting with his blacksmith, Wilson Reed. "It pays to have some sand," said Wright with some satisfaction.

"Yes," Reed said, "sand is all right in some places."

Then, looking out the door, Reed saw two men approaching the bridge over Otter Creek. "Who is that?" he said.

Outside, someone said, "Here they come."

"Let them come," said Wright. He picked up the rifle from behind the door and hurried down to the bridge.

What happened next was observed, at close range, by only two men; an Ottawa Indian named Joseph Pomigishick and a "Swede" named Charley Anderson. They were piling lumber near the bridge. Pomagishick spoke no English but could understand a little.

Wright met Marshall and Thurber just south of the bridge and for a time walked beside them, talking in a loud voice (the two workmen could not hear the words over the noise from the mill). Then Wright jumped in front of Marshall and raised his rifle. The big man reached for the gun and grasped it just below the muzzle. Wright jerked the rifle out of Marshall's grasp and shot him through the chest, just below the heart.

Marshall staggered, uttered a loud groan and fell face downward in the dust.

Thurber, a pace or two behind Marshall, cried, "My God, my God! What has he done!" Then he leaped forward and grabbed for the gun while Wright was trying to lever in another shell.

The two men locked in a death struggle, fighting for the rifle. Swaying from side to side, with the rifle muzzle pointed up over their heads, they fought back along the road. Just before they reached the bridge, some thirty feet from where Marshall's body lay, Wright put one arm around Thurber's neck, drawing him close to his chest. With the other hand he took a pistol from his right hip pocket, put the muzzle to Thurber's ear and pulled the trigger. Thurber released his hold on the rifle and fell dead.

Wright walked over to Pomagishick (Charley Anderson had fled) and asked him if he had seen what happened. The Indian, badly frightened, nodded his head. Wright told him to say nothing about it, and the Indian nodded again. Then Wright walked a short distance from the road and sat down on a scantling.

While he was sitting there, Newman Clark, one of his teamsters, came up and sat down beside him. Wright remarked that it seemed to be getting cooler. Clark asked if he could have some money, and Wright said, "My God, Clark! Can't you wait until this excitement dies down?"

But Clark was gently insistent and so the two men walked down to the company store, where Wright had his office, and Wright made out a check for Clark's wages. Wright's bookkeeper and brother-in-law, Fred Crosset, came in and asked Wright what had happened.

"Oh, those two crazy fools pitched into me and I had to shoot them," Wright said. "I feel sorry for them and their families, but they shouldn't have done what they did. A man has a right to protect his own property."

Wright stayed around the mill and the store until six o'clock, paying off his men. Then he disappeared into the woods.

Meanwhile, someone had covered each body in the road with an umbrella to shield them from the hot sun. Later, the bodies were brought in and laid on planks in one of the sheds at the mill. A cursory examination was made, and it was discovered that there was a flesh wound about an inch and a half long on Thurber's chest. Evidently the rifle bullet, after passing through Marshall's body, had inflicted this minor wound on Thurber.

Around 4:30 a telegram was sent from Aral to Sheriff Case in Benzonia. It said merely that there was trouble at the Mill. Half an hour later, a second telegram arrived, saying that Marshall and Thurber had been shot and killed and warning the Sheriff and Prosecutor Covell not to come alone, as they might be waylaid and killed.

This galvanized the Sheriff into action. He telegraphed his deputy in Frankfort to secure a boat, deputize 20 men and await his coming. Then with a fast team and accompanied by Covell and a reporter from the *Benzie Banner*, he covered the seven miles between Benzonia and Frankfort in record time.

There he and a posse of deputies boarded the steamer *Dewar* and reached Aral, 20 miles to the north, at 10:00 just as the summer sun was setting behind Lake Michigan and a full moon had risen.

In the meantime, news of the killings had spread like wildfire all over the county, and men had been coming into the town of Aral on horseback and afoot, and there was much talk of lynching. Upon the arrival of Case and his men, a search was made of all the houses and mill buildings and the barge *Seymour*, tied up at the dock; but Wright was nowhere to be found.

A young Ottawa Indian, Peter Lahala, who seemed to some of the crowd to be acting suspiciously, was seized and dragged to a pine tree nearby. A rope was secured from the barge, and someone in the mob knew how to tie a hangman's knot. The noose was placed around Lahala's neck and the other end of the rope thrown over a convenient branch. The Indian was told that unless he revealed Wright's hiding place, he would die.

Lahala protested that he knew nothing and was hoisted off his feet—Sheriff Case having told him to shake his legs vigorously if he wanted to talk. Lahala was hoisted off the ground and lowered at least three times. On being hanged for the third time, he said hoarsely that he would talk. He told the Sheriff that Wright was waiting at a sand hill near the beach about a half a mile north of Aral. He also said that Wright had arranged with him and Pomagishick to meet him there with a skiff after the barge was loaded, and take Wright out to the *Seymour*. Lahala said that he and Pomagishick were too frightened to do it. (That delightful teller of tales, Herman Bayne, said in his memoirs that he felt sorry for the poor Indian, who had to go through life with a crooked neck. The *Benzie Banner* reporter, on the other hand, called Lahala a "wretch".)

After the hanging and confession of Lahala, a game warden named Krouse, who lived at a rival lumber town a few miles south, was patrolling the beach north of Aral with a companion, Ernest. Krouse told the story at the hearing as follows:

"We heard a crackling of twigs and, as we were old hunters, we stopped to listen. Ernest said he could see a man with a light summer hat dodging from tree to tree. I saw him, too, and covered him with my Winchester, calling, "Come out of there."

I heard the man answer and couldn't make out the words, but I recognized the voice. I said, "Is that you, Charley?" and he answered, "Yes, Ed. For God's sake don't let them shoot me." I had him covered all the time, saying, "Do you want to surrender?" He said, "Yes, but I ask your protection. Don't let them kill me." I said, "Charley, hold up your hands, no foul play. Step out and show up. Are you armed?" "No," he said, and came out towards me with his hands up, saying, "Ed, where is Sheriff Case. Can you protect me?"—

Krouse hallooed for the Sheriff and a part of the mob came running up, yelling for blood. Among them was William Marshall,

160

brother of the slain deputy, carrying a rifle. "Are you the man who killed my brother?" he said.

"No, sir. I ain't," said Wright nervously.

"You ain't, eh," Marshall said, and pointed the rifle at Wright's head.

Krouse jumped between the two men and disarmed Marshall. "Just cool down and let the law take its course," he told Marshall. "This man is my prisoner and I will protect him."

Other deputies formed a circle around Wright and kept the crowd away, while they handcuffed the prisoner and searched him. They found a .44 caliber bulldog revolver in his hip pocket.

Wright was taken to his house and given an hour to take care of his business affairs. His wife had returned that afternoon on the stage coach from Frankfort after spending several weeks with relatives in Racine. She had seen the bodies in the road and had been told what had happened. But she had not seen her husband until he was brought in by the Sheriff. One can imagine that the meeting was an anguished affair. Wright left the operation of the mill in the hands of his wife and his brother-in-law, Fred Crosset. Then he was taken aboard the *Dewar* and, along with the Sheriff and his men, arrived at Frankfort at sunrise and was locked up in the Frankfort jail. Also aboard was the body of Neil Marshall.

The Frankfort jail was a rather flimsy affair and all day on Sunday there were threats of violence, and toward evening a small mob skirmished around the building. They scattered after someone fired a shot. Nevertheless the Sheriff decided, after Wright's entreaty and his lawyer's demand, that he be moved to the Manistee jail; and he was taken there aboard the *Dewar*. (A part of the mob, with plenty of rope, rode as far as the State Hospital grounds on the outskirts of Traverse City some 30 miles away, on the strength of a rumor—possibly planted by Sheriff Case himself—that Wright was being moved to the Grand Traverse County jail.)

Neil Marshall's funeral took place on Monday in Benzonia, and was attended, it was said, by the largest number of people ever to gather in Benzie County. He was buried on Cemetery Hill over-

161

looking the town; the inscription on his headstone reads:
"Faithful unto death
and while performing
his duty, fell'd by the
murderers hand."

Dr. Thurber's body was taken south to Holland, Michigan and buried there near his boyhood home.

A hearing was held on Wednesday at Bailey Hall on the Benzonia College campus before Justice W. L. Case—there being no suitable county building for the purpose. (The Benzie Coroner was Morris Case. The Cases were numerous and influential in Benzie County and they still are.)

Wright's brother from Wisconsin, his wife and her brother, and his two lawyers were admitted to the court room before the general public. Mrs. Wright went to her husband and clasped his manacled hands.

Mrs. Marshall and her four daughters, ranging in age from five to twelve, entered in the company of her mother, brother and brother-in-law. A reporter for the *Grand Rapids Press* describes her as "rather frail lady, appears to be very intelligent, and although she does not look to be more than thirty or thirty-five, her hair is quite gray."

Her brother-in-law was Louis Sands, a lumber mogul from Manistee. As he approached the bench where Wright was sitting, he turned and said to Mrs. Marshall, "This is the man who killed your husband." Then, turning to Wright, "Look at this woman whose husband you killed and these children whom you have orphaned."

The four little girls clung to their mother, crying, and she said, with tears running down her face, "Oh, why did you kill my husband?"

The hearing lasted four days, and Wright was then bound over to circuit court next spring on a charge of murder in the first degree. He spent the ensuing months in the jail at Traverse City.

Wright's trial opened in the second week in April, 1890, after an exhausting ten days of selecting a jury. Wright's lawyer had said he was going to drain the County and he very nearly did. The defense used up all its preemptory challenges, and 270 talesmen were examined before the 12 jurors were selected. (Some prospective jurors hid out in the woods; Sheriff Case had to send out deputies to round them up.)

The long, drawn-out process of selecting a jury was not without its moments of humor. Upon being asked about his knowledge of the case, John McMillan, of North Ireland birth, replied that he believed that half the lies he heard were not true. (The *Detroit Free Press* reporter called this remark "an Hibernicism".) A cross-eyed man was excused for no other reason than that he made both defense and prosecution lawyers nervous. Also excused was a sleepy man who was known to nod in church and even at work. During one of the longest recesses, the court officials began a baseball game on the college grounds, with the jurors watching from a raised bandstand. The game was interrupted by the arrival of half a dozen fresh candidates for jury duty.

The Wright murder trial began on April 17 and lasted two weeks. The State called a dozen witnesses who had either witnessed the killings or had heard Wright threaten to kill the two deputies. Most damaging to Wright was the testimony of Charley Anderson and Pomagishick. The defense called two men who claimed to have seen Deputy Marshall reach behind as if to draw his pistol; but their testimony was largely discredited upon cross examination.

Pomagishick's testimony was interpreted by his Indian friend, John Jacobs, while the defense had retained Joseph Blackbird to check on Jacob's interpretation. (Joseph Blackbird was the son of Andrew J. Blackbird who in 1887 published a history of the Ottawa-Chippewa Indians including a grammar and glossary of the language. His Indian name is Mackaw-de-be-nessy, which means black hawk.)

In relief from their arduous duties, the jury after breakfast on April 23 went fishing at Crystal Lake and returned an hour later with a half dozen suckers, knocked out of the water with bamboo poles; they said they had caught 17 in all.

After being charged by Judge Aldrich on May 1st, the jury deliberated only two and a half hours before reaching a verdict: guilty of murder in the first degree. Wright showed no emotions; his wife went into hysterics and his sisters were similarly prostrated.

Judge Aldrich sentenced Wright to imprisonment for life at hard labor, and on the following day Sheriff Case and his prisoner departed for the State Penitentiary at Jackson. They stopped for dinner at Cadillac, and the weekly newspaper there reported that the "hotel's festive board was joined by a congenial prisoner, the millionaire lumberman C.T. Wright; a former female candidate for the Presidency, a reverend minister, and several plebian innkeepers."

Sheriff Case bade his prisoner goodbye at the prison gates, and Wright told him to drop in whenever he was in the neighborhood, that he was almost certain to be at home. (Case did visit him several times.)

Wright was employed in the prison shirt-making shop and later as bookkeeper for that department. It was said that he became a great favorite of the warden, who let Wright drive the horse on outing buggy-rides together.

Twelve years later, despite the bitter protests of the widows and their friends—including former prosecutor George Covell— Wright was set free by Michigan Governor Pingree. The governor, for reasons best known to himself, commuted Wright's sentence to 17 years, and with time off for good behavior, he was paroled in May of 1902.

Wright paid a brief visit to Benzonia and Aral. His wife had divorced him and had married a carpenter. One story has it that she came to Wright and begged to be taken back, but he had turned her down. According to another version, Wright visited his former wife and her new husband. She asked him to sing one of her favorite songs, and Wright, who had a beautiful baritone voice, obliged. The lady was so overcome with emotion that she dissolved in tears; the carpenter, likewise affected, gave her back to Wright with his blessing. And all lived happily ever after.

Anyhow, that's the story as related by our old friend Herman Bayne, and if it isn't true, it surely ought to be. In any case, with or without his wife, Wright went back to Racine and was never seen or heard from in Benzie County again.

The "frail" widow Marshall—J. Marietta was her given name—outlived her husband by 28 years, dying in 1917 at the age of 72. Her oldest daughter lost her mind soon after her father's death and was committed to the State Hospital at Traverse City, where eventually she died.

Aral was a sawmill town—a town created by the mill—and when the mill died, the town died. It had a brief respite when, in 1903, the mill was taken over by members of "King" Ben Purcell's House of David cult. (One old-timer remembers the long-bearded ones with affection and respect—how when any two of them met in woods or village street, they would always stop and shake hands.)

But by that time, the timber of all kinds had pretty nearly run out, and the "Israelites" gave up around 1910 and moved south to Benton Harbor. The town lost its post office in 1905; people died or moved away; some of the buildings burned or were torn down; and by 1918 the town had ceased to be.

Now, all that remains to show that men and women once lived and worked there are a few spiles of old dock, the big concrete block that was foundation for the mill steam engine—and the "hanging tree".

A TRAVERSE CITY TRAGEDY

Grand Traverse County's biggest murder trial grew out of the same classic circumstances that Theodore Dreiser made famous in his novel, *An American Tragedy*.

Few Michigan murders have aroused such intensity of feeling as that of Julia Curtis in 1895. It is only a slight exaggeration to say that the good people of Traverse City literally thirsted for her killer's blood.

It all began on a sunny spring afternoon in April. Julia, 22-year-old daughter of Mark Curtis, a well-to-do farmer on Old Mission Peninsula, told her parents after dinner that she wanted to go looking in the woods for trailing arbutus. She left home shortly after one o'clock, carrying a small wicker basket. That was the last time anyone saw her alive—anyone, that is, except the murderer.

Her parents grew anxious when suppertime came and Julia had not returned. Dusk came on, and still no Julia, and they became frantic with worry. Her father alerted the neighbors and a searching party hunted the woods and fields by lantern light until almost daylight. No trace of Julia was found.

That morning, word having been sent to town, a party of 40 men

167

under S.C. Despres joined the search. A few hours later, the girl's body was discovered in a thick hemlock swamp.

She lay in an easy and graceful position, her feet crossed and her hands lying naturally on her breast. Her skirts were tucked neatly beneath her legs. Nearby was her basket, containing a few wilted flowers, and a half-filled bottle of laudanum. The gentle farm lass looked as peaceful as though she were sleeping.

Word was sent to Coroner Verly in Traverse City, who impaneled a jury and, accompanied by Dr. E. Corbin and Sheriff Vinton, came at once to the place. After a hasty examination of the surroundings, the girl's body was carried home to her weeping parents. There the doctor made a preliminary post-mortem and discovered that Julia was pregnant. For a time, this satisfied Verly that the poor girl, unable to bear her shame, had taken her own life by swallowing half a bottle of laudanum.

Only for a time. A further examination disclosed that she had met her death as a result of strangulation. There were red marks on her throat and the inner tissues of the throat were badly lacerated. Clearly, this was a case of murder.

The search for her killer or killers began at once. Vinton and his deputies questioned everybody who knew the girl—her parents, neighbors, friends, relatives, including a brother, Milo, who lived in Traverse City. No one could think of any good reason why anyone would want to kill this quiet and gentle farm girl. As far as anyone knew, she hadn't an enemy in the world. The doctor confirmed that she had not been molested sexually.

Two young men who boarded at the Curtis home came under suspicion for a time. But neither had been intimate with Julia and both had iron-clad alibis.

Also questioned was Woodruff Parmalee, a carpenter and small fruit grower who lived on a farm nearby. Parmalee, in his middle thirties, had been married twice, and had a sixteen-year-old son by his first wife. His son, Louis, lived with Parmalee at the farm, and the records do not show what happened to his first wife, Eliza Brinkman. His second wife, Euretta McDermott, had divorced him in 1893 after two years of marriage and no children, charging extreme cruelty. In her petition for divorce she said that on several occasions he had dragged her into the bedroom and beat her up. On one occasion he had tried to smother her by holding his hand over her face. He had a quick and violent temper, she said.

(Woodruff's father, George Parmalee, was a pioneer in fruit farming in the Grand Traverse area. He came here in 1865 from Grand Haven where he had planted the first peach orchard in that area. In 1867 he purchased a partially cleared farm near Old Mission and planted one of the first fruit orchards. When in failing health he sold it in 1883 to O.H. Ellis, it was the largest fruit farm in the Grand Traverse area. He died in 1885.)

Woodruff Parmalee and Julia Curtis had been "seeing" each other for several months. Parmalee accounted for his doings on the previous day by saying that he had worked all afternoon cutting brush for a new road adjacent to his farm. Witnesses confirmed his story.

The police got their big break about a month later. A farm laborer named John J. Staggs came to the Sheriff with the following story:

"On the afternoon of April 29 I was working on Barney Anderson's place, trimming trees. Parmalee came over about a quarter to one and we talked for a while. Then he started away down the ravine that runs southeast toward East Bay. I saw him a few minutes later still going southeast.

"I saw him again about 4 o'clock the same day in the same ravine, coming back. I was about 50 rods away from him. I am positive it was Parmalee. I thought he was looking for his tools. He was dressed in light pants, shirt-sleeves and a straw hat."

He went on to say that he saw Parmalee again the next morning. "He seemed very much excited. He was with McCool. They said they were going to form a line and look for the girl. I saw him that evening, too, at Schoolcraft's grocery. He bought some cheese. I rode home with him. He looked and acted very nervous. He said, 'Don't it beat you that Miss Curtis was two months gone?'

169

"On Wednesday he came where I was working. I didn't ask him about what was going on. He said: 'They are investigating pretty close. They had me before them today again.'

"He said you fellows were ferreting it out. He said it was a mystery to him how she was laid out so nicely. I asked him how close he came to where the girl's body was found and he said he was in the clearing north of the place one time, and then south of it later."

Asked why he had not come forth earlier with his story, he said he hadn't thought too much about it at the time. Then later, when he'd had time to think about it, he became suspicious. (It turned out later that his motive may not have been a simple desire to see justice done—but let's not get ahead of our story.)

On the strength of this story, and other information obtained from the Curtises, Parmalee was arrested and taken to jail in Traverse City. At his arraignment in June, he was bound over to Circuit Court on a charge of murder in the first degree.

Julia was the youngest daughter of the Curtises. She was a quiet, retiring girl—not pretty, but sweet-tempered and well liked. She and Parmalee had been keeping company for about a year. Her parents did not wholly approve, but they did not interfere. They felt that Parmalee was too old for their daughter, and they didn't like the idea that he'd been married twice before. But Julia was old enough to know her own mind, and perhaps they felt that, at age 22, her chances of marriage were fading.

On one occasion, several days before the murder, her mother had found them talking quietly near the kitchen door and had told them to come inside. They came in and sat down at the kitchen table, but in a few minutes he said goodbye and went out the door.

On other occasions she had seen them on the hill behind the house, sitting together and holding hands. Several times Parmalee had taken dinner with them. He had also met Julia at her brother's house in town and brought her home very late at night.

But it seemed to the Curtises that Julia's pregnancy was not sufficient motive for Parmalee to murder her. They shook their heads sadly.

Parmalee's trial was scheduled for Monday, July 8, his lawyers having requested the earliest possible date so that Parmalee could get back to his fruit farm, which urgently needed his attention.

A few days before the trial, Mark Curtis and a friend, Charles Garland, were talking together on Front Street when John Staggs came up to them. Staggs said to Curtis, "Don't forget. I'm your best witness and you must keep me posted."

"You're a hell of a witness," Garland said contemptuously.

Curtis told Staggs that he must tell the truth exactly as he knew it, and nothing more.

In retrospect, Staggs seems to have been a small-time grifter trying to work both sides of the street. At the trial, he testified that he had been approached by a member of the defense team and offered some money to leave town. He said he told the lawyer that every man has his price. He said the lawyer came to him later and said he couldn't raise the money.

At the trial, the defense declared that they had set a trap for Mr. Staggs and that he fell into it. They sought to capitalize on this by trying to impeach Staggs as a witness, but Judge Corbin demurred and Staggs stuck to his original story.

The trial opened as scheduled at the courthouse in Traverse City on July 8, Judge Roscoe L. Corbett on the bench. The defense had somehow been able to secure the services of Odell Chapman, a noted criminal lawyer from Owosso; he was assisted by the local firm of Gates & Turner. Prosecuting Attorney W. H. Foster and his assistant, L. Roberts, presented the case for the people.

The following men were selected for jury duty: Henry Workman, Wilfred Batey, A.R. Curtis (no relation), Addison Gray, John Bartley, Oscar Jefferson, J.W. Lane, Fred Rial, Eugene Norton, George McClellan, C.M. Potter and A.H. Jackson.

On Wednesday morning, July 10, when the State formally

opened its case, a huge crowd had gathered at the courthouse and the courtroom was full to overflowing. During the next few days, Prosecutor Foster put on a parade of witnesses—56 in all. Mrs. Curtis testified to the intimacies she had observed between Parmalee and her daughter. Other witnesses corroborated her testimony. Among them was her son, Milo Curtis, who testified that many times Julia and Parmalee had met at his house in Traverse City. On one occasion, he said, Julia had stayed all night, and Parmalee had come the next evening and they left together at about 11:30 p.m. He said that many times the visits were of a somewhat secretive nature.

A map was produced by County Surveyor H.F. Northrup showing the geographical relationship of the Curtis and Parmalee farms, and the route Parmalee was alleged to have taken to the final trysting place. The defense asked that the jury be allowed to go over the ground and the prosecution agreed. This was done later.

Other witnesses testified that the tracks found in the ravine by the searching party were those of Parmalee. They were peculiar tracks, Sheriff Vinton stated. He said that Parmalee's tracks in the jailhouse yard were identified with the ones found in the ravine.

Dr. Corbin stated that death was by strangulation. He had found marks on the face, throat and abdomen; the windpipe was crushed and blood vessels ruptured. Chemical expert, Professor Gomberg of Ann Arbor testified that he had failed to find any traces of poison in the stomach, making it virtually certain that death was the result of violence at the hands of some other person than herself.

After direct testimony by John J. Staggs as to his seeing Parmalee on the afternoon of the murder, cross examination produced the following testimony:

> Defense: Do you know Mr. Vanderlip?
> Staggs: I do.
> Defense: About the 18th of June did you have the following conversation with him; did you say: "I

am the main witness in this case and if I can get anything worthwhile out of it, I will get out of the country"?

Staggs: I did not.

Defense: Did you not then say, "If I can get $400 or $500 out of it, I will go to the State of California, where I have a son-in-law"?

Staggs: I did not.

Defense: Mr. Staggs, turn around and look at the jury. Did you have that conversation with Mr. Vanderlip?

Staggs: No, Sir. I did not.

Defense: Did you not say that in substance?

Staggs: They came at me.

Defense: Very well. Give the jury your version of the story.

Staggs: Well, Mr. Vanderlip came at me and asked me if money would have me go away. I said I was like anybody else and had my price. And then he went to you fellows as you say and he came back and talked a little in favor of it at first, but he said he couldn't raise the money.

Defense: What did you say then?

Staggs: Nothing.

Defense: What was your price?

Staggs: I didn't set no price.

By far the most damaging to Parmalee was the testimony of Julia's father, Mark Curtis. He said that he had been at Parmalee's house for a few minutes on March 27. Parmalee complained of a toothache and he, Curtis, asked why he didn't try laudanum or something. Parmalee remembered he had some in the house and produced a bottle and asked Curtis if that was laudanum. Curtis examined it and said it was and told him how to use it. Parmalee put the bottle in his pocket.

Prosecutor Foster held up the half-filled bottle found at Julia's side.

"Is this the same bottle you saw on March 27?"

"It is," Curtis said, firmly.

Defense attorney Chaplman objected but was overruled by Judge Corbett.

"You're very sure that this is the same bottle?"

"Yes, it is the same bottle," Curtis said, adding that it appeared to have about the same quantity of laudanum when found as when he saw it in March.

The State rested its case on Saturday, July 12.

In his opening statement for the defense, Chapman said that the prosecution had failed to show that the accused was within a mile of the spot where the body was found; that no evidence had been given to show that Parmalee had been in the vicinity; that the motive was lacking since the disclosure of illicit relations with the girl was not sufficient for a charge of murder; that the identity of the bottle was not proven beyond doubt.

Parmalee was his own chief witness for the defense. He appeared cool and collected. He testified in substance to the friendly relations between himself and the Curtis family. He said that he had gone home with Julia on several occasions, from Milo Curtis's especially, and that his son Louie usually accompanied them when he took her home.

Asked the direct question whether he had anything to do with the death of Julia Curtis, he promptly replied he had not.

He swore he had never been intimate with Julia. He denied ever seeing the laudanum bottle until it was found by the body. His whole testimony, in short, was a practical denial of that of the witnesses for the prosecution.

The defense rested on Tuesday, and, after being charged by Judge Corbett, the jury retired at 4:30 p.m.

The crowd hung around the courthouse grounds in anticipation of a speedy verdict of guilty, but at 9 p.m. the jury was still out. They were then sequestered for the evening at the City Hotel. After supper, the baliff took them for a walk and juror George

McClellan was approached by his wife and given a clean shirt. (The defense made an issue of this incident later at its motion for a mistrial.)

Wednesday morning the jury was still out and at 9 a.m. Judge Corbett called them in and asked how they stood. Foreman Curtis announced that they stood 11 to 1.

This news went quickly through the crowd and there was angry talk of lynching. Through the open window of the jury room, the jury heard one man shout: "What are they holding out for? Let's hang the fellow that's holding out! If they don't convict, let's mob Parmalee. Let's hang the son of a bitch!"

Whether this made any impression on the jury one way or another is not known; but at eleven o'clock they announced they had agreed upon a verdict. The prisoner was brought in, the attorneys were notified, and the courtroom at once filled with a great crowd of people. When quiet was restored, the Clerk asked the jury if they agreed upon a verdict.

"We have, your honor," said Foreman Curtis.

"What is your verdict?"

"We find the defendant guilty of murder in the first degree."

After a momentary hush, the courtroom exploded in a burst of applause, which was checked immediately by Judge Corbett, who reprimanded the crowd.

According to the Traverse City *Evening Herald* reporter, Parmalee sprang partly from his chair and faced the crowd with the expression of a hunted tiger, then dropped into his seat, put his hand to his face and partly covering his mouth sat quiet, with his eyes downcast while the jury was polled. Judge Corbett announced that the sentencing would take place at four o'clock.

Long before that time there were hundreds of people on the courthouse grounds waiting for the doors to open; about one-third of the number were women. When the doors were thrown open, the crowd surged in and filled every available seat.

At precisely four o'clock, Judge Corbett rapped for order. "Woodruff Parmalee," he said, "stand up. What have you to say why the judgement of the law should not now be pronounced against you?"

In a clear but somewhat tremulous voice, Parmalee said, "Your Honor, I don"t know as anything I might say would make any difference, but there has been a terrible mistake made. I have been robbed of my home, robbed of my family; I have been robbed of everything except a clear conscience. I have never committed murder."

Parmalee was sentenced to solitary confinement at hard labor for the rest of his life. Next morning, in the custody of Deputies Spangle and Taylor, Parmalee boarded the train for Jackson Prison.

Thus ended the greatest murder trial in the history of Grand Traverse County. The crime was a fearful one, and the punishment was quick. The case was purely circumstantial but the evidence was strong. The feeling in the county had been intense, so intense that several times during the trial noisy demonstrations had broken out in the courtroom and outside.

Parmalee served almost 20 years in prison. On May 19, 1915, he was paroled by Governor Ferris and returned to Traverse City where he took up residence first at a boarding house on Washington Street and then on State. For several years before retirement in 1928 he worked as a carpenter for the Hannah, Lay Lumber Company. He died at the Traverse City State Hospital on February 10, 1942, of senility and pneumonia at the advanced age off 89.

Author's Note: Judge Corbett died three years after the trial under circumstances that for a long time remained mysterious. He was killed by a rifle bullet while hunting deer in the Upper Peninsula with his son, Charles. At first, the son came under suspicion that he had accidentally killed his father. But an autopsy disclosed that Corbett was shot with a .45 caliber ball, whereas Charles was carrying a shotgun loaded with buckshot.

Nevertheless, some doubt remained in the minds of many people, and for 20 years the son lived under that cloud of suspicion. Then, in 1915, a man in Alpena confessed on his deathbed that it was he who had accidentally fired the fatal shot.

MURDER BY THE DOZEN

Saturday, May 2, 1903, was cold and blustery with snow flurries—typical early spring weather in Springfield Township, Kalkaska County. Farmer Joe Battenfield had come in late from the barn and was sitting in an easy chair, reading the weekly *Kalkaskian,* when there was a knock on the door. He got up to answer it, wondering who in the world could be calling at this time of night.

It was old Sarah Murphy, a neighbor, gasping for breath and obviously distraught. "Come quick!" she said. "John is terribly sick. I think he's dying."

Mrs. Battenfield came up beside her husband. "What can we do?" she asked anxiously.

"Do you have some camphor? We have none at home. Mary told me to bring some."

Mrs. Battenfield ran to get the camphor while her husband put on his shoes and a mackinaw coat. Then he and Mrs. Murphy hurried down the road to the Murphy farmhouse, a quarter mile away.

When they arrived, Mrs. Murphy led Battenfield to an upstairs bedroom. The small room contained only a bed, a wooden chair and a washstand. There was a washbowl and pitcher on the stand,

and a kerosene lamp burning smokily. At the foot of the bed sobbing into a handkerchief, was widow McKnight, John Murphy's sister. John himself lay across the bed with his feet on the floor. He was a tall slender man with thick black hair. He wore a grey flannel nightgown.

His body had been racked by convulsions. His face was red and glistening with sweat, and the corners of his mouth were flecked with foam. His eyes were closed.

Joe Battenfield moved to his side and held the open bottle of camphor to his nose. The tormented man opened his eyes.

"It's no good, Joe," he said. "I am dying."

"It can't be that you are dying, John," said Battenfield

"Yes, John said. "I am gone." Then he cried, "Hold me down, Joe. My feet will come up."

Battenfield pressed his knees against the dying man's legs. The spasms came again, one after another. They lasted for what seemed to Battenfield a very long time. Then the body grew quiet; mercifully, John Murphy was dead.

"Is he gone?" asked his sister. "Oh, God, is he gone?"

Battenfield nodded and lifted John's body back full length on the bed. Old Sarah Murphy, John's mother, wept quietly in the bedroom doorway.

On the way home, Battenfield's thoughts were troubled and confused. He was shocked at John's death, but somehow he wasn't surprised. It seemed that an evil cloud hung over the Murphy family. Less than a week ago, John's pretty young wife Gertrude and his baby daughter, Ruth, had died, both on the same day—the baby of spasms, the mother of an epileptic fit. And now John was gone. It was too much, Battenfield thought. It was more than any family should have to bear.

The Murphy's, Sarah and Isaiah, were Canadians; they came to Alpena in northern lower Michigan in 1871. They raised a large family—five girls and five boys. Isaiah was a lumber camp worker—a teamster and cook. All the boys and some of the girls worked in lumber camps when they grew up.

The family moved from camp to camp. There were lumber

camps all over northern Michigan in those days. It was said that a man could travel from the timberline in Michigan, across the straits and down into Wisconsin without a penny in his pocket: it was a tradition in the camps that a travelling stranger was entitled to at least one night's lodging and meals. All camps paid the same wages—a dollar a day. The difference among them was in the food. A good cook could keep the lumberjacks happy; a poor one would drive them away.

In 1873 Isaiah Murphy bought a tract of land in Springfield Township and built a house. The family lived there together until the sons and daughters were married—farming in the summer and working in the lumber camps in winter. Now there were only old Sarah; the widowed sister, Mary McKnight; and Ann Mullin, a mentally retarded niece whom Mary had taken in out of the goodness of her heart. Mary's father, Isaiah, had died in 1894.

Everybody loved Mary. She was the kindest, gentlest person in the world. She was warm and outgoing, plump and pretty, with an engaging personality. Everybody said she looked far younger than her forty years.

But her life had been full of sorrow. She had buried two husbands and all of the children from her first marriage had died young—three in infancy and two of dyptheria at ages 5 and 17.

Mary was a trained nurse and midwife. As a young wife she had learned practical nursing from an older woman in Alpena. It was there that she met her first husband, James Ambrose, a well-to-do house painter. He died of consumption in 1887.

Shortly after his death, Mary married Ernest McKnight, also a painter and an associate and friend of the Ambroses. The couple moved to Grayling in 1889. McKnight, a big, jovial Irishman, was a kind and indulgent husband; he and Mary got on well together, and both were great favorites in the Grayling community. As a practical nurse, Mary was on constant call to care for the sick.

But death dogged Mary's footsteps, and Ernest McKnight died in 1897 of spinal meningitis. After that, Mary sold the property and moved in with her mother on the farm near Fife Lake. By reason of her mother's age and ill health and Mary's financial position, (both husbands had left her well fixed) Mary assumed the role of head of the household.

In the late winter of 1903, Mary's brother John and his wife and their baby daughter, 3 months old, moved in with Mary and her mother while John was building a new house. The John Murphy's had been married a little over a year; she was a Ward from over by Waters.

On Monday, April 24, Gertrude left the baby in Mary's care while she was helping her husband in the new house. When they returned, early in the afternoon, the baby was dead. It had died of spasms, Mary said, terribly broken up.

After trying to console his wife and Mary, John left for Fife Lake to buy a coffin. Five hours later, John returned and found his young wife dead. She had died of an epileptic fit, Mary told him, undoubtedly brought on by the baby's death. Probably it was all for the best, Mary said; Gertrude would never have gotten over the death of her baby. John died five days later.

A few days after John's death, Mary brought a mortgage in her favor to the county clerk in Kalkaska for filing. The mortgage was drawn on John Murphy's 40 acres—he had borrowed $200 from Mary to build his house. What aroused the clerk's suspicions was that the mortgage had been clumsily altered from $200 to $300, and there were other erasures, corrections and interlineations. He took his suspicions to County Proscecutor E.C. Smith. Next day Smith and County Sheriff Creighton drove out to have a talk with Mary.

Mary told them that she had loaned John the extra $100 for a well and other improvements. She said that John himself had made the alterations and that John had taken the mortgage to Justice A.T. Kellogg for notarization.

That seemed plausible enough, but somehow Smith and Creighton didn't like the look of it. Something here was wrong. Something smelled rotten in Springfield.

After talking with Joe Battenfield, Smith obtained a court order for the exhumation of John Murphy's body. On May 18 he and

Creighton and Dr. Pearsall, the coroner, dug up John's body at the Springfield cemetery. The internal organs were removed and sent to Ann Arbor for examination. Meanwhile, Smith launched an investigation into Mary McKnight's past. What he found was appalling.

It seemed that Ernest McKnight had not died of spinal meningitis after all. On the day of his death, one Saturday in 1897, Ernest McKnight drove his wagon out to a piece of property he owned just outside Grayling, to cut some hay. He invited his wife and his niece to go along, but they decided against it. That evening he came home sprawled out in the wagon-box in agony, with the horses finding the way.

He told Dr. J.A. Leighton, a neighbor, that he had become violently ill after eating a lunch that his wife had prepared for him. (According to family tradition, the lunch included a piece of rhubarb pie, McKnight's favorite.) For a while, he said, he thought he was going to die on the spot, but after an hour or so he managed to get the team hitched to the wagon and headed home.

Dr. Leighton, a good friend of the McKnights, thought his chances hopeless but treated him as best he could.

To the physician's amazement next morning, he found the rugged Irishman sitting up in bed, smoking a pipe. Dr. Leighton went home, delighted at his friend's recovery.

But the next morning a screaming Mrs. McKnight summoned the doctor. Her husband, she said, had died in his sleep.

Dr. Leighton could not explain the sudden change. Puzzled, he wrote out a death certificate, listing the cause as spinal meningitis. But even as he did so, he felt that this was an error because there had been no rise in temperature when he first examined his friend.

"My inability to diagnose that case bothered me," he told Prosecutor Smith. "I believe now that Mary McKnight poisoned her husband in his lunch and then gave him a second dose that night."

Moreover, there was reason to believe that Mary's first husband, James Ambrose, had not died a natural death. He was known to be suffering from consumption, but he died in agony, his limbs twitching convulsively. And there were other sudden and mysterious deaths in Mary's past.

Meanwhile, after a week, the report came back from forensic laboratory at Ann Arbor: there was enough strychnine in John Murphy's stomach to kill an elephant.

That was enough for Prosecutor Smith. He got a warrant for Mary's arrest and drove out with Sheriff Creighton to the Murphy house. Mary wasn't home, her mother told them. She had taken her niece Mary Mullin with her to Traverse City on some legal matter.

Mary McKnight was arrested at Walton Junction on the evening of May 31. She had gone to Traverse City to get help from Parm C. Gilbert, a rising young attorney, to prevent the exhumation of John Murphy's body. (She told Gilbert that just before he died John told her, "Please, Mary, don't let anyone dig me up after I'm gone.")

She was apprehended while waiting in the GR & I depot at Walton Junction for a change of cars to take her home. Sheriff Creighton took both Marys to the Kalkaska jail for questioning. The child Mary Mullin was released after two days of interrogation.

Mary did not take well to jail living. She refused all food and spent her nights pacing the cell, her days in simulating rest or sleep. Smith urged her to unburden her conscience with a statement, offering her flowers and sympathy, but on the advice of her legal counsel, Gilbert of Traverse City and Joshua Boyd of Kalkaska, she refused to talk.

Meanwhile, the bodies of Gertrude Murphy and her baby were exhumed, and large amounts of strychnine were found in both.

On June 5, in an interview with a staff correspondent of the *Detroit Journal*, Sarah Murphy and the two younger brothers Charles and Dan, emphatically declared their belief in the innocence of Mrs. McKnight. They said they were sure that the baby died of convulsions, that Gertrude died in a fit, to which she was subject, and that if John himself died of poison, it was through suicide which they claimed he had threatened.

"That's all rot," said Sheriff Creighton. "It's not even a possibility in view of the evidence we have picked up in the last few days."

He went on to say that he had known Mary McKnight since she was a little girl and had never known anything good about her.

On Monday, June 8, after seven days of fasting and sleeplessness, Mary McKnight was at the end of her rope. She broke down and sent for Prosecutor Smith. "I have something to say," she told him.

Then, in what surely must be one of the weirdest confessions in the history of crime, she said: "I had the strychnine and some quinine mixed together in capsules. When Gertie's baby died, I thought it would soothe her if I gave her one of the capsules. I didn't mean to harm her. Then Gertie died. I did the same with John. I did not intend to hurt my own brother. I thought the capsule would soothe him. It seemed to kill him though. I didn't give the baby anything. I don't know how it came to die."

Next evening, Mary made a full confession: "I didn't mean to harm anyone. I did give the baby the strychnine. It woke up and cried with its mother gone, and I made up a little of the strychnine in a glass, with some water, and gave a spoonful of it to the baby. I didn't mean to harm the little thing at all. I confessed all I did to the Lord this afternoon and I feel he has forgiven me.

" When Gertie came home and found the baby dead, she got awfully nervous. She knew she was nervous and all worked up and she came to me and said, 'Mary, can't you give me something to quiet me, something that you take yourself?' I said I would and I really didn't think it would hurt her if I gave her one of the capsules."

(It should be pointed out here that in those days strychnine was used medicinally in very small quantities as a tonic and stimulant.)

"She had spasms right after that," Mary continued, "and I suppose it was the strychnine that killed her. I really didn't mean to hurt her though. I loved Gertie and I was really sorry to see her go.

"Then John seemed to feel so badly about it, so broken up, that I often thought, after Gertie died, that it would be better if he were to go, too.

"John was feeling bad and he came to me and said he wanted something to quiet him. He was suffering from asthma, too. I had two or three capsules filled with strychnine and quinine in the cover of a pill box on my dresser, and he went up and helped himself. I don't know whether he took one or two.

"Then he went to bed and I went to bed, too, and by and by I heard him and went to his room. He said that he was having a chill. Mother came, too. By and by he came to have those same spasms, and I suppose that was the strychnine working. I suppose that is really what killed him, thought I didn't intend to hurt any of them.

"I loved John. He was always a good brother to me. I loved Gertie, too. I was sorry to see John go, but I suppose it was all for the best. John has come back to me and Gertie too, since I have been in jail, and they have told me that they forgive me, and I told the Lord all about it, too, and I am sure that he has forgiven me."

Her lawyer, Parm Gilbert, discounted the confession and said, "The real truth of her confession is this: She gave the babe what she considered was a soothing potion. She allowed the mother and father to take medicine that she herself used, and in each case they took too much of the medicine and death resulted." The defense was not giving an inch.

He said further that Mrs. McKnight looked like a kind and gentle person and one who would not be willing to hurt anyone. He said that her every action indicated good breeding and thoughtfullness of others, and that she would be the last one that he would consider guilty of any crime.

At her arraignment before Justice A.T. Kellogg in Kalkaska on June 27, Mrs. McKnight pleaded not guilty. After two days of testimony, she was bound over to circuit court on the charge that on the 2nd day of May, 1903, *in the Township of Springfield,

Kalkaska County, Mary McKnight did feloniously and with malice aforethought kill and murder one John Murphy.

The trial began on November 9 before Judge C.C. Chittenden but because of the difficulty of securing an impartial jury, the Judge granted a petition by Parm Gilbert for a change of venue, and the trial was adjourned to the next session of the circuit court in Cadillac. During the proceedings Mary had sat with bowed head, her face drawn and haggard. According to the Traverse City *Evening Herald* reporter, "She appears to have aged ten years in the past few months. At the time of the hearing she was very plump, smooth-faced, and by no means a bad looking woman. Now her face plainly shows her keen suffering, whether from remorse or confinement is not known. She almost continually rolled her eyes, which were open very wide, the whites plainly showing. She was dressed in black, with gloves and a fur collarette around her neck. Her appearance physically was that of a woman continually suffering."

When she accompanied the deputy sheriff to the conveyance to take her back to jail, she had to be assisted somewhat. Her teeth were tight shut, but her lips were widely parted, which plainly showed both rows of her teeth, and she kept her lips in this position as far as could be seen. She has an expression bordering on the idiotic, part of which, at least, seems to be assumed."

Mary's trial opened in Cadillac before Justice Chittenden on December 1, after several days of jury selection. Three quarters of the spectators were women, some of whom brought their knitting—in a scene reminiscent of *A Tale of Two Cities* with Madam Defarge knitting at the foot of the guillotine, waiting for the heads to roll. Some of the ladies brought lunch in a brown bag so as not to lose a ringside seat, while others left the courthouse at eleven o'clock for an early lunch at home so as to be on hand when the afternoon session began.

According to the custom of the day, the jury was kept sequestered at the courthouse: cots were set up in an adjoining room and their meals were sent in.

As she had done at the hearing, Mary sat with head bowed,

apparently taking no interest at all in the proceedings. From time to time she would throw her head back, baring her teeth.

The prosecution opened with the testimony of Joe Battenfield, who described the circumstances of John's death. He also testified that a few days before John died, Mary asked him to buy some strychnine for her. She told him she needed it to kill some mice in the cellar. He said he bought five cents worth of the poison at LaBarr's drugstore in Fife Lake and gave it to Mary Mullin who came running out from the house as he drove up in his buggy.

A particularly damaging witness to the defense was a Mrs. Dyne, a neighbor of the Murphy's who had been present when Gertrude and the baby died. She said that Mrs. McKnight gave the baby what she supposed was antifebrin, but that the baby went into spasms and died almost immediately. Shortly after this, Mrs. Dyne said, Gertrude complained of being sick and nervous and Mrs. McKnight placed her feet in a tub of hot water and gave her a capsule for her nerves. Fifteen minutes later, Gertrude stiffened and went into convulsion after convulsion until she died. Asked whether Mrs. McKnight showed any emotion, she said yes, that Mary had cried and carried on and said, John will take this hard. It will kill him in two weeks."

Mary's confession was introduced and it was admitted as evidence in spite of the bitter protests of the defense, who claimed that it had been obtained through fraud and trickery.

Reed, a Kalkaska undertaker, testified that John's body was so stiff and rigid that he had to use two hands to straighten out the arms. He said that Gertrude's body was also stiff and rigid. (One of the characteristics of death by strychnine poisoning is prolonged rigor mortis.)

The State rested its case on December 5, and Parm Gilbert made the opening statement for the defense. He said that the defense would show that John died of an attack of asthma, and suggested that the poison was introduced in John's body in the embalming fluid—leading one reporter to write that the defense "would go to any length to secure an acquittal."

186

Although he did not make a formal claim of insanity, he introduced several witnesses—relatives and friends of Mary—who testified that Mary was subject to fits of despondency, and a doctor from the Ionia Mental Hospital testified that, given this kind of medical history, Mary would sooner or later have spells of insanity. (The prosecution countered with their own mental physicians, who said that this was not true; and the net effect was that both sides cancelled each other out on this issue.)

Final arguments were made on December 9, and that same morning Judge Chittenden charged the jury. At one-thirty the following afternoon, after deliberating 27 hours, the jury brought in its verdict: guilty of murder in the first degree. (It was learned later that five members of the jury held out for several hours for a verdict of not guilty by reason of criminal insanity.)

With a slight trembling but otherwise showing no emotion, Mary received her sentence from the judge that she must spend the rest of her natural life in Jackson State Prison. Asked if she knew any reason why such sentence should not be pronounced, she said, "I am innocent. I did not kill John. I did not give him the medicine with the intention of killing him."

Next day, in the custody of the Wexford County Sheriff with the delightful name of Billy Huckleberry, Mary boarded the GR & I passenger coach for State Prison. (There she would be transferred to the Detroit House of Corrections, there being no women prisoners at Jackson.)

Of all her immediate relatives, only her sister, Ruth Chalker, was on hand to bid her goodbye. Ruth was the only one who stood by her during the many months of her ordeal.

Mary told reporters at the depot that she wanted to thank the officers of the court for their kind and courteous treatment. She said that all she remembered was that she never intended to harm anyone.

There was a final moment of parting, described by a Cadillac reporter as "a pitiful scene, with the bent little prisoner sobbing in her sister's arms."

During the course of his investigation, Prosecutor Smith had made a list of the people that Mary McKnight had probably "soothed" to death:

> —James Ambrose at Alpena in 1887. Suffered from consumption but died in agony, his limbs twitching convulsively;
>
> —Mrs. McKnight, first wife of Ernest, in July 1887, at Alpena. Partial paralysis and convulsions. Limbs twitching as in case of poisoning;
>
> —Baby Teeple, Mrs. McKnight's niece, died two days later at the same place. Died of convulsions in Mary's care;
>
> —Eliza Chalker, Mrs. McKnight's niece, died in Grayling in May 1892. Partial paralysis, foaming at the mouth and convulsions after taking tea with Mrs. McKnight;
>
> —Sarah Murphy, Mrs. McKnight's sister, died in Grayling, February 1893. Case precisely similar to above;
>
> —Ernest McKnight, Mary's second husband, at Grayling 1898;
>
> —Mrs. Curry, a relative, died in Saginaw in 1896;
>
> —Dorothy Jensen, in Grayling, Good Friday, 1902. Convulsive twitching and foaming at the mouth. Child was in Mrs. McKnight's care at the time;
>
> —Baby Murphy, at Fife Lake in May 1903;
>
> —Gertrude Murphy, baby's mother, same date, same place;
>
> —John Murphy, Mary's brother, same place, 5 days later.

Prosecutor Smith said that there were several other possible victims—friends and relatives of Mary.

Joseph Murphy, who with his wife Carolyn lives on a farm near Frederic, is one of the few living descendents of Isaiah and Sarah Murphy. (Mary McKnight was his great aunt.) Joe's father, James Ray Murphy, told him that for years Mary's name was never mentioned in family circles. His father also told him that he,

James Ray, almost became one of Mary's victims. It happened after a family funeral. His father, fifteen years old at the time, complained of a headache. Mary suggested that he go to her bedroom and get a headache powder in a capsule container on her dresser. His father James—Mary's brother—told the boy not to go.

Why did Mary McKnight kill? What made her tick? So far as we know, she had nothing against any of her victims, and, except for her husbands and possibly her brother John, she did not stand to profit a penny from the death of any one of them.

That she was insane in the true clinical sense of the word seems clear beyond the shadow of a doubt. Today she probably would have been sent to a mental hospital instead of prison—though one cannot be sure about this, since the legal litmus test of sanity (the ability to know right from wrong) is almost as simpleminded today as it was then.

Was she, then, a child by tiger—one of those monsters, mentally bright but emotionally crippled, to whom a human life is of no more consequence than that of a fly—psychologically, if not temperamentally, akin to the quiet, dutiful son who without warning and for no apparent reason suddenly goes berserk and slaughters the whole family in cold blood?

Perhaps it was Jennie, wife of James Murphy and sister-in-law to Mary, who years ago came up with at least part of the answer.

"Mary liked funerals," she said.

Somehow it has the ring of truth. Mary was a friendly, gregarious person. She loved to get dressed up for social occasions. And there were few social occasions in backwoods Michigan in those days to equal a family funeral. It brought the whole family together. And after the funeral there would be an Irish wake.

One can imagine that Mary was in her glory then, dressed up in her finest black taffeta, black hat and veil, grieving as loud and long as anyone, in an orgy of emotion. And who is to say that her tears were not real?

Mary McKnight served 18 years before she was paroled. A Mrs. Robert Y. Ogg, a member of the board of the Michigan Training

School for Women, opened her house to her. She died there several years later.

Thus, Mary Murphy shuffled off this mortal coil and went to take up her abode in whatever place in hell is reserved for mass poisoners—along with such female monsters as Sarah Jane Robinson, Christiana Edmunds, Jeanne Weber, Belle Gunness and Madeleine Smith. In terms of number of victims, Mary had outdone them all.

THE BENZONIA MYSTERY—
Murder of Suicide?

The women of the hilltop hamlet of Benzonia in northwestern lower Michigan were suspicious of W.H. Thacker from the beginning.

Not that they foresaw his wife's death, although some said later that they did.

At first it was "just the way he called his hired girl, 'Girlie'." (She called him "pa".)

Ora Bunker, who worked in the Thacker home before the turn of the century, was a rather buxom farm girl in her 'teens, with a tendancy to giggle and primp. Maybe she hadn't done anything wrong yet, they said, but they were convinced it was only a question of time before she did.

They voiced their opinions to Mrs. Thacker at church one Sunday. She told them Ora was "a silly girl" who "disgusted her" at times, and that she was thinking of letting her go.

But Ora stayed on, caring for the Thacker children and preparing the meals, and life in the little village overlooking Crystal Lake went on as usual.

It was hard to keep secrets in a quiet, churchy little place like Benzonia, and leading a double life was next to impossible. William Henry Thacker was a well-to-do Benzonia businessman.

He lived on a little farm just south of the town, and he sold farm implements and life insurance. As befitted his station in life, he was also a Sunday School teacher and a trustee of the church.

One summer he attended a Sunday School convention in Lansing, and it happened that Ora Bunker was there, too.

Mrs. Shaw, the minister's wife, came home and said she saw them walking "arm in arm".

George Jones, the undertaker, said he saw them together in Frankfort one day when Mrs. Thacker was known to be ill. Ora left for Benzonia on the evening train, and Thacker drove home his buggy.

Gossip began to flow across the backyard fences and at ladies' socials. Many had observed the pair at evening prayer meetings—how close they sat together on the wooden bench, how they kept a little apart from other folks. Their actions seemed to indicate an intimacy far beyond that of master and hired girl.

Then there was Miss Spencer. She was Mrs. Thacker's sister—an invalid, often bedridden. She had been living in the Thacker household ever since losing her health while serving as a missionary in Turkey four years earlier. She had ample opportunity to observe their conduct, and she thought it disgraceful. At least a dozen times she had come upon Ora and Thacker in whispered conversation in the kitchen—with Ora pressing Thacker against the wall. Once, when Thacker was sitting on the foot of her bed chatting, Ora came in and curled up at his feet, resting her head against his knee and fondling his hands. Another time Ora caught hold of Thacker's beard and tugged it playfully. "You remember what you told me," she said; and Thacker said, "Yes, I remember." They acted as intimate as man and wife, Miss Spencer said. Curiously, they did not seem embarrassed by her presence. She didn't like the look of things at all.

Finally, she had gone to Thacker and remonstrated with him. He ought to be ashamed of himself, she told him, carrying on like that with a hired girl under his wife's very nose. Had he no regard for her feelings at all? But Thacker insisted there was nothing wrong. Ora was like a daughter to him, he said. He was almost as fond of her as he was of his own daughter Lottie. But that was all, he said. There was nothing wrong in that.

Miss Spencer wasn't convinced. But when, later on, she broached the subject again, Thacker wouldn't listen to her. He turned his back on her and stood at the window, saying, "Let's have no more of these insinuations."

Everyone agreed he was old enough to be her father; that made it all the more scandalous. Poor Mrs. Thacker, the women whispered. Why didn't she send Ora Bunker packing? The affair was a disgrace to the community and a bad example to the young people. Something would have to be done, they said.

They prevailed on Dr. Shaw, the minister, to have a word with Thacker. He took Thacker aside one Sunday and talked to him like a Dutch uncle. He found it hard to believe, he said, that the gossip about Thacker and Ora Bunker was true. Nevertheless, as a trustee of the church, Thacker must, like Caesar's wife, avoid even the appearance of evil. The church would be compelled to take steps if the situation persisted. A word to the wise, he hoped, was sufficient.

Again Thacker declared his innocence. But he promised to be more circumspect in the future.

That should have satisfied the ladies but it didn't. They wanted Ora Bunker out of the Thacker home. Two of them drove out to the Bunker farm, twelve miles away, and warned Ora's mother of "what was going on"; and Mrs. Bunker told Thacker she believed it would be best for him to stay away from her daughter.

Ora ceased working for the Thackers.

After a short stay on a farm she went to work for the Shaws, who had rooms above Mott's drugstore—a quarter mile up the hill from Thacker's place. This pleased the ladies. That Dr. Shaw was above temptation they hadn't the slightest doubt, and with Mrs. Shaw to keep an eye on the girl, she couldn't be in better hands.

That's what they thought. But Ora and Henry Thacker continued to see each other.

Mrs. Shaw told about it later in court:

Mr. Thacker would come around to see Ora at least once or twice a week, she said. "Sometimes he had letters for her that he said were dropped in his box; sometimes he brought messages from her folks—or so he said."

She went on to say that they visited together on the back porch with the door closed so she couldn't hear what was said. They usually spent at least ten or fifteen minutes together out there, she said. Once when Ora was ill and couldn't come to the door, Thacker told her that Ora's monthly periods were very hard on her, she said.

Dr. Shaw testified that on Sundays Ora would keep watch out the window until she saw Thacker coming up the hill, then run downstairs in time to enter the church with him.

One Lawrence Mahn said he saw Thacker coming down the back stairs from the Shaw apartment one night around eight o'clock when he knew that nobody was home except Ora Bunker and the Shaw baby. Thacker saw him, too, and hastened to explain that he was keeping an eye on the drugstore to see if he could "catch Dr. Mott selling liquor". Thacker was a deputy sheriff, he explained.

So things stood one day in early May, 1894, when a friend and neighbor dropped in to see Mrs. Thacker. Mrs. E.C. Bailey described herself in court as a long-time friend of Mrs. Thacker. The latter's husband called her "a meddler".

At any rate, Mrs. Bailey came in response to a note from her friend, delivered by the Thacker's fifteen-year-old daughter, Lottie. She found her friend lying on the sofa in the sitting room, desperately ill.

Mrs. Thacker said she had not felt well that morning and had not joined her family at the breakfast table. Instead, her husband had brought the meal to her in bed. She became violently ill, she said, after eating her usual morning dish, graham mush. She suffered a terrible nausea, and felt "as though she was burning up".

While they were talking, Mrs. Thacker was seized by another attack. She rolled off the sofa and crouched on the floor on her hands and knees, retching and heaving. After it was over, Mrs.

Bailey helped her back on the couch and went to find her husband.

Mrs. Thacker was very ill, she told him. Didn't he think they ought to call a doctor?

"Well, if you think best," Thacker replied, curiously unconcerned.

Mrs. Bailey sent word to Dr. David Dean, and the young physician arrived at the Thacker home shortly after supper. Dean was puzzled by Mrs. Thacker's illness. He diagnosed it tentatively as a case of the 'flu, with serious stomach disorders. But, although Mrs. Thacker complained that her body felt "like it was on fire", both her temperature and pulse were normal. Dr. Dean gave her some medicine to soothe her stomach and departed.

Next day, finding his patient no better, he suspected something else. He asked Mrs. Thacker if it was possible she had taken some poison by accident, and she said, "No, we do not keep it in the house."

The doctor wasn't satisfied. Her symptoms—intense thirst, persistent vomiting and retching—indicated acute poisoning. Her medicine seemed to have no effect. Twice more he asked her about poison, but she insisted there was no poison in her house.

A week later, his patient sinking fast, Dr. Dean called for a consultation. Thacker demurred, saying that Dean seemed to be doing all that could be done and that he did not see the necessity for it. But the doctor urged, and Thacker gave his consent provided his wife were willing. She consented, and Dean summoned Dr. Kinne of Frankfort. The consultation was held the next day.

They found the patient in very weak condition, suffering from nausea and intense thirst; the features pinched and shrunken, the tongue dark and swollen, the skin assuming a bronze hue, the hands and feet cold and clammy—classic symptoms of arsenic poisoning. Pathetically Mrs. Thacker appealed to them: "My condition is not so very bad. Why don't I get better?"

Dr. Kinne told Thacker that his wife was very ill and suggested that he hire a nurse; but Thacker said his wife would not hear of it and that he and Lottie could manage very well. He said that from the first he had had grave doubts about his wife's recovery. He told them his wife must have had some kind of presentiment, too, because shortly after she became ill she signed the deed to the property over to him. She had inherited the house and land from her father, Thacker said.

Meanwhile, Miss Spencer had gone to live with the Baileys. Ostensibly, she wanted to relieve Thacker and Lottie of the additional burden. Actually, she left the house in fear for her life.

On several occasions she had found a strange white powder in the food that was brought to her. She had taken some samples of it—in the prunes and the graham mush—wrapped them in white paper with her name and date written on it, and had given them to Dr. Dean.

Mrs. Thacker died on May 16, twelve days after the onset of her illness. Thacker, Lottie and Dr. Dean were with her when she died.

Thacker arranged to hold the funeral next day—without waiting for Mrs. Thacker's brothers, who lived in Minneapolis. When undertaker Jones suggested that might be a bit soon, Thacker said he wanted to get it over with as soon as possible. Mrs. Bailey offered to help lay out the body of her friend, but Thacker rebuffed her, saying the family could take care of its own dead.

Meanwhile, Dr. Dean had sent the food samples given him by Miss Spencer to Ann Arbor for analysis. Back came the report, a week later, that the white powder in the prunes and graham mush was arsenic.

Ten days after the funeral Anna Thacker's body was disinterred and an autopsy was performed by the coroner, Dr. Powers, in the presence of Dr. Dean and Sheriff Chandler. Portions of the vital organs were removed—including the stomach and brain—sealed in glass jars, and sent to the chemical laboratory at the University of Michigan.

In due course, a report was received from Professor Gomberg, head of the department of forensic medicine. Arsenic had been found in the stomach, liver and brain—indicating that the poison had been ingested over a considerable period of time. Gomberg found one sixth grain of arsenic in crystalline form in the stomach. This indicated that the woman had received additional poison no more than twelve hours before death.

A coroner's jury, after hearing the doctor and Mrs. Bailey, blamed Thacker for his wife's death. Thacker said he was certain he would be cleared in court, but added:

"It looks as if I will have to go to jail."

Thacker was confident there was no evidence to hold him for trial but his sister-in-law quickly provided it.

Miss Spencer said during her sister's illness she had kissed her once and later got a dry and burning sensation when she moistened her own lips. She said she had found in her own food a pile of white powder beneath the graham mush. A pit had been removed from one of the prunes and the cavity filled with the same white powder. After she went to live at the Bailey's, she gave the samples to Dr. Dean. In deference to her invalid condition, Miss Spencer's testimony was taken at the Bailey home.

Dr. Dean said death was due to arsenic poisoning.

Lottie Thacker said she and her father had eaten the mush, too, without becoming ill, but Thacker was ordered to stand trial for murder.

The things that happened then did little to soften the townswomen's attitude toward Thacker. He sent word to Ora Bunker to come and care for his children. A committee of women called on Thacker's lawyer and demanded Ora be ordered out of the house. Thacker refused, saying it was the children's wish she be called, and that his wife told him to get Ora if anything should happen to her. The women then went to the Judge, who had a talk with the lawyer—and Ora left.

The Thacker trial opened before Judge Aldrich at Case Hall in Benzonia in mid-July and lasted ten days. The people were represented by prosecutors Warner and Pratt, Thacker by attorneys Wilson and Covell.

Prosecutor Warner charged that Thacker had killed his wife to get control of her property, and to be free to "carry on" with another woman.

Dr. Dean testified that his attention had been called to some food prepared for Miss Spencer before her sister's death, and had found "some grey powder under the graham pudding and inside one of the prunes". Professor Gomberg said it was arsenic.

Miss Spencer swore to having found the powder in her food four different times. She said the various kinds of food prepared for her made her sick until at last she was reduced to eating nothing but crackers and raw eggs.

She believed that Thacker wanted to do away with her, but when she left for the Baileys she said she "didn't think her brother-in-law was so dastardly as to give his wife enough poison to kill her". She said she made out her will in Thacker's favor, "hoping for some commendation", but he gave her none and she destroyed the will after going to Mrs. Bailey's.

Several witnesses—including Dr. and Mrs. Shaw, Mrs. Bailey and Lawrence Mahn—testified to having seen "certain intimacies" between Thacker and Ora Bunker.

The defense introduced half a dozen witnesses who testified as to Thacker's good character and standing in the community.

In summing up, Covell scouted the idea of Thacker's guilt, and suggested that Mrs. Thacker died a suicide.

"The people would have you believe," he said, "that Henry Thacker has murdered his bosom friend, the woman he swore to love, the woman who bore him five children. If there is a reasonable doubt, he is entitled to it.

"Let us see," he continued, "Dr. Dean suspected it. Mrs. Bailey was aware of it. Miss Spencer knew it. My God, three of the citizens of Benzonia sat down while Henry Thacker poisoned his wife."

It was a masterly argument, but to no avail. The jury deliberated only five hours and found Thacker guilty. Thacker broke down and sobbed, while his children tried to comfort him. "There is something wrong here," he kept saying as he was led back to his cell.

A friend had offered to put up his hay for him, but Thacker thanked him and told him he would be free to do it himself the next day.

Judge Aldrich sentenced Thacker to a life term but gave him a few hours to wind up his affairs and say goodbye to his children. Before leaving for Jackson State Prison Thacker told the Judge:

"I have said all along, and I say now, that I am an innocent man, I loved my wife as your honor loves yours."

Next day the Jackson *Patriot* reported: "W.H. Thacker, the Benzonia wife poisoner, arrived at the prison accompanied by Sheriff Chandler and a deputy. The trio came on the Grand Rapids express at 9:05. The prisoner was not handcuffed and when they alighted from the train he preceded the two officers into the depot, walking a firm step. He gave no indication of anything out of the ordinary, and few of the bystanders recognized him as the prisoner. A hack was secured and the party drove immediately to the prison."

And that should have been the end of the Thacker murder case—but it wasn't.

In August, 1894, Thacker's lawyer announced an astonishing discovery. A suicide note, signed by Mrs. Thacker, had been found in the Thacker home. On the basis of this new evidence and several errors made during the trial, they won a new trial for Thacker by order of the State Supreme Court.

The suicide note, written in pencil on a sheet of her husband's stationery, read as follows:

> *Dear Husband, I am tired of life. I have been*
> *tempted ever since you bought that arsenic for*
> *dogs to use some my self, have taken some*
> *three times. will take some more now. take*
> *good care of the children and do as I told you,*
> *you remember. My head feals badly. Goodbye,*
> *Anna.*

The note was dated May 15, the day before Mrs. Thacker died.

The new trial opened on July 30, 1896, and lasted two weeks. It was held in Frankfort rather than Benzonia because the county seat had been moved from Benzonia to Frankfort in 1894.

The Benzie *Banner* reported that "no case in the history of

The suicide note.

A known specimen of Mrs. Thacker's handwriting, introduced for comparison at the trial.

Benzie County has attracted the attention of the public as the present trial of Thacker. The court room is packed to suffocation for every session of the court, and as is usually the case in trials of this kind, the women are in the large majority, all straining every nerve to catch any piece of evidence that smacks of scandal and will give them a prominent topic for the next sewing circle.

"In fact," the *Banner* continued, "on one or two days of the trial and until the judge finally came down on it, a stranger coming into the court would have taken it for a kindergarten, as every mother who had a baby brought it with her."

The same witnesses appeared as had testified in the previous trial—except Thacker himself, who elected to take the stand and testify in his own defense; and Professor Gomberg, who was on a sabbatical in Germany. His evidence was admitted by deposition.

Miss Spencer said that for two years prior to her sister's death, Thacker "had not talked with her in the same brotherly manner as was his custom". This she attributed to the fact that she had reprimanded him about Ora Bunker. Thacker explained it by saying that "Miss Spencer, soon after she came home from the hospital, came to me and said, 'Henry, I find I am growing much too fond of you, and I think the thing to do for the good of us both is for you not to come around to where I am. Every time you come into my presence I feel a thrill pass over me, and I grow more and more to look for your return when you are away from me, so I think you must not come where I am.'"

The women in the courtroom gasped with astonishment at this.

The defense introduced the suicide note and called a dozen witnesses who asserted its authenticity. They included Lottie and Roy Thacker, who were familiar with their mother's handwriting, and others—like bank teller W. Cunningham and newspaper publisher Thomas Bates, both of Traverse City—who had compared the note with samples of Mrs. Thacker's writing.

The prosecution called the note a clumsy forgery. They introduced as many witnesses of their own. They pointed out that there had been erasures where the date and the word "dogs" appeared. Dr. Dean said it would have been impossible for Mrs. Thacker to have written the note or anything the day before she died; that she was then in a semi-comatose state.

Miss Spencer testified that her sister was college educated and would never have made the grammatical errors or misspelled the word "feel".

Since none of the witnesses was a handwriting expert (the study of graphology had yet to be established), the net effect of this testimony was probably to cancel out—though Miss Spencer's testimony was certainly damaging to Thacker.

Then came the moment everybody had been waiting for.

Prosecutor Pratt asked Thacker: "Did you have dreams during your stay at Jackson, and did you at one time dream for three nights in succession that within the covers of a certain medical book kept in the family there was a suicide note written by your wife?"

Thacker professed surprise at having been asked this question. He really could not remember whether he had such a dream, he said.

"You wrote the details of this dream to Roy and Lottie Thacker, did you not?"

Again Thacker said he just couldn't remember if he had done that. He said his mind was so overcome with horror at being confined in solitary for thirty-one days to a cell three by eight feet that his memory failed him. Pratt hammered at him for almost an hour, but did not break him down.

The prosecution then called Roy Thacker to prove the receipt of such a letter from his father. He admitted having received the letter, and said that Ora Bunker had stolen it from the house. Ora testified that she heard Roy read such a letter and had seen him put it in the stove and burn it up.

Lottie testified that she had failed to find the note from her mother on her first search, but later discovered it when she was showing the home medical book to her little sister Josie, who was ill. She said it was inside one of the folding pictures in the book.

The case at this time came to an abrupt end—much to the surprise of many in the courtroom.

George Covell's final argument was even more masterly than that of the previous trial. Or so the Benzie *Banner* reported; "He delivered a strong and masterly rhetorical plea in behalf of his client, many passages of oratorical flight visibly affecting not only the jury, but also bringing tears to the eyes of the spectators, whose previous conduct was conspicuously in opposition to the defendant."

This time, Covell's argument worked—or something did. After deliberating only a short time, the jury returned a verdict of not guilty—proving once again the old adage that you never can tell what a jury will do.

Thacker arrived at home on the evening train once more a free man.

There is no record of how the women of Benzonia treated Thacker after he came home. But the Congregational Church, which had excommunicated him after his conviction, did not receive him back in its bosom after his acquittal.

It didn't make much difference, though, because a few weeks later Thacker married Ora Bunker and blew town together with the Thacker children in a cloud of dust.

That was vindication enough for the Benzonia women. After all, they had suspected W.H. Thacker from the start.

THE LAST BATTLE

They called him Old Soldier, but he'd never done much fighting, except with his wife. At the age of 27, Branson L. Gardner enlisted with the 147th Indiana in February, 1865, and, with the Civil War ended, was mustered out in August of that year. The regiment had done garrison and guard duty in various places in the Shenandoah Valley, but had seen no action.

After the war Branson returned to Lafayette County, Indiana, got married and worked at his trade, which was carpentry. The Gardners had one child—a daughter, Nettie. In the 1880s they moved to Traverse City, and later, Nettie married Elisha J. Fulghum, who owned the Fulghum Manufacturing Co. (flooring) and served as mayor of Traverse City in 1904.

Gardner and his wife began to have trouble when, in his fifties, he developed a roving eye and a disposition to match. A traveling theatre company came to town and played several weeks at the Steinberg Opera House. Gardner was smitten with one of the young actresses and when the troupe left town, Gardner left with it.

His wife did not hear from him for ten long years. She moved in with her daughter and husband at the Fulghum residence at 310 East Eighth Street.

Finally, word reached her that Gardner had checked into the Indiana State Soldier's home at Lafayette, and that he had started divorce proceedings. She consulted a lawyer, decided to contest the suit, and filed a claim in Washington for half of her husband's $8-per-month pension.

That was too much. Gardner was furious. Here he was, a poor, broken-down old soldier with heart trouble, and his wife Matilda wanted to steal half of his paltry pension. He decided that something drastic would have to be done.

He borrowed $15. from an old friend in Lynn, Indiana, got permission to leave the Home for a few days, and took a train for Detroit and Traverse City.

When he got there, apparently he did nothing much except wander around town. An old acquaintance, A.J. Helm, recognized him, but Gardner pretended not to know him and hurried off. Two days later, Helm ran into him again at the doorway of the Briggs apartment building on East Front. This time, Gardner greeted him warmly and talked volubly, pouring out his troubles. He said he was going to make trouble for Elisha Fulghum for coming between him and his wife.

That night, Helm went to the Fulghum house and alerted Elisha, saying that Gardner had talked "kind of wild". Fulghum thanked him and said he'd keep a sharp lookout, as he was expecting trouble with Gardner over the divorce. Helm watched at the Briggs apartments for several nights, but did not see Gardner again.

Neither did the Fulghums and Mrs. Gardner. Apparently, his temper had cooled. He was known to be an irritable and sometimes violent man; sometimes he seemed almost crazy.

Branson had indeed gone back to Indiana, after pawning his gold watch.

Gardner's next trip to Traverse City, three weeks later, was carefully planned. He left the Soldiers Home on Sunday, May 8, 1905, posting a letter to the sergeant major at the Home, William P. Stump. The letter read as follows:

> *Mr. Stump: Over domestic difficulties I have gone to make away with myself and I wish you would box up the few things I have in the bottom drawer and send them to A.C.H., Lynn, Ind. You will hear of me later. I can't wait any longer to do this and I will leave a*

note telling you all about it. So goodbye.

Gardner arrived in Traverse City on the 8:30 train, Monday evening. He went straight to the Fulghum house on 8th Street. It was already dark when he got there. He donned a pink mask, climbed the porch steps and knocked roughly on the door. Waiting, he put both hands in his coat pockets.

Mrs. Gardner and her daughter were in the sitting room. As was her habit in the evening, Mrs. Gardner was reading her Bible. Elisha Fulghum was not at home. He had gone to attend a Board of Trustees meeting at the Methodist Church.

Mrs. Gardner got up and went to the door. Opening it, she gasped at the sight of the masked man. Gardner asked if the man of the house was in. He spoke gruffly as though to disguise his voice, but his wife recognized it. She ran to the sitting room where Nettie was waiting — she, too, had recognized her father's voice.

Branson followed close behind. Calmly he shut the sitting room door and took a .38-caliber pistol from his pocket. His wife fled to the kitchen in terror. Gardner caught her there and shot her through the head. Then he took another .38 pistol from his pocket and, putting a gun to both his temples, pulled the triggers simultaneously. Man and wife were reunited at last—in death.

Nettie had run screaming from the house for help. As she came down the porch steps she heard the pistol shot and the heavy fall of a body. She ran across the street to the home of C.A. Hurly, a butcher. He telephoned Chief of Police John Rennie and waited outside the Fulghum house until the Chief arrived a few minutes later. They entered the house together.

They found the bodies in the kitchen. Mrs. Gardner lay with her head close to the cooking range, Gardner with his head towards the other side of the room. Their feet were almost touching. Gardner's hands were stretched above his head and the pistols lay near his shoulders. One pistol had two empty cartridges, and the other, one.

Drs. Swanton, Garner and Gauntlett were summoned and, after an examination of the bodies, said that death was practically instantaneous in both cases.

In Gardner's pockets they found the following items: a pocket-book containing $6.07, a watch and chain, a pair of glasses, and two letters.

One of the letters, from Washington, read as follows:

You are hereby notified that the claim of Matilda Gardner for one-half the pension granted to Branson L. Gardner had been approved on the ground that pensioner deserted claimant, his lawful wife, who is a person of good moral character and in necessitous circumstances...

The other letter, addressed to Nettie Fulghum, was in Branson Gardner's hand:

Well, Net, I am going to stop all of this trouble at the point of a revolver. I have seen enough of it and I will stop it in this way. You won't know me when I come in your house until I have done the deed. I will go with her and if I can, I will take Elisha with us. He helped to make the trouble and I blame you for causing her to put in for half of my pension. Andrew Parmenter has got the gold watch that I had and if you want it, go pay him $5.50. Net, bury me with this suit. Don't take it off. I have nothing on my person but what is in my pockets.